"Lo   all-out civil war."

"Destabilizing U.S. interests here," Bolan concluded.

"Right," Fonesca agreed. "That would also give the conservative elements in Washington ammunition to talk the President into adopting a military solution."

That idea was unthinkable, although Bolan knew that a civil war in Puerto Rico would leave the Man no choice but to send military forces to restore law and order. The small National Guard presence on the island would never be enough to quench the fervor of an all-out armed conflict between civilians.

Civil war in Puerto Rico? America having to intervene with its own protectorate by means of military force? The end results of such a thing would be tragic and horrific, at best.

"I'll start by sending a message to the Independents, letting them know if they are responsible this won't go unchecked."

"Fair enough," Fonseca said. "What do you need from me?"

"A place to deliver it," the Executioner replied.

Don Pendleton's Mack
Bolan®
Diplomacy Directive

A GOLD EAGLE BOOK FROM
WORLDWIDE®

TORONTO • NEW YORK • LONDON
AMSTERDAM • PARIS • SYDNEY • HAMBURG
STOCKHOLM • ATHENS • TOKYO • MILAN
MADRID • WARSAW • BUDAPEST • AUCKLAND

Recycling programs
for this product may
not exist in your area.

First edition January 2010

ISBN-13: 978-0-373-61534-6

Special thanks and acknowledgment to
Jon Guenther for his contribution to this work.

DIPLOMACY DIRECTIVE

Printed in U.S.A.

Though force can protect in an emergency,
only justice, fairness, consideration and cooperation
can finally lead men to the dawn of eternal peace.
                              —Dwight D. Eisenhower
                                        1890–1969

My use of force is always as a last resort.
Unfortunately, it's the only thing that terrorists
understand, and sometimes without it we can never
know peace.
                              —Mack Bolan

PROLOGUE

Guadalupe La Costa knew a break when she saw it.

It wasn't every day the director of the local Associated Press affiliate in Puerto Rico handed out juicy assignments to reporters—especially to a young woman who refused to sleep with him—let alone a rookie reporter with a penchant for being a might too ambitious. In any case, some might have viewed covering the upcoming election to appoint a new governor as one of the more mundane assignments. La Costa saw it as a challenge with a gem of a story behind it: a human interest story that focused on the two opponents.

The director had issued an order that La Costa not broach personal issues with the candidates, and keep the parameters of her story confined to the issues. La Costa got the gig, which would include a two-minute live segment on the nightly news channel feed out of Miami. And if she played her cards right, she'd get an exclusive with each of the candidates during the little soiree being held later that night. That last detail had cost her plenty, namely a Gucci leather handbag she was still sure was a knockoff and some very expensive French shoes. The gifts went to the respective PR chiefs of the two candidates, both of whom happened to be women, and felt like cutting a sister a break if it meant she could get ahead. They had required her to present her questions in advance, and to her surprise the candidates agreed. The campaign had become as much a race of personalities as it was one of competent leadership.

Then again, many elections founded on basic democratic principles were more of a popularity contest than about the election of someone who might actually be able to *do* the job.

La Costa shook her head every time she thought of that. Well, she didn't give a rip who got elected. Her only connection to Puerto Rico was she'd been born there while her father, an American career diplomat, was assigned to the area. The family headed back to the States, and her father continued his career in various posts.

Securing a job with the Associated Press as a foreign affairs journalist posed no challenge. La Costa's Masters in journalism certainly helped, and she hadn't minded using her father's connections, either.

The man seated next to her in the van didn't come up quite the same way. No, definitely no silver spoon in Julio Parmahel's past. Parmahel had been raised the hard way in Little Havana, scraping and fighting his way into a decent college where he could study photography. Journalistic photography had a limited scope, though, since most reporters were also expected to be decent photographers. With a lack of work, Parmahel turned to camera operations. It wasn't his first love, but at least he got to use some of his creativity.

"Man, I am bored out my skull," he said in his heavy,

Cuban accent. He leaned back as best he could manage, given the size of the driver's seat of a studio van. He yanked a toothpick from his mouth and pointed it at La Costa to make his point. "And sweet Mama, why do the nights always got to be so damn hot?"

La Costa shook her head and laughed. "Julio, I'm going to assume that's a rhetorical question, since we've been together down here almost a year. I'd think you'd be used to it by now."

"I'll never be used to it. Guess I'm just homesick."

The appearance of a sponsorship member on the platform they had erected for the speeches diverted her attention from making a reply. As he introduced the first candidate, La Costa and Parmahel transferred to the back of the van and began checks on their equipment. They weren't there to cover the actual speeches; somebody else had that part of the assignment. La Costa was there only for the interviews and to present her live recording after the speeches were concluded. They'd already gone through their checks twice, but she insisted they do it one more time.

Parmahel responded to her obsessive-compulsive whims without grumbling, which was one of the reasons she liked to work so much with him. By the time they finished running through the checklist, the second candidate had stepped up and was about halfway through his speech. The sponsors had allotted each candidate a total of fifteen minutes to present.

La Costa helped Parmahel unload the equipment from the back. They did a quick test run of the remote feed, then stood by as the second candidate completed his speech. As the cheers went up from the crowd, they locked the van and moved into position near the dais, where they would begin the segment once things started to break up. The crowd started dispersing shortly after the announcer concluded with the sales pitches for each sponsor.

The production supervisor showed up at the last minute, just like he always did—about the only thing in which the guy seemed consistent—and shortly thereafter the countdown began. The supervisor began a countdown from five, then used his fingers to silently tick off the last two seconds before the lights came up, the dome on the camera went red and he pointed to La Costa to begin her spiel.

"Thank you, Cassandra. We're here tonight in beautiful downtown San Juan, where the candidates have just completed their speeches and are now shaking hands with their constituents. The city is afire with the pending vote to elect a new governor, and you can feel the excitement here. Later this evening we'll have the unique privilege of getting to chat personally with each of the candidates, who have graciously granted us exclusive interviews. You won't want to miss these interviews as the candidates will be talking candidly with us about their individual views of the upcoming election. The huge show of support here tonight was impressive. We—"

The area around them exploded in sounds of shouting, screaming and gunfire.

The stage lit up like a fireworks display, and the podium where the two candidates had stood just minutes earlier exploded. Pandemonium erupted and people scattered in every direction. Security and police officers nearby rushed the stage, struggling to pick their way past the dead or dying bodies, and debris littered the explosion site.

More shooting ensued as law-enforcement officials began to trade fire with a small band of armed men who rushed the wall of people surrounding the two candidates. The aggressors wore assorted military-style fatigues and bandannas of red, white and blue—colors of the territorial flag—while triggering semiautomatic pistols and assault rifles. The paramilitary police force split up, some staying to move the candidates out of harm's way behind the dais and into the adjoining government building, while others fanned out to form a defensive perimeter.

La Costa dived for cover and shouted at Parmahel to follow her lead, but the cameraman kept shooting footage. She screamed at him, but her objections were overridden by the crazed crowd looking to escape death and the production supervisor, who yelled at Parmahel, "Keep rolling! Keep rolling!"

The new arrivals in fatigues appeared to be indiscriminate in their shooting, seeming more intent on terrorizing anybody in their path than at actually assassinating one of the candidates. La Costa glimpsed Sallie Manzano, the Popular Democratic Party's candidate, go down as rounds ripped open her belly. La Costa emitted an involuntary scream and felt tears gush from her eyes and her face flush. The shooters weren't firing even close to them and yet La Costa couldn't extinguish the fire of terror in her gut.

The battle continued to rage for several minutes before the few remaining gunmen spent the last of their ammunition, then turned and ran in the opposite direction. People were still scrambling over one another—some had been trampled nearly to death—while others stayed frozen behind whatever cover they could find.

In less than five minutes it was over.

But for Guadalupe La Costa, it would never be over. It would be something she'd remembered for the rest of her life.

CHAPTER ONE

Mack Bolan deplaned from the Gulfstream C-21 belonging to Stony Man Farm, one of America's top covert special operations units.

The vulcanized neoprene soles of his combat boots held firm on the rain-slickened tarmac at Luis Muñoz Marín International Airport. Balmy winds off the North Atlantic tugged at his black hair and filled his nostrils with its salty scent.

Jack Grimaldi poked his head out of the cabin and took a deep breath. "Ah, there's nothing like the tropics."

Bolan looked up the steps at Grimaldi and produced a half smile. The two men had been friends for what seemed like an eternity, their initial meeting more fate than chance for both of them. Grimaldi had been working as a chopper pilot for a Mafia casino boss, and meeting the Executioner had created a paradigm shift in his life neither of them would soon forget. Now Grimaldi served as ace pilot for Stony Man and served Able Team and Phoenix Force—Stony Man's elite counterterrorism teams—with the occasional "loan out" to Bolan's officially sanctioned missions.

"You need help with the equipment?" Bolan asked.

"Naw, but if you can get our wheels that would be sweet."

Bolan nodded and headed across the tarmac toward a solitary hangar close by. Inside he knew he'd find everything he requested: a sport utility vehicle, a briefcase containing assignment information, military uniforms, credentials and official-looking military orders. Since Puerto Rico was a commonwealth and protectorate of the United States, and there was no official military presence here other than a contingent of National Guard, any potential acts of terrorism fell under the jurisdiction of the Department of Defense. Bolan had used the alias of Colonel Brandon Stone many times, and would do so again.

"You'll have the full cooperation of the governor's office," Hal Brognola had informed him.

While Bolan had maintained a strictly informal alliance with his government, Brognola was a friend and wouldn't hesitate to call on him in the direst circumstances. The violent attack on political candidates perpetrated by a paramilitary guerrilla unit qualified, and the president had agreed when Brognola brought that fact to his attention.

Bolan drove the SUV to the tarmac and, despite Grimaldi's protests to the contrary, helped offload equipment into the back. Normally, Bolan would have preferred to operate alone and leave Grimaldi with the plane, but he needed the time to review the paper and electronic files provided by Stony Man, so the pilot agreed to be his chauffeur.

"So what's the gig, Sarge?" Grimaldi asked as he left the airport and headed for the downtown area. The ace pilot was the only person from the Executioner's past who called him that.

Bolan's eyes never left the file he was reading by a red interior lamp. "Unknown aggressors engaged police and civilians at a political rally two days ago. Total of nineteen victims, four were fatalities."

"Terrorists?"

"Not sure," Bolan replied. "Although if this were a terrorist group I'd have trouble buying politics as a motive."

"Why's that?"

"There are easier ways, Jack. Politically motivated terrorists don't usually operate so openly. They tend to favor well-placed bombs or hit key targets. This was entirely random. To march into a crowd and simply start shooting doesn't sound political."

"I thought I heard Hal say they blew something up, too," Grimaldi replied.

"Yeah. They threw a grenade at the stage. It wasn't a bomb."

Grimaldi sighed. "Grenades and automatic weapons. Sounds like a paramilitary group, maybe militia or rebels."

Bolan nodded. "Exactly."

The drive to the hotel took less than thirty minutes. Once they checked in, Bolan traded his civilian garb for a class B army uniform. As Bolan emerged from the bedroom bedecked in olive-drab trousers and a light green, short-sleeve shirt adorned with military decorations and the appropriate rank insignia, Grimaldi returned from the restaurant with two cups of coffee and a half-dozen cheese Danishes. Bolan gratefully took the coffee, but shook his head at the pastries.

"Just leaves more for me," the pilot said.

"Which I'm sure you had planned," Bolan replied.

Grimaldi nodded with a wink as he stuffed half a Danish in his mouth. Around a mouthful of the food he said, "Don't you look dapper."

"I have a meeting first thing this morning with one of the governor's security advisers."

"You need me for that?"

Bolan shook his head. "The office is only a few blocks from here. I'll walk."

After a few minutes of small talk, Bolan secured his Beretta 93-R in a standard military holster, donned his utility cap and headed outside. The streets were coming alive with morning commuters, but it was still early enough that Bolan didn't encounter many passersby. It took him ten minutes to reach the government building, and a secretary immediately showed him to the office of the security adviser. Bolan had read the brief on his contact, a native-born Puerto Rican named Alvaro Fonseca, who'd served with the Central American desk of the CIA and as a Foreign Affairs adviser to the U.S. Senate before taking this assignment. Fonseca had a reputation as a no-nonsense type with a dubious background in foreign intelligence. Still, Bolan had every confidence the guy knew his stuff, which was affirmed upon meeting the man, who offered a strong handshake and polite smile.

Fonseca asked his assistant to bring coffee and then took a seat on a comfortable sofa across from one of a couple chairs he offered Bolan.

"I hate meeting with folks behind my desk," he told the Executioner. "It's too impersonal."

"I understand. I know you're busy so I won't impose on too much of your time, sir," Bolan said, easily shifting into his role as a military man accustomed to extending full diplomatic courtesies.

"Are you kidding, Colonel? Hell, you're doing me a big favor by being here. I'm sure you can understand the governor wants this situation resolved as soon as possible. It's resulted in a lot of political unrest."

"That's one of the things I wanted to ask you," Bolan replied. "What are your thoughts about this attack being politically motivated?"

"I'm not buying it. And frankly, by virtue of the fact you even bothered to ask that question I'm thinking you aren't, either."

"Not really."

Fonseca settled into the sofa by crossing his legs and draping one arm over the backrest. "As I've already told the president, I believe this indicates a move by militant members of the Puerto Rican Independence Party calling themselves *Los Independientes*. The Independents."

"That's a serious charge," Bolan observed. "Especially seeing they're an officially recognized party of government."

"True, but not all of their members necessarily speak for the PIP. Please bear in mind this particular faction does not have any official position or support by the party. In fact, the PIP leadership denounces any actions by the Independents, and has further implemented both political and legal sanctions against them. Moreover, the views of this group are diametrically opposed to the New Progressive Party."

Bolan furrowed an eyebrow. "Afraid I'm not familiar."

"The New Progressives also support independence for Puerto Rico, but by means of ratification into U.S. statehood rather than adoption of territorial autonomy. If I might be blunt, it surprises me that the Oval Office would choose to respond to this incident by sending a military man rather than a full ambassadorial party."

Bolan thought fast. "My position is…unique."

"Really? In what way?"

"My function is actually as military liaison to the Diplomatic Security Service. Because of my particular background, someone thought I'd be of more use than a politician or DSS agent alone."

"I see," Fonseca replied, poker-faced. "You are, um, attaché to some sort of special operations group."

Bolan smiled. "If it allays your concerns as to my qualifications."

"Fair enough. I won't press with uncomfortable questions. I'm sure the president's decision to send you was well thought out, and that's good enough for me, Colonel. And I can assure you that you'll have the full cooperation and authority of my office as well as that of the governor's while you're in Puerto Rico."

"Thank you. What else can you tell me about the militant group you suspect was behind this?"

"Well, you'll recall I mentioned the New Progressive Party, or PNP as they are often referred to. They have their own entourage of violent radicals, whose actions are also fully sanctioned. The PNP has had considerably more success disavowing this group than the PIP has of the Independents, since there's never been any evidence that ties the PNP cell to any violent actions in Puerto Rico, political or otherwise. Or anywhere in the Western Hemisphere for that matter."

"Peaceful political extremists?" Bolan frowned. "Doesn't feel right."

"It may not be after what happened the other night," Fonseca replied in a matter-of-fact tone.

"What do you mean?"

"Nobody's claimed credit for the attack, yet, but if the Independents *do* come forward this might very well spurn their enemies into a counterresponse. A violent one. And that won't be good for either the current political state of Puerto Rico or the upcoming elections."

"You think the Independents might try to foment the PNPs folks into armed rebellion under some flag of solidarity."

"The thought had merited my concerns for just such a possibility, and the governor agrees. In either case it's a threat we cannot afford. We must stop the Independents, guilty or not, before there are any further acts like this."

He paused for a time, probably to let the Executioner chew on that statement for a bit.

After a time, Fonseca continued, "There's always been a level of political unrest here, Colonel. Most individuals in the general populace have very personal and impassioned views about what should be done to solidify Puerto Rico's political sovereignty and economy. If such incidents continue to occur, warring between the Independents and their enemies could well become the least of our problems. It could cause Puerto Ricans to utterly lose faith in our system of government and, quite honestly, result in a full-scale civil war."

"Thus destabilizing U.S. interests here."

"Right. That would also give the more conservative elements in Washington ammunition to talk the president into adopting a military solution."

That idea was unthinkable, although Bolan knew that a civil war in Puerto Rico would leave the Man no choice but to send military forces to restore law and order. The small National Guard presence here would never be enough to tamp down the fervor of an all-out armed conflict between civilians. The circumstances leading to the very founding of America had proven that. Democratic society only worked as long as the people had faith in the system of representative government. The moment they lost that faith, it wasn't hard to believe they would take matters into their own hands by organizing an opposing force. Civil war in Puerto Rico? America having to intervene with its own protectorate by means of military force? The end results of such a thing would be tragic and horrific.

"I think I'll start by sending a message to the Independents, letting them know if they are responsible this won't go unchecked," Bolan said.

"Fair enough. What do you need from me?"

"A place to deliver it," the Executioner replied.

CHAPTER TWO

Bolan got a delivery address, and after returning to his hotel room and changing into civvies, he drove across San Juan to a poverty-stricken east side neighborhood. Grimaldi would pick up another rental vehicle and be on standby in case the Executioner needed backup. The houses were really shacks; gutters and sidewalks were in disrepair, and filth covered the streets and cluttered the curbs. Weeds or mud took up space where green lawns should have been. The cars parked in the yards or along the narrow streets were so old and rusted that most didn't look like they could be moved, and if they were they might well fall apart before traveling even half a block.

Bolan had seen squalor like this before, and it left him understanding why elements within Puerto Rico were dissatisfied with the current state of affairs. Not that the Executioner believed an independent Puerto Rico could fair better. Sometimes there were political elements that chose to let things continue like this, to permit certain segments of the populace to live in these conditions, so they could justify some higher political gain.

Why would it seem out of place, then, for the Independents to set up shop in a neighborhood like this?

Bolan studied his target through the binoculars from his position a half block down. He didn't take long to get the lay of the area. His vehicle stuck out like a sore thumb, and he knew if he stayed too long it would draw some unwanted attention, which he couldn't afford. He would have to hit the place hard and fast.

Only one problem. Nothing moved around the house. No sign of sentries or a roving patrol. There were no vehicles parked in the narrow drive or in front of the property on the street. The house looked utterly run-down, almost as if it had been unoccupied, and something in Bolan's gut told him it was empty and had been for some time. The only thing he'd learned from his recon so far spoke of abandonment and disuse.

Bolan considered his next move, deciding if a closer look on foot would be worth it, but he didn't get the chance to act on that thought. A flash of light reflecting off metal winked in his side mirror and drew his attention. He spotted a quartet of motorcycles with black-clad riders as they rode up on his vehicle with the muzzles of wicked-looking machine pistols leveled in his direction. Bolan went horizontal in the seat in time to avoid a maelstrom of autofire. High-velocity rounds shattered the front and rear side windows and left shards of glass to rain down on Bolan in their wake. The soldier folded up the center console, slid over to the passenger door and went EVA.

By the time he'd rolled to the relative safety of cover behind the SUV and gained his feet, the four motorcycles were making their turn for a second pass. Bolan reached into the glove box and came away with his

Desert Eagle. The massive, stainless-steel pistol had become a faithful ally in moments such as these. Since Bolan didn't have easy access or time to get to the heavier weaponry, the .44 Magnum hand-cannon would fill the void.

Bolan took up position just forward of the A-frame post, leveled the weapon in a two-handed Weaver grip and sighted on the closest rider. He squeezed the trigger and the weapon thundered as a Cor-Bon 305-grain full-metal-jacket round left the barrel at 1,600 feet per second. The round struck the motorcyclist in the chest as he was triggering his own weapon. The motorcycle seemed to shimmy a moment beneath the rider before the impact drove him from the saddle. The motorcycle continued on an erratic path for another twenty yards or so before crashing to the pavement about the same time as did its rider.

Bolan had already tracked on another rider and triggered his second round. The big weapon boomed again in the noonday air with equally satisfying results. The man's head exploded inside his helmet, and a crimson spray washed over the face shield. The handlebars appeared to become wrenched from the rider's grasp, and the bike made a sudden and awkward turn to the right before sliding against the pavement and dragging the deceased rider along with it for a fair distance.

The remaining two motorcyclists were now even with the Executioner and opened up simultaneously. Bolan ducked behind the SUV, which protected him from the volley of fresh rounds. He heard them slap into the metal and fiberglass body of the SUV, absorbing the impact with a noisy chatter of protest as round after round chewed through the thin skin of the vehicle and lodged deep in its frame or pebbled the safety glass of the windshield.

Bolan waited until they passed, then climbed inside the cab and cranked the engine. He whipped the steering wheel into a hard left as he gunned the engine. The vehicle left its spot at the curb, tires smoking as Bolan powered into an intercept course. Or at least that's what he'd planned. But the riders no longer appeared interested in sticking around. With their numbers halved they seemed more concerned with escaping their enemy's fury. Bolan meant to see to it they didn't get off so easy with their hit-and-git; the Executioner wouldn't be anybody's target for a sucker play like that.

The soldier put his foot to the floor and kept one eye on the motorcyclists, who were rapidly widening the gap between them. If they decided to split up, the entire pursuit might turn out to be for nothing, but he couldn't worry about such petty details. As long as he could keep at least one of them in sight, he'd be in good shape. At the moment he wished he could get Grimaldi into the air. With air observation he could follow their course without having to keep them physically in sight at ground level.

To his surprise, the riders slowed down—whether forced by the thickening traffic on San Juan's busier streets or by simple design—which allowed him to keep them in sight. Bolan figured they probably planned to lead him into a trap. They could have killed him back there if they'd exercised a bit more caution in their approach, but instead they had chosen to come at him like gangbusters. Maybe their intent had been to lead him away from that neighborhood all the time, which meant either he'd come closer than they liked or they had been prepared for his arrival.

A leak inside Fonseca's office? Possible, but highly unlikely. Fonseca had told him when he first gave up the address it might not lead Bolan to much. Their intelligence on the Independents was sketchy, at best, and was practically nonexistent on the enemies of the political guerrillas and sworn enemies of the group. So if Bolan had barked up the wrong tree and wasn't really presenting any sort of threat, why not simply let him go about his business until they had reason to interfere? No, Bolan's arrival in Puerto Rico had obviously shaken up someone and the warrior meant to find out just who it was.

The pursuit continued along the narrow backstreets, and as traffic increased it became a more perilous journey. Within ten minutes they were back in the heaviest urban sections and the chase hadn't lost any intensity. It seemed almost surreal as other drivers who passed him looked at his bullet-riddled vehicle with expressions that ranged from mild curiosity to utter shock. A few more minutes elapsed and the motorcycles suddenly turned onto a side street that led south out of the city. Bolan continued following at a distance, now curious more than intent on catching the motorcyclists and dispensing some good old-fashioned street justice. Obviously they wanted him to tail them, and they were doing a good job of keeping far enough ahead so he could follow them, but not so close as to arouse his suspicions.

More trouble seemed to appear out of nowhere as Bolan realized he'd picked up a tail. He wondered for a moment if they had put a car on him in the rear position, but then he dismissed it. This driver was no professional. If the enemy bothered to set up a way to box him in, they wouldn't send anyone so sloppy. His pursuer had little to no experience in the fine art of inconspicuously tailing a vehicle. An amateur all the way, and that meant someone who could get in harm's way.

Bolan's eyes alternated between the motorcyclists and the tail. Eventually they got off the highway exit and proceeded along a dusty road. The Executioner figured if he was headed into an ambush, this would be the perfect spot, and this time he meant to be prepared. He waited until the dust obscured his vehicle at both front and rear, then steered off the road and maneuvered into a thick stand of brush. Bolan bailed from the driver's seat and scrambled over the rear seat to the storage area. He saw the trail of the vehicle that had been following him continue past without slowing—the driver hadn't even spotted him.

Yeah, definitely an amateur.

Bolan retrieved several 30-round detachable box magazines loaded with 5.56 mm NATO rounds. They fit the next item he withdrew from the weapons bag, a carbine version of the Fabrique Nationale FNC. The weapon packed the versatility of a full-auto assault rifle in a virtual submachine gun profile. In fact, the FNC was often mistaken for the HK33 at first glance, but the two were quite different in a number of ways. Bolan had come to prefer this assault weapon above almost all others because of its reliability in close-quarters combat.

The Executioner performed a final check on the weapon before locking and loading. Then he placed it on the seat, backed from cover and onto the road, and proceeded in the direction he'd been heading. Now he had both the enemy and the unknown tail in front of him; they would either be surprised to encounter each other or realize both of them had been duped. In any respect, they had made the mistake of putting the ball in play.

And the Executioner was a veteran of this particular game.

THE RED-CLAY ROAD, pockmarked with ruts and divots, terminated at a copse of tall pinnate palms that formed a natural canopy over it. From this point it appeared to end, but through the windshield Bolan observed the fresh tire tracks that seemed to pass into the dark, variegated brush beyond that point. The soldier put the SUV in Reverse, traveled roughly fifty feet, then downshifted to Drive and gunned the engine.

The tires churned rocks and dust in their wake as the SUV lurched into motion and crashed through the brush into a natural, jungle darkness beyond. As Bolan had suspected, there was a man-made road beyond the concealed entrance and through the gloom ahead he could see a wood-and-barbed-wire gate positioned between thick, makeshift posts. The soldier poured on the speed and would have crashed through the gate, but was stopped short by the sudden appearance of the vehicle that had tailed him.

Bolan swung the wheel to the right to avoid crashing into the side of the car, but the move put him on a collision course with a massive tree trunk. He leaned on the brakes, but the tires found no purchase on the slick, mossy ground and the front end of the SUV slammed into the tree hard enough to deploy the air bags. Bolan snatched the FNC off the seat and exited the vehicle at the same time as the other driver bailed. He turned the weapon in the driver's direction.

The Executioner took in the entire scene within a

heartbeat and his combat senses negated the petite, dark-haired woman as a threat. The half-dozen armed men approaching from the opposite side of the gate, however, were another matter entirely. Bolan managed to reach the young beauty just in time to drag her down behind the cover of her sedan. The air around them came alive with a metal storm of rounds that whizzed overhead like a horde of angry bees.

"Who the hell *are* you?" she demanded.

Bolan grimaced. "Later. Now get in."

She tensed at first, standing her ground, but let Bolan haul her into the front seat. The woman got her legs in under her own power before Bolan slid behind the wheel and whipped the nose of the sedan into a collision course with the gate. As he picked up speed, Bolan stuck the FNC out the driver's window and triggered it one-handed to keep the gunners' heads down. The sedan, while small, did a fair job of smashing into the makeshift gate and ripping the pine frame from the uprights, which were obviously dry-rotted from the elements.

Bolan rammed into one of the gunmen who didn't get out of his path quite fast enough. The guy's head connected hard with the windshield at an awkward angle and produced an audible crack. Bolan swung the muzzle of the FNC into acquisition on two more targets and snapped off a few short bursts. Brass shells ejected from the weapon and tinkled against the metal body of the sedan, followed by screams of agony as the pair fell under the Executioner's marksmanship.

The soldier ordered the woman to keep her head down as he rolled out of the seat and away from the vehicle. He landed on his feet, pivoted in the direction of the remaining trio of shooters and swept them with a sustained volley. One man took three rounds to the pelvis and another took two rounds to the abdomen. The remainder of the 5.56 mm slugs cut through the chest, neck and head of the last target, and a gory, crimson mess exploded through midair as the man's corpse folded to the jungle floor.

Shouts and the sounds of booted feet approaching signaled it was time for the Executioner to make his exit. Under normal circumstances he would have stayed to fight, but he now had a bystander to consider, one who obviously had no idea upon what sort of mess she'd stumbled, and he couldn't risk getting her killed. There would be another place and time, another battleground on his terms. Bolan entered the SUV, grabbed the weapons bag and sprinted for the sedan.

The woman had taken her place behind the wheel now, and Bolan managed to leap through the open window of the passenger door just as she jammed the stick shift into Reverse and hauled out of there. His head ended up in her lap, but she seemed oblivious, apparently more intent on getting out of there as fast as the four-cylinder engine could take them. By the time Bolan had righted himself in the seat, the woman had cleared the tree line and picked up speed as she struggled to keep the wheels on the slick, dusty surface of the road. Twice she almost lost it, and Bolan finally looked over his shoulder to verify they weren't being followed before he spoke to her.

"You can ease off. We're in the clear."

"You want to tell me who you are now?" she demanded. "And what the hell all that was about?"

"It depends," Bolan replied easily. "You want to tell me why you were following me?"

"I didn't know I was following you," she snapped. Then she looked at him, noticed his easy smile and added, "I mean…at least until I realized you were following the guys on the motorcycles."

"What's your business with them?" Bolan asked.

"Uh-uh," she countered. "I've given you something, now you tell me what you're doing here and what your beef is with those men."

"I'm afraid that's classified."

"So you're with the American government." She smacked the steering wheel. "Hot damn! I *knew* I was onto a scoop!"

"You're a reporter?"

She nodded. "Guadalupe La Costa, AP out of Miami. I'm here on temporary assignment for a couple of years."

"Let me guess. You were at the rally the other night."

"You're damn skippy we were," she said.

"We?"

"My cameraman and I. We were right smack-dab in the middle of that shooting gallery. Hell, my producer even added a few gray hairs being down there. Oh, Julio's going to pass a rainbow-colored Twinkie when he finds out I went on this excursion without him." She patted a digital camera on the seat next to her. "Boy, did I get some good shots."

Bolan reached down, popped open the camera's flash drive compartment and removed the memory card.

"Hey!"

"The name's Stone," he said.

"What the fu—?"

"And I'm sorry, but I can't afford to have my mug splattered all over the front page. You can have whatever's left back once I've removed any images of me. I promise."

"Ever hear of freedom of the press?"

Bolan's voice took an edge. "Not when it interferes with my op, La Costa. And this is too important to let you screw it up so early in the game."

"How about giving me the scoop?"

"If there's one to give, I'll see what I can do," Bolan said. "Why not tell me what you know about our friends back there? Are they part of the Independents?"

La Costa expressed suspicion. "What makes you think those animals were part of *Los Independientes?*"

"That's a question, not an answer. Try again."

"Look, I'm not sure who they are, but I'm positive they're not with the Independents."

"My intelligence contacts say otherwise," Bolan replied.

La Costa shrugged. "You asked my opinion, I'm giving it to you. Those guys are bad, no doubt, but they aren't part of the Independents. I've been following up on a whole lot of leads since the other night, and everything I can come up with says they're not part of any political party in the country, official or unofficial."

"What do you mean?"

"I don't know yet," La Costa replied. "I was trying to find out when you got in the middle of investigation."

"There is no investigation," Bolan said flatly. "Not anymore. It ends now. Whoever's behind this attack has created a political and social firestorm, one that could turn ugly for everyone in Puerto Rico. The situation is too hot for me to allow you or anyone else to get in the way."

"How do you propose to stop me?"

"Tie you up, if necessary."

"Sounds kinky," La Costa replied. "But it'll have to wait."

"Fine with me. But you still haven't explained where you came up with the idea someone on the outside is behind this."

"Because neither of the radical politicos in this region operates this way," she said. "They've protested, even turned riotous and been squelched by local police, but an outright act of violence is totally out of character. Plus the fact, I know the head of the Independents personally. He would never do anything like this."

"Maybe his people planned it without his knowledge?"

La Costa shook her head with a snort. "Not likely. Believe me, Stone, I've been here for over a year reporting the news. I know everyone who's anyone. This isn't his style."

"Then maybe you can help me after all."

"How?"

Bolan grinned. "By making an introduction. Maybe if I hear it from this guy myself I can help clear him and his people."

"I'm not sure he'd meet with you."

"Never know until you try," Bolan replied. "Besides, it's better than being tied up in some strange hotel room until I can clear this up by more indirect methods."

La Costa laughed. "Says who?"

CHAPTER THREE

Despite Guadalupe La Costa's reservations, Mack Bolan eventually convinced her to take him to the leader of the Independents.

Something made him admire this young, spirited reporter. She didn't take any sass and gave out plenty, and she seemed genuinely concerned about reporting the truth no matter how brutal it might seem. Bolan could admire that kind of gutsy determination and devotion to duty; he understood those traits because they were so much a part of what made up his own identity. He related to La Costa and in large part that contributed to her attractiveness.

"The Independents are led by a man named Miguel Veda," La Costa told him as Bolan drove them to the man's seaside home northwest of San Juan.

It seemed Veda lived off the coast. Although he had other business interests to the degree that his political interests seemed more entrepreneurial—or those of a raving lunatic who really cared little about the future of Puerto Rico—La Costa's description of Veda's estate left Bolan with the impression business was good. When they finally arrived at the place, about a thirty-minute drive from the hotel, the big American's assessment was confirmed.

Two uniformed security men checked their credentials and La Costa's vehicle, including looking in the trunk and running a mirror the length of the undercarriage, before an escort team in a golf cart led them up the driveway. More armed security ushered them into the house. They were shown to a spacious office and library. Most of the furniture looked early twentieth century, although some peculiar-looking pieces were interspersed among the predominant decor. Everything here looked as if it had been chosen with regard to functionality, with very little gaudiness apparent. Everything had to serve some practical purpose; Veda obviously didn't buy anything for its artistic value.

"You're damned right he doesn't," La Costa replied in agreement when Bolan verbalized the sentiment. "Miguel's the kind of man who doesn't feel he should squander his hard-earned money on overpriced trinkets while his people are starving."

"Miguel," Bolan echoed. "You're on a first-name basis?"

La Costa looked abashed. "Have been. He gave me my first big break down here. It's not easy being both a woman and a minority in the press, even today. Especially working in Puerto Rico, where the male ego is fragile enough that machismo is still a mainstay of the culture."

"I'd think something like that would prove a real turnoff for someone as strong-willed as you."

La Costa smiled and winked. "You have no idea."

A set of double doors on the far side of the office, opposite from where they had been shown in, swung open and cut short their dialogue. The man who stepped into the room walked slowly with a visible limp. From what little La Costa had told him about Veda's activities, Bolan didn't figure that the man could have been a day over fifty, but *this* man looked twice that age. Unkempt white hair grew in tufts along the sides of his head and yet curled oddly into neatly trimmed sideburns that ended midear level. Liver spots were visible on his exposed arms and the once-dark skin had taken on an odd, yellowish tint when the light hit it a certain way. His face possessed a gaunt quality, but still had more health and glow than the rest of his body appeared to have, which was a bit of a surprise to Bolan.

Two muscular men wearing pistols in shoulder holsters followed Veda and took up positions where they could react quickly should any threat present itself.

"Lupe," Veda cried, shuffling over to her and bending to accept a kiss on the cheek.

Veda turned to Bolan, then extended his hand.

Bolan felt as if he were shaking the limb of a skeleton. "I'm—"

"Colonel Stone, U.S. Army," Veda finished. "Yes, Colonel, I knew of your arrival practically from the moment you stepped foot in Puerto Rico."

Bolan held an impassive expression. "You seem well-informed."

Veda chuckled as he sat behind his desk. "It's a job requirement in my business."

"Which is?"

"Come now, Colonel, there's no need to be coy," Veda said pleasantly. "I know who you are, so it stands to reason I would know why you're here."

"And why's that?"

"Because of the incident the other night at the rally."

Bolan nodded in way of prompting him to go on.

"I'm sure that Governor Hernandez's advisors are telling him that either the Independents or our contenders are to blame," Veda continued, "but I can assure you that such allegations are entirely false."

"Really," Bolan interjected. "Why?"

"Because despite whatever rumors you might have heard to the contrary, we are not violent militants. In fact, I do not believe in violence as means to an end, whether for political purposes or otherwise. I believe in peaceful resolution to conflict."

"You can't ever hope your views will be recognized through standard political channels while your group is sanctioned."

"On the contrary, it is *because* we are under sanctions that is at the very heart of these matters. You see, Colonel, supporters for the idea of statehood for Puerto Rico have dwindled over recent years for a good number of reasons, the instability of the economy and devaluation of the U.S. dollar not the least of them. This has caused significant increased support for our cause. The current party in power knows that, just as they know that their own influence falters."

"So if you know that they're touting propaganda about your efforts and the Independents, why not set the record straight through peaceful means?"

Veda laughed outright this time. "We do, Colonel Stone, we do! And that's why I can promise you that we had nothing to do with this. Someone is out to destabilize Puerto Rico because it is a commonwealth and protectorate of the United States."

"And?"

"What sense does it make for a group like ours to conduct violent acts against the established government, when by their nature those same acts would topple our wish to be independent and promulgate further interference by the United States? In fact, I surmise such acts would force the president to invoke emergency powers by military means. Your presence here is proof enough of that. Is it not?"

Veda gave pause there, probably so Bolan had some time to absorb it.

The soldier locked gazes with Veda. He'd learned long ago how to spot deception in people. What he saw now made him wonder if Veda was one of the biggest liars alive or if he actually spoke the truth. Bolan decided to give the guy the benefit of the doubt, play a card and see what happened.

"I never really bought the whole political motive from the start," Bolan ventured.

"And well you shouldn't, Colonel."

Bolan didn't miss a beat. "But what I haven't heard you do is offer any hard evidence your people aren't behind the attack."

"From where I stand, I can offer no such proof," Veda conceded. "Only my word. And assurances that those you encountered earlier today are not members of the Independents."

"How did you know about that?" La Costa asked.

Veda's expression softened and he offered La Costa an ingratiating smile. "My dear, you know I have eyes and ears everywhere in Puerto Rico. Why should this surprise you?"

La Costa didn't have an answer for him.

Veda turned to Bolan. "Colonel, when I first heard of your arrival I wasn't the least bit inclined to cooperate with you. But now that we've spoken and I've seen you're only interested in getting to the truth, I offer you every resource at my disposal."

"I appreciate that," Bolan said warily. "But I think you'll understand if I decline your offer for the moment."

"I understand. You must maintain some air of neutrality. But consider the offer standing for the duration of your time here."

Bolan nodded, "Thanks."

"As to other places to look, might I suggest you start within the very place this thing started?"

"The governor's office?"

"You sound surprised," Veda said. "Is it so hard to believe? Who else stands to suffer considerable losses if political parties pressing for an independent Puerto Rico gain popularity? The idea of becoming a country of our own is known in many circles as progress. But I and my colleagues wish to do this peacefully and legally. We still lack resources and the support of the strongest backers, those with the money and political clout, primarily due to the current government's disinformation campaign against any group preaching independence be it by nationalism, secession or otherwise."

"You're proposing the government's in bed with terrorists," Bolan said evenly.

"I'm proposing that *someone* inside Governor Hernandez's office is in bed with terrorists," Veda countered.

Bolan grasped the tight, aching muscles on the back of his neck and considered Veda's proposal. In other circumstances it would have sounded utterly preposterous, but in this case he could see its feasibility. Whoever hit the rally, and Bolan was fairly convinced he could rule out anyone working for Veda at the moment, would have given an insider exactly the leverage they needed to point the finger at the Independents or another group like it, not to mention all the political ammo they needed to take the attention off themselves. That left just motive and Bolan could think of only one.

If terrorists could get Puerto Rico out from under American control, it would provide them not only with a significant financial resource, but would also establish a strategic stronghold and base of operations from which to launch strikes against the continental U.S. and her allies. It was unthinkable, but not implausible.

"Let's suppose your theory has some merit," Bolan finally said. "Where would I start looking? I can't very well start poking my nose into the affairs of the Puerto Rican government's office without raising eyebrows. I'd be demoted and transferred to some remote post for the duration of my career."

"Having once been a soldier myself, I can empathize with the predicament such actions might cause you, Colonel. So in good faith, I would like to suggest that you look in Las Mareas."

Bolan looked askance at La Costa.

"On the other side of the island," she offered.

The soldier returned his attention to Veda. "That's all?"

"It is, I am afraid, all that I can offer you," Veda replied. "To say any more would violate the…ah, air of neutrality we spoke of. Now if you don't mind, I have a tremendous amount of work here that demands my attention."

Veda looked to the two guards, who took a couple of

steps forward. Bolan knew the conversation was over, so he nodded at La Costa and the pair rose.

As they turned to leave, Veda said, "My men will conduct you safely back to your vehicle and off the premises."

"We can manage," Bolan said.

"It's our pleasure," Veda replied in a nonnegotiable tone.

When they were off Veda's estate and on their way back to the hotel, Bolan said, "Well, he told us something but nothing."

La Costa smiled. "That's Miguel. Do you trust him now?"

"No." Bolan glanced at her. "But I'm not sure why. Not yet."

"Well, I tried," La Costa said. "I'll admit he *was* acting a bit strange."

"He's sick, isn't he?"

La Costa nodded. "Very. Pancreatic and liver cancer. The doctors have given him less than a year. So was it something he said, maybe, that makes you mistrustful of him?"

Bolan shook his head. "Instinct."

"That's all?"

"That…and the fact there's someone following us," Bolan replied as he scanned the rearview mirror.

AS SOON AS THE VISITORS departed, Miguel Veda considered his options. He hadn't wished to tell the American as much as he had, but he also knew if he'd refused to cooperate that Stone would hound his every waking moment. He didn't need those kinds of distractions. Not now. Not when the time was coming so close to his plan. His final plan. The plan that would bring independence to Puerto Rico, make her a free nation.

Not that he stood much chance to see that day. The cancer had eaten at his internal organs so rapidly that even the best physicians on the island couldn't offer much hope. By the time they detected it, he'd already advanced to late-stage sarcoma that had metastasized to most of his abdominal organs. He'd spent hundreds of thousands of dollars to fly in some of the greatest oncologists in the world, but even they could offer little comfort. None of that really mattered now, however. The only thing that mattered was going through with his plans.

Veda felt sick having to lie to La Costa. He didn't really give a damn for the man named Stone or his precious American government. America. Why the very word was like a monosyllabic curse that left the same foul aftertaste as if he'd imbibed sewer water. But La Costa had been straight with Veda from the beginning, and he couldn't imagine what she would say—even what she would do for that matter—if she uncovered his deceptions. Well, best to put it from his mind. He had an important call to make.

Veda ensured none of his staff were within eavesdropping range and then secured the doors to his office. He returned to his desk, picked up the phone and dialed a number from memory. A gruff voice on the other end answered with a "Yeah" on the third ring. Veda identified himself and a few minutes ticked by before another voice came on the line.

Veda recognized the smooth, cultured tones of Siraj Razzaq. Still, they had to exchange their code words for the day. Veda felt foolish playing these silly games of secrecy, yet he knew the importance of pleasing Razzaq.

"What have you to report?" the terrorist leader asked.

"Well, you already know the attack in the square was successful," Veda replied. "But I think someone may be onto our plans."

"Who?"

"A U.S. Army colonel by the name of Stone. He's been to the governor's office, and he's engaged some of my men firsthand."

"You mean my men," Razzaq interjected. "The Americans have a saying—'don't forget where your bread is buttered.'"

Veda considered a flippant reply at first, but bit it back in afterthought. It hadn't been easy making alliances with a member of a cell within the New Revolutionary Justice Organization. He hadn't lied when telling La Costa and Stone he abhorred violence as a means to gain a political end, but the cancer eating away at his body had transformed Veda's optimism into pragmatism. The fact the NRJO stood to benefit significantly from this unholy alliance was too obvious to even bear mentioning, but it had come to the point that Veda saw this as the only way to get things done. Once he'd left this life, he didn't think any of his subordinates would be able to hold things together for long. There would be infighting after his death, followed by a complete breakdown in order. Ultimately, that would lead to dissolution of the Independents. Veda saw the NRJO and its offer as the only remaining option.

It wasn't a decision he'd come to lightly, and it had proved most difficult because he had to maintain a business-as-usual air around his people. They could never know about this alliance. Never.

"As you prefer," Veda finally said. "My point is that this new development stands to create a complication for both of us."

"I've just received word that one of our subposts near the city did not check in at their appointed time."

"Yes, I was led to believe he had a violent encounter with one of your small-ops units."

"And how did he connect them back to you?"

"I'm not sure," Veda lied. Thus far, he'd managed to keep La Costa's existence under wraps and he intended to keep it that way.

"What did you tell him?"

"Nothing, of course, other than that I do not believe in using violence to gain political advantage."

Razzaq produced an almost scoffing laugh. "Yes, that tired old story. However, I do know it is a conviction you're passionate about. That should have been convincing enough for him. What do you think he will do next?"

"I know exactly what he'll do." Veda paused, savoring the moment. "I sent him to Las Mareas. I'm sure he'll travel there by vehicle. That will give you time to implement a reactionary plan and take him down before he gets there."

Razzaq didn't say anything for some time. Then, "That should do nicely. Yes, my friend, well done."

Veda felt sickened by the mere intimation he could be friends with a man like Razzaq. "I figured whether you send someone to intercept or simply order your people there to await his arrival, which I believe will be imminent, you should have no trouble eliminating him."

"And what of the rest of our plan? Are your preparations nearing completion?"

"I should need a few more days, at most, which is still well ahead of your timetable."

"That is good news. Very good news, indeed."

Veda considered not even bringing up the last thing, but he felt there wouldn't be a more opportune time, particularly since he had Razzaq in good spirits.

"You are still committed to our agreement, yes?"

"You refer to your longevity."

"You know I am."

"No need to go on the defense, my friend. I may not have the most endearing virtues, but one of them is that I'm a man of my word. Your personal affairs will be addressed when the time comes."

"I would hope so. And now if you'll excuse me I have other matters that need my attention. I will be in touch when all is readied."

Veda hung up without waiting for Razzaq to say goodbye, then leaned back in his chair and rubbed his eyes. They burned and itched, partly from exhaustion and partly from the pain medication. He checked his watch and realized the time had come to take what he'd christened his "comfort cocktail." He reached into his desk drawer to remove the pill bottles. He poured a glass of water from the crystal set on a nearby tray, then dutifully swallowed the three-pill combination that enabled him to function.

What Veda appreciated more about the medication was it masked some of the internal feelings, not those derived from the disease ravaging his organs, but the more foul aspirations of his soul. To have allied himself with the NRJO went against nearly everything he'd fought for these many years. This only served to remind him just how desperate he'd become to see it through.

One day his countrymen would curse him, but he saw a bright future—one beyond the boundaries of the short-term—where a united and independent Puerto Rico would one day immortalize his name.

CHAPTER FOUR

The tail initiated when Bolan and La Costa were no more than a mile outside Veda's estate and maintained a discreet distance on the return trip to San Juan. As Bolan swung into the small drive and stopped beneath the overhang in front of the hotel, the other vehicle edged to the curb about half a block back. It was still early afternoon, so traffic didn't clog the thoroughfare, and a minute adjustment to the side mirror earlier afforded the soldier a direct line of sight.

"Are they still there?" La Costa asked, tension in her voice.

"Yeah." Bolan unbuckled his seat belt. "Stay here."

"But—"

"No buts, stay here."

Bolan left the car, walked around the front of the vehicle and pushed through the revolving door that led into the hotel foyer. He walked straight to the courtesy phone and dialed his room. Jack Grimaldi answered on the first ring.

"It's me," Bolan said. "I've picked up watchers."

"Friendly?" Grimaldi asked, voice immediately alert.

"Not sure yet," Bolan said. "I need to know their real interest. They're in a late-model, silver Toyota. I've also picked up a reporter named La Costa. I need you to come down here, go straight out front where her car's parked. Blue Toyota. Get behind the wheel and drive away. Keys are in the ignition."

"Where to?"

Bolan thought on it a moment. "Airport. When you get there, requisition us a light chopper. Where's your rental?"

"Hotel garage, ground floor. White Ford Escape. Keys are under the front wheel well in a magnetized case. What's your angle?"

"If they follow you, they're after La Costa. If they don't, then their only interest is in me. Either way, any contact will be on my terms."

"Understood."

"Out here."

The soldier dropped the phone in the cradle, already formulating a plan of action as he went out the back door of the hotel to the open-air, two-story parking garage. He went straight to the SUV, retrieved the key, got behind the wheel and left the garage. Bolan checked his watch, confident in the timing, and swung in behind the enemy's sedan just as Grimaldi pulled from the curb. The enemy's sedan left the curb to enter the flow of traffic. Bolan saw his opportunity and pulled out behind it; obviously, their interest lay in La Costa, and the soldier felt a bit of responsibility for her since she'd agreed to take him to Veda.

Bolan waited until their vehicle had entered the thoroughfare before driving the nose of his SUV into the rear of the fender at the seam of the driver's door.

The jolt caught the wheelman off guard, the surprise evident on his face even as Bolan backed up a foot, then went EVA with Beretta in fist and leveled the pistol at the driver's head. He'd hit that target with a very specific purpose in mind. He'd damaged the sedan in such a way that the door would jam against the fender if the man attempted to open it. The pair were effectively trapped since the passenger's door would not open as it was now wedged against the rear bumper of the car behind, which they had parked.

"Stay right there, hands clear!" Bolan ordered.

The two men complied and Bolan quickly sized them up. Both Hispanic males, about equal in physical size, clean-shaved and with hard expressions that spoke of experience combined with training. If he hadn't known better, Bolan would have sworn he was looking at a couple of federal agents—maybe FBI or U.S. Marshals—given the way they carried themselves. Well, at least they weren't extremists, because if they had been Bolan knew his warnings would have gone unheeded. No, these weren't fanatics; they had too much of a sense of self-preservation to try anything while he had them at gunpoint.

Bolan ignored the honking of angry motorists who had to maneuver around the crash site. He kept his eyes on the pair, watchful for movement while he occasionally scanned the area surrounding them for any sort of backup. Convinced they were operating alone, Bolan approached the driver's door until the muzzle of the Beretta came within a few yards of the man's head but still afforded Bolan a clear field of fire in the passenger's direction.

"Which of you boys would like to explain?" Bolan said.

"We mean you no harm," the driver replied.

"Could have fooled me. I saw you the moment you picked up my tail. You obviously aren't interested in me, so that means you're after the woman. I want to know why."

"We work for the Internal Security office," the passenger protested.

"Fonseca sent you?"

He nodded. "We're just following orders, Colonel."

Bolan gestured toward the driver. "Show me ID. Slowly."

The man reached into his jacket pocket. If these guys were legit—and Bolan had the sneaking suspicion they wouldn't have made up such a ridiculous story on the fly—neither of them would try drawing down on him. The driver held his ID card out the window for inspection. Bolan took it from him, perused it for any hint of forgery, then flipped the holder back through the window, satisfied it was the real thing.

Bolan holstered his pistol. "What's Fonseca's interest in the woman?"

"She's been consorting with known political criminals," the passenger answered.

Bolan frowned. "I wouldn't put it that way."

"What way would *you* put it?"

"That you should drop it," Bolan replied with a hard edge to his voice.

"Mr. Fonseca—"

"Is out of line sending you to tail her. I'm here operating under the authority of Governor Hernandez. You go back and tell your boss I said to remind him of that. And no more covert ops against the woman."

"We got orders."

"Like I said, drop it."

Bolan didn't wait for any further arguments. He returned to the SUV, reversed easily from his contact with the sedan and swung into traffic. He checked the side mirror once and caught the pair of stony faces watching him go, glanced again in the rearview to make sure they didn't follow him and then pointed his vehicle in the direction of the airport. He turned on the wipers as an early evening rain had begun to fall while the sun dipped toward the horizon.

Something didn't make sense here. Why would Fonseca tell Bolan about Veda and the Independents and then put a pair of his men on La Costa's tail when he knew his tip would have to lead Bolan right to her? The soldier didn't believe for a second that Fonseca didn't foresee his information would lead the Executioner straight into a hornet's nest. For one, he could hardly have called Fonseca's intelligence leads solid. If he knew about Veda already, why not just send Bolan straight to the source? Moreover, why wouldn't he mention someone like La Costa as a potential lead? No, Bolan was beginning to see a lot more at work here than met the eye.

From this point on, he knew he couldn't afford to take anything in Puerto Rico at face value. It wouldn't have been the first time the corruption went deep within the halls of political power. Bolan's instinct told him somewhere along the way something, or *someone,* had gone awry inside Governor Hernandez's political circle. Maybe the tale Veda had spun for him about the disinformation campaign within the present governing body wasn't such a preposterous idea after all. Well, one way or another he'd get to the bottom of it.

And then Mack Bolan would deal with it in his own unique way.

"ANY IDEA WHY the governor's security advisor would have an interest in you?" Bolan asked La Costa as the pair stood on the tarmac at Marín International.

"No."

"Those the cats who were following us?" Grimaldi asked.

Bolan nodded to his friend and then pinned La Costa with a searching gaze. "If there's something you know and you haven't told me, it's time to come clean."

La Costa's expression hardened. "I've told you everything I know. Okay? I told you about the Independents, I took you to see Veda and I've even risked my job, since I've been out carousing with you and I'm three hours overdue at the studio. I don't know what the hell else you want from me."

"Nothing, not a thing. I appreciate all your help, as does your country." Bolan handed her a card. "In fact, if you get any trouble with your employer, just tell them to call that number and ask for Hal."

La Costa stared at it a moment and then looked up. "The U.S. Justice Department?"

Bolan shrugged. "I have a few friends."

"Yeah."

"Now I have a plane to catch."

Grimaldi took the cue and climbed into the requisitioned civilian version of the OH-58 Kiowa on which he'd done a preflight while waiting for the Executioner.

Bolan put out his hand. "It's been a pleasure, La Costa. Good luck with your story."

"What?" La Costa looked at his hand and blinked. "You mean that's it?"

"What's it?"

"I mean, that's just it?"

"What were you expecting?" Bolan asked.

"Something," she replied. "Maybe some solid leads on my story, an exclusive…something!"

"Listen, La Costa, if Veda is right about someone high up in the government being dirty, and that same someone's on to you, that makes you a liability to my mission. I appreciate your help, but I didn't promise you anything and I don't have time to be yanking your butt out of harm's way at every turn."

Yeah, that was for sure. The numbers were running down, Bolan knew it, and he didn't have time to explain it to La Costa in detail. He couldn't allow her to get in any deeper.

"I'm sorry if I've somehow affected your sensibilities of fair play," Bolan told her, "but time is a resource luxury I don't have. And every minute we stand here arguing could turn into a cost in more human lives. Understand?"

La Costa stared him in the eyes a moment, then nodded. "Oh…yeah. I understand perfectly, Colonel."

She whirled on her heel and stomped toward her car. Bolan watched her a moment, then turned and boarded the helicopter. He pushed thoughts of the reporter from his mind. He really did feel a twinge of remorse because while he hadn't made a direct promise, he had implied a potential reward for her cooperation. Now he was taking to the skies and telling her she couldn't go along like an older brother telling the younger sibling she couldn't hang out with him.

By the time Bolan dropped into the copilot's seat and Grimaldi had the helicopter moving, La Costa's vehicle was nowhere to be seen. He donned the headset so he could communicate with the pilot.

"Whoa, Sarge," Grimaldi said immediately. "She did *not* look happy."

"She wasn't," Bolan said.

"Didn't like the travel arrangements, eh?"

"No."

"Well, Hal called while I was in preflight. Needs you to contact him ASAP."

Bolan nodded as he turned the receiver channel on his headset to the frequency that interfaced with a secure, onboard communication satellite uplink. He could only hope that Fonseca's goons would carry the message back to their boss and lay off the woman reporter. Deep down, his gut told him they would. It was the same gut feeling that told him that somehow he had neither seen nor heard the last of Guadalupe La Costa.

BY THE TIME La Costa arrived at the AP offices, Julio Parmahel had already packed the van and departed.

La Costa could see by the stern look on her producer's face, visible through the blinds spanning the office windows, that she'd really blown it this time. Well, who the hell gave a damn? She felt betrayed by the man she knew only as Colonel Stone and just rebellious enough that if her producer confronted her she'd likely lose her job for telling him exactly where he could shove his disapproval.

Fortunately, she managed to get to her desk, retrieve a bag from the bottom drawer where she kept a spare change of clothes and a toiletry bag, and beat feet out of the office before the man saw her. La Costa knew *exactly* where to find Parmahel as he'd probably gone with a sub—or by himself—to cover a small, red-carpet political fund-raiser. It took only one time circling the block before she spotted the van. To no surprise, she found her friend and colleague slumped with his head against the window and snoring loud enough for it to be audible outside the news van. She found more amusement in the fact he'd been sleeping long enough to fog part of the driver's window he used as a pillow.

La Costa rapped her knuckles on the van and startled Parmahel awake. He immediately rolled down the window when he recognized her.

"Well, where in the hell have you been?" he asked. He looked at his watch as he smacked his lips, his mouth dry from his nap. "You realize we were supposed to be on a segment almost half an hour ago?"

"Screw the segment," La Costa said through clenched teeth. "We got a much bigger story."

"Says who?"

"Me," she said. She tried to look over the window to see the gas gauge, but the angles were wrong. "How's this thing fixed for gas?"

"Just topped her off before I left."

"Good, we got a long trip ahead of us," she replied as she dashed around the front of the van.

When she'd jumped into the passenger seat, Parmahel asked, "Trip to where?"

"Las Mareas."

CODE NAME: AD-DARR. Mission: eliminate the American military officer attached to the Diplomatic Security Service.

For lesser men it would have been potentially impossible, but for Afif Ad-Darr—an expert in the killing arts—it was simply another job. Not that he underestimated the man calling himself Colonel Stone. Siraj Razzaq's spies inside the U.S. military hadn't been able to come up with a thing on Stone. According to their records, there was no Colonel Stone in any of the four major branches of the military or the U.S. Coast Guard. That meant either a covert, military operative or civilian black ops using a military cover.

As he stared through the open window of the bar at the rain-streaked streets of downtown Las Mareas, Ad-Darr wondered how this Stone's people could be so sloppy. After all, when providing a cover it seemed only natural that cover would be in place, so if someone did a routine personnel check they would find the person existed. By virtue of the fact this enigmatic Colonel Stone allegedly didn't exist at all troubled Ad-Darr. Would the American intelligence community be so careless? He didn't think so.

Maybe the record had been removed permanently from U.S. military personnel files when Stone went to work for the DSS. Unfortunately, Razzaq's connections didn't go wide or deep enough to get *that* kind of information, and Ad-Darr didn't consider it important enough to pay the hefty price it would probably require, not to mention he didn't have the time. Already the Americans were apparently ahead of the game and only Razzaq's puppet, the man named Veda, had managed to divert this Stone to Las Mareas, where he would be out of the way and Ad-Darr could deal with him neatly.

Although why Razzaq had agreed to work with that imbecile Veda was anyone's guess. Ad-Darr had been in the employ of this cell of the New Revolutionary

Justice Organization for many years now. Razzaq was legendary for spearheading such operations, and this one had proven to be no exception. A fully equipped base nestled in the swamplands of the East Gulf Coastal Plane of Georgia—the name of which escaped him at the moment—that boasted an army of nearly thirty men. Razzaq had ears all over America, with satellite areas spread throughout the United States that consisted of maybe one or two members, at most. Once firmly ensconced, Razzaq had turned his sites toward his plan for Puerto Rico. The independence of this island territory would prove to be a major coup for Razzaq. Perhaps he would be able even to unite the disaffected among their ranks and restore the former glory of their cause.

For now, Ad-Darr would draw consolation from performing the duty for which he'd earned his name. "Professional assassination" and "Ad-Darr" were practically synonymous terms. Whenever the NRJO wanted to make sure a mission succeeded, they called on him. It was a compliment to his craft, and one Ad-Darr didn't mind exploiting to maximum benefit. And benefit, he had. By his twenty-second birthday Ad-Darr had become a millionaire; by his twenty-fifth, a multimillionaire. What was the old saying: he was in the business of killing and business was good? Something to that effect.

Ad-Darr had also turned out to be the perfect tool because he'd been born in the United States. Technically, he was an American citizen, but in the depths of his soul he knew that was only a birthright of pure circumstance. No, at the very core Ad-Darr was Lebanese, and a Muslim. His brothers in Hezbollah were still in need. The war against the Americans, British and Israel had to survive, and their ability to set up a massive base in Puerto Rico from which to strike would indeed provide them distinct advantages in their war, not to mention the rich natural resources of this sizable island.

The NRJO was operating in America's own backyard, and they didn't even know it.

Ad-Darr smiled at the thought as he watched the rain consume everything, washing the streets clean of dirt and detritus from the lives of squalor lived here. Somewhere out there he would find this Colonel Stone, then Ad-Darr would conclude his business for the glory of his faith and heritage.

And the American would die a slow, painful death.

CHAPTER FIVE

While Jack Grimaldi would have preferred better weather, he managed to land the helicopter safely with only minutes to spare before the skies overhead released a warm and thunderous tropical downpour.

"Remind me next time to bring an umbrella," he told Bolan.

The Executioner didn't really have a retort, as his conversation with Brognola, albeit brief, had put him into a deep contemplation.

"We may have a problem," Brognola had told him.

"Lay it out," Bolan said.

"One of Bear's sniffer programs picked up that a computer query was performed on the military jacket we provided for your Colonel Stone cover." "Bear" was Aaron Kurtzman, Stony Man's resident computer wizard.

"You flagged it?"

"Well, we did what we would normally do, and that's simply to say the jacket is restricted only to eyes with a class six or higher security clearance. The troubling thing here is that this query came from *inside* a military facility, and what's worse is that because of the odd way the hacker tried to move around the system to get the information it came up as a null."

"In other words, I never existed."

"Right."

Bolan could hear the grimness and regret in Brognola's tone, and decided to go easy on the guy. "It's water under the bridge, Hal. I'd concentrate on finding out who made the query and not worry about my cover. I'd have to guess after my little run-in with some hostiles earlier today my cover doesn't mean much now anyway."

"Sorry, Striker," Brognola said.

"Don't be."

"What about you? Everything okay?"

"Peachy if I can just figure out what's really going on here."

"Anything we can do to help?"

"I'd like Bear to dig a bit deeper into the staff in Governor Hernandez's office, particularly Alvaro Fonseca."

Bolan then elaborated on his encounter with Fonseca's men and his meeting with Veda.

"That doesn't make sense," the Stony Man chief said when Bolan had finished. "Governor Hernandez requested this intervention and in complete agreement with the president. Why would Fonseca try to undermine that?"

"I don't know, but I need you to give me something more," Bolan said. "Preferably something I can use for leverage if the need arises."

"We'll get on it right away."

"I'll reconnect for it when I can."

"Be careful, Striker."

"Roger. Out."

Bolan now reconsidered his conversation with the Stony Man chief as he and Grimaldi walked from the chopper to the small office east of the runway. They needed some wheels and spotted a row of cars, identical makes of American Chevy Aveos, aligned against one side of the makeshift tower and airport office.

Grimaldi jabbed his chin at them. "Wonder if any of those are for rent."

"Guess we'll find out," Bolan said.

"I imagine anything's for rent or sale here at the right price," the Stony Man pilot replied.

They stepped into the comparative coolness of the office that was divided into a few spacious cubicles against one wall, a row of offices opposite that and a long service counter just inside the double-door foyer. The furnishings were modern and the rooms spacious. There were also a few private areas where travelers could hook up to the Internet or make a phone call by credit card.

"Gentlemen, good evening!" the proprietor said. "How may I help you?"

Bolan held the man with an expression that implied he didn't have time for any nonsense. "Those cars out there for rent?"

"Of course, sure," the guy answered, rubbing his hands. "How long will you need one?"

"Not sure," Bolan replied. "Not more than a couple of days."

The man perfunctorily reached beneath the counter and brought out a few forms. It took only ten minutes to fill in the forms, pay the rental fee by cash and load the weapons bags from the chopper into the trunk. The rain began to let up as they headed toward Las Mareas, a mere five minutes away.

"So what's the plan?" Grimaldi asked after a few minutes of riding shotgun in silence.

Bolan's reply seemed a bit grim. "Truthfully, I don't have one yet. Veda didn't give me any indication as to who or what to look for, but I got the impression from the way he said it we wouldn't have to look hard."

"You think one of his people will make contact," Grimaldi said.

"Yeah."

"Can we trust Veda?"

Bolan shook his head. "No. But then again, who can we trust? The fact someone in Hernandez's office might be involved in this supports one of two theories. Either the local government here is planning a coup or Veda's lying to throw me off his trail."

"What's your gut tell you?"

"That theory two's the most plausible," Bolan replied. "But then my run-in with two of Fonseca's goons gave me pause to wonder. Now I have to at least consider the possibility Veda's on the level and there's an internal conspiracy at work here."

"Well, Veda does seem pretty well-informed, Sarge. He managed to know you were involved from practically the moment we arrived here."

"A guy like Veda has far-reaching contacts. His information could have come from anywhere."

"Yeah, except for the fact that only a few people outside of Stony Man even knew about your mission here, and all of them were inside Hernandez's office."

Bolan nodded. "Yeah, I thought about that, too. That's why what Veda told me makes so much sense."

"You think La Costa will be okay?"

"If Fonseca gets my message and backs off her, she'll probably be better off than we will."

They rode the remainder of the trip in silence. When they reached the town, the two men could see why the dinky airport didn't have much business. Las Mareas couldn't have been comprised of more than five or ten streets. As a barrio in Guayama—a municipality of less than fifty thousand—only one of those streets even sported a commercial section. Bolan almost drove past the half-lit sign that boasted "—OTEL" and swung precariously in the damp breeze. He slowed and gently pulled over, careful to pump the brakes so he didn't skid the vehicle into the high curb. The sharp, jagged edges that protruded from years of disrepair would have torn those cheap, economy tires to shreds like cat claws through tissue paper.

Grimaldi gave the place a once-over, peered at the sidewalk and then grinned at Bolan. "Think I'll wait here."

Bolan nodded and left the car. The rain had stopped, but the mock flagstone steps leading up to the narrow house were still slick with water. Bolan ascended them carefully and rapped on a screen door that had metal bars mounted to it. He didn't get any response, then noticed a thick piece of twine dangling to his right he hadn't seen before in the gloom. He gave it a yank and somewhere inside a bell jangled. Two minutes passed before Bolan signaled again and just about that time the inner door opened and a heavyset, middle-aged Hispanic woman stepped onto the porch.

"I'm coming. What you want?"

"I'm looking for someone," Bolan said, not even sure he knew why he was doing this. Something just told him it was right.

"You no want room?"

"No."

"Then go on, I don't want know your business."

As she started to turn and go inside, Bolan called, "Miguel Veda sent me."

The woman froze in her tracks. So, he'd been right about Veda—the guy had connections everywhere. She'd obviously been told to expect him; either that or he had a name the poor and disheartened of the country knew all too well. Whatever the case, she turned and cocked her head. She had an entirely different expression, a smile, and in one sense it almost creeped Bolan out.

At least she hadn't slammed the door in his face. "You come inside. It's wet out there." As she opened the door to admit Bolan, she nodded at Grimaldi, who she obviously noticed still sat in the car. "What about you friend? He come inside, no?"

As he followed the woman inside, Bolan shook his head. "He's kind of shy."

The woman led Bolan through a cramped hall littered with tables of knickknacks and other cheap junk. It took some flexibility and catlike grace to avoid knocking over something on at least one of the tables. After negotiating the obstacle course they made it into an equally cramped kitchen, where Bolan discovered a young, fair-skinned male sitting at a two-seat table in the corner. The man didn't even look at Bolan, but was satisfied to grunt and wave Bolan to the unoccupied chair.

As he sat, Bolan glanced at the woman, who didn't meet his gaze. Instead, she turned her attention to whatever she was cooking on the stove. The young guy looked like a first-rate hood, between the tattoos adorning both arms from the knuckles to the shoulders, and the gold tooth that glinted through slightly parted lips. A two-inch-wide line of hair ran Mohawk-style from front to back on an otherwise bald head. He wore baggy jeans and a white muscle shirt that was yellowed and tattered with age.

"You Stone?" he asked.

Bolan nodded.

"Okay, like, I got told that if you managed to find your way here that I was to tell you what you wanted to know."

The soldier considered that for a moment and then replied, "You work for Miguel Veda?"

The guy half laughed and half belched and then took a deep pull from the sweating, long-neck bottle. "Why do you care?"

Bolan tried an easy smile. "I like to know where my information's coming from."

The young man tried to look puffed up, his wiry frame all but puny against Bolan's combat-honed mass of sinew and muscle. He might have intimidated lesser men, but the Executioner didn't see him as a threat. The possibility existed, of course, the guy had ten or fifteen guns waiting in the next room, but Bolan knew if he gave even the slightest impression of weakness he would lose all respect. And maybe get his throat cut, too. He thought about an additional rejoinder, but he decided a steady look would suffice.

When the guy sensed Bolan wasn't a pushover, he said, "Yeah, okay, so who doesn't work for Miguel?"

"That isn't an answer."

"Yeah, okay. I work for Miguel. Whatever gets you through the day. Okay, man?"

The guy made some kind of gang sign, but Bolan let it pass. "You were going to tell me something."

"Yeah, sure," the guy said, taking another drink as if trying to build up courage. "You want to know who did the deed the other night in San Juan, no?"

"Yeah."

"It was them dudes down here. Guys over on the north side of town."

"What guys?"

"I don't know, man," the young man said irritability. "They some guys from the States, man. Guys from your home turf, man."

"Americans?"

"No, these no Americans. These guys aren't even white, man. These dudes are like al Qaeda or something."

The hairs stood on the back of Bolan's neck. "You're saying these men are terrorists?"

"I guess so, if that's what you say."

"It's not what I said, it's what *you* just said."

Bolan found this guy more frustrating by the moment. Right now, he didn't have time for games. He couldn't understand why Miguel Veda would have sent him on a wild-goose chase to Las Mareas if he didn't have anything to hide. Unless Veda was stalling, in which case that would've clinched the party leader's guilt. For now Bolan knew he'd have to find a way to work with this guy. Yet something deep in the Executioner's gut told him he could be walking into a trap.

Bolan shook his head. "Look, if you have information for me then spill. Otherwise, I'm out of here."

"Look, man, all I do is what Mr. Veda says. I tell you

only what I see, which is all I can tell you, 'cause I don't know nothing else."

"All right," Bolan said. "Tell me where I might find these terrorists."

"They have a club on the north side of town, I think." He leaned back in his chair and scratched his belly thoughtfully. "I can give you an address, but if you want it you got to pay."

"First the address and then the money," Bolan replied coolly.

The man stared at Bolan for a time and then finally shrugged, leaned forward, grabbed a pen from the table and quickly scribbled a barely legible address on a scrap of paper. He then set the pen down with a pronounced movement and promptly held out his hand. Bolan scooped up the paper, made sure he could read the address and then dug into his pocket. He handed the guy a fifty-dollar bill as he rose and turned to leave. Under other circumstances he might not have turned his back on a crew like this, but he didn't think they would try to burn him at this point. They had plenty of opportunities to take him out, and neither of them had given him any reason to suspect they would try something now. Bolan traversed the hallway as quickly as possible, went out the door and within a minute he and Grimaldi were headed for a barrio in uptown Guayama.

"FOR PITY'S SAKE!" Guadalupe La Costa snapped. "Will you step on it already, Julio? At the rate we're going I'll have grandkids before we get there."

"I've got it pegged now," Parmahel protested. "These things won't go over fifty-five miles per hour. If you'd like to get out and push, that might help."

La Costa thought about cursing him out with a string of obscenities, but she knew it wouldn't do any good. She considered apologizing, but then simply sighed, slid down the seat and closed her eyes. She was acting like a bitch and she knew it, but in her defense that damned Colonel Stone had utterly messed with her head. La Costa knew better than to have trusted him; she learned many years ago that most men eventually lied, cheated or just simply broke hearts. They couldn't help it—it was in their blood.

Julio had always been different though, which is probably why their partnership had worked out so well over the past year. In one way, she regretted the thought of parting company with Stone, but this story would make her career and she wasn't about to let anyone hold her back. Especially not some cocky and arrogant military type with a Neanderthal protective instinct.

Of course the possibility remained that she wouldn't find Stone in time, in which case she'd not only be out of a story, but also most likely a job. It still made sense on some level, however, to risk it. Beside the fact, she stood a pretty good chance of finding out what was going on without Stone's help, and if she came back with exclusive news and videotape her producer couldn't possibly be angry with her. Yeah, that was the answer. She had to come back with something really big and really juicy. How else to keep her job?

She opened her eyes just in time to catch the sign marking the city limits of Guayama.

At long last they had arrived!

"Well, it looks like we finally made it. Now all we have to do is find Stone."

"What's so important about this Colonel Stone?"

Parmahel asked. "I mean, it's not like the guy's going to tell you anything. He already screwed you over once. What makes you think he won't do it again?"

"My goodness, Julio. Haven't you learned anything working with me? You don't honestly think I'm going to let Stone rip me off from my story, do you? He told me I had to stay in San Juan, but you see how that worked out."

"Why do I get this strange feeling that you're getting us into something really messy and really dangerous?"

"I don't think it is dangerous," La Costa replied. She batted her eyelashes at Parmahel. "You don't honestly think I would jeopardize your life and mine on a whim."

Parmahel scratched absently at his neck. "Well, after working with you for this long I'm not exactly sure what kind of crazy stunts you might pull. And the last time I checked, there were guys with guns shooting at us."

"They weren't really shooting *at* us."

"Okay, my bad, they were shooting *around* us! Which is pretty much the same as shooting at us in my book."

"Where's your sense of adventure, Julio?"

"Guess I'm just addicted to breathing," he said.

La Costa chuckled and punched his arm. "Just stick with me, my friend. I'll show you the time of your life."

CHAPTER SIX

Guadalupe La Costa knew of only one person in all Guayama who would answer to Veda, and subsequently have the kind of information that Stone would seek.

La Costa knew him only as Frederico, a drunken and tattooed fool living in Las Mareas who would do anything for a quick buck. And usually did. Not that a little cash didn't go a long way in Puerto Rico—certainly way more than it did in the States. And if there was anything La Costa had it was cash. Actually, the AP compensated her pretty well. In addition to providing her travel expenses while she worked, they had also arranged for very affordable housing through coop apartment homes and condos. La Costa shared a two-bedroom apartment with another reporter who handled the night beat. This way, she was able to sock away a lot more than if she had a place on her own.

They found Frederico in his usual place, doing his usual drinking and scratching his rear and avoiding anything resembling hard labor, seated on the front porch of the run-down motel owned by his aged mother.

Frederico didn't look terribly happy to see her, and he seemed even less enthused when setting eyes on Julio Parmahel. La Costa would never have admitted it but she figured Frederico had somewhat of a crush on her, and he probably viewed Parmahel's presence as an infringement on his territory.

"Hello, Frederico," she said.

"What do you want?" He was slurring his words, and even in the dim porch light she could see his eyes were bloodshot.

She nodded toward the whiskey bottle on the small table next to his chair. "I see your tastes have moved up in the world. You must have come into some money recently, because you're not drinking that rotgut you normally do. And Canadian whiskey no less. Fancy, fancy. I don't suppose that money happened to come from a tall American who asks too many questions, did it?"

"What kind of a businessman would I be if I talk too much about my clients?" He belched.

"Frederico, you are disgusting," La Costa replied. "But unfortunately, we don't have time to go into proper etiquette and manners around a lady."

Frederico squinted. "Yeah, man, especially since I no see a lady here."

"I think I'll just let that one go by, since I know it's a bunch of false bravado anyway. What I need to know from you is real simple. What did he ask you and where did you send him?"

"Why should I tell you? Huh? What you do for me?"

"First, I won't ask any of my friends on the Guayama police to kick your head in the next time they catch you downtown." She produced a roll of money.

"Second, I have here what I'd bet is at least twice what he offered you."

Frederico grinned broadly as greed filled his eyes. "What was the question again?"

MACK BOLAN DROVE SLOWLY past the address he'd been provided and scoped out the area.

The address happened to be a club of some kind nestled in what he quickly surmised to be Guayama's red-light district. Pedestrians of every ethnicity hung out on the sidewalks, a good number of them obviously out to do nothing more than take in the sights. However, that left plenty who clearly had another purpose in mind. Some wore the clothing and colors and stances of gang members; some were out to sell flesh; some were simply out to peddle their wares, be it drugs, guns or knockoffs.

The soldier knew this scene all too well, but he wished he could have said otherwise. The vices of this area were no different than they would have been in any mid- to large-size city in America. Those who had spent their lives in unemployment and squalor—usually without equal access to opportunities in jobs and education—typified the majority of the denizens in this part of the world. Bolan knew it wasn't all bad. Puerto Rico boasted many beautiful and prosperous areas.

This just didn't happen to be one of them.

As they rolled past the club, Bolan pointed toward two big men who weren't standing close enough to the door to be bouncers. No, these men had been waiting, and to Bolan's trained eye had been waiting for some time. The fact they wore sunglasses and had rather long black hair, coupled with their custom-tailored suits, marked them as out of place as a pair of hippos in a petting zoo. Neither Bolan nor Grimaldi could tell if the pair of watchers had taken more than a casual interest in their car.

Bolan continued along the thoroughfare without changing speed and proceeded another two blocks. He turned right onto a side street, drove one block and made another right. Along this part of the north side commercial area all the businesses were dark. Bolan pulled to the curb and stopped. He killed the engine before going EVA and opening the trunk. From the weapons bag he retrieved his Beretta 93-R nestled in the shoulder holster. He donned the leather rig and fastened it down, then procured an MP-5 K machine pistol.

By the time Grimaldi had joined him, Bolan had also withdrawn a Benelli M-1014 combat shotgun. Adopted by the Marine Corps in 2001, the weapon had proved itself as a reliable and powerful ally against the war on terror. And in the hands of Grimaldi, it would do so once again.

"I take it this means you have a plan in mind?" Grimaldi asked, arching an eyebrow.

"I'm thinking soft probe," Bolan said. "But I want to be ready if it goes hard."

"What's my role?"

"You're going to take the wheel, give me fifteen minutes and then drive past the front of the club. Have the window down and be ready in case I have to come out swinging."

"What's the shotgun for?" Grimaldi asked, as he took the Benelli from Bolan.

The soldier smiled. "A hasty exit."

Bolan turned and crossed the street, heading for the back of the club. He wasn't exactly sure what to expect, but he couldn't think of a better way to get answers. If the information he'd bought didn't pan out, it would mean a dead end. Still, he knew only one of two possibilities lay in wait beyond the walls of that club—there were terrorists operating in Puerto Rico or Miguel Veda had managed to dupe him into a trap. Something about this setup told Bolan he was walking into a trap anyway. It didn't bother him—he'd walked into them before.

The waist-high cinder-block wall didn't pose any obstacle to him any more than the ten-foot wrought-iron gates beyond it. Within a minute, Bolan reached the rear entrance of the club. The door was locked, so the soldier went to work on jimmying the catch using his boot knife. It didn't take long before he gained access; the door didn't even have a dead bolt. Apparently, the proprietor didn't worry about break-ins. That told Bolan whoever owned the club relied more on human security.

The rear door opened onto a dimly lit, narrow hallway with a red carpet, red walls and overhead blue lightbulbs. A number of doors, all of them closed, lined both sides of the hallway. Before Bolan could investigate further, he spotted two behemoths heading toward him.

As the first guy got close, he reached inside his jacket and Bolan reacted with an offensive posture. Knife still in hand, the soldier rammed the razor-sharp blade straight through the breast pocket of the man's coat and subsequently through his hand. The guy let out a blood-curdling scream as the weapon penetrated cartilage and nerves, and continued with a three-inch intrusion of his chest wall. Bolan followed with a kick to the groin that doubled the man over and exposed his partner to the MP-5 K Bolan swung into target acquisition. As the first man fell and his weight drove the knife deeper into his heart, the Executioner squeezed the trigger and delivered a short burst to the second man's chest at nearly point-blank range. The 9 mm Parabellum rounds made neat, red holes in the target's breastbone and lungs before the impact lifted him off his feet and dumped him flat on his back.

Bolan pressed his back to the wall and held the MP-5 K in ready position, muzzle leveled at the door on the far side of the hallway. No further threats presented themselves. Bolan heard the heavy, steady beat of what sounded like rave music emanate from beyond the door. He waited a full minute before trying the handle on the door nearest to him. To his surprise it turned without resistance. Bolan opened the door onto a small, cramped room containing only a bed and a sink. He went to work immediately—dragging the two bodies into the room—but since there wasn't enough space to hold them both side by side he had to stack them. Oh, well, it wasn't as if neatness counted.

Bolan locked the door before closing it behind him. If this back hall served the purpose he thought it did, it would be some time before anybody got curious and made forced entry into the room. By that time he planned to be long gone. He proceeded along the hallway until he reached the far door. He'd consider checking the other rooms just to make sure he covered his flank, but quickly dismissed the idea as too time-consuming. While they might not come looking for their colleagues immediately, Bolan knew he still didn't have a lot of time and especially not if he was forced to deal with other enemies inside the club proper.

The soldier opened the door, keeping the MP-5 K held low against his leg, muzzle down. Near blackness accompanied the deafening music, and people took scant notice of him. The place was wall to wall with bodies and Bolan figured many of those faces—what he could see of them anyway—were dazed by too much loud music, noise and chemical stimulation to be focused on him. This kind of crowd actually proved fortunate, allowing the soldier to move through the club with relative anonymity.

Bolan passed beyond the crowds until he found another door set in a wall just beyond where the curved bar ended. The two bar attendants were so busy filling orders that neither even noticed him as he approached the door. They also didn't notice him raise the MP-5 K and stick it into the gut of the lone monster in the silk suit standing guard. The guy started to look in their direction, but a nudge of the weapon and shake of the head proved adequate in squashing any designs he entertained to warn them. Bolan inclined his head toward the door, and the man seemed all too happy to comply.

Not that he had a choice.

The soldier followed the man into the room, which actually turned out to be a very large office, and closed the door behind them. Against a far wall, a man sat busily typing at a computer keyboard, his lithe body wedged between the massive desk and credenza. The guy barely looked up from whatever held his attention on the computer screen and mumbled something about leaving whatever it was he'd been expecting on his desk.

Bolan cleared his throat and the man looked in their direction, an expression of surprise melting the stony sculpture of his features.

"Leave your hands where I can see them," Bolan ordered. He followed the command with the jab of the muzzle into the guard's back, prodding him in the direction of the sofa. He returned his attention to the guy behind the desk. "You running this operation?"

At first the guy didn't make a response and Bolan began to wonder if he spoke English. Finally, he replied, "Yes."

The Executioner thought he detected a slight Southern accent in the man's voice, but other than that this one didn't possess any striking features. Something about him didn't seem quite right, but Bolan couldn't exactly put his finger on what it was. Maybe the way he held himself or the look in his eyes or just a simple calm with which he carried himself. Whatever the case, it seemed plainly obvious that barring his initial surprise, he didn't seem overly concerned. Bolan detected the unusual way in which the man sized them up.

"It would seem," the man said as he was careful to keep his hands in view, "that you are under the mistaken impression you have us at a disadvantage."

"You mean I don't?" Bolan quipped. He waved the MP-5 K. "Seems to me this gives me the advantage."

"Don't believe for a moment that brandishing a weapon necessarily puts you in a position of authority, neither does it grant you automatic consideration. In fact, I've had a weapon pointed at me many times before…and yet here I am, still alive."

"I'm not really interested in killing you," Bolan replied. "If that were the case you'd be dead already. The only thing I'm here for is information, and if you give it to me, then I'll leave here and nobody else needs to die."

"You're saying you've already taken the life of one of my men?"

"Two men. And only because they left me no choice."

"That is unfortunate," the man replied.

"And why's that?"

"Because you will not leave here alive."

"Who are you exactly and why are you here?"

"You don't think after admitting to killing two of my men that I'm going to answer any of your questions. If you do, you are crazier than I anticipated."

Bolan considered the statement a moment before replying. "It sounds like you were expecting me."

The man inclined his head slightly. "Very perceptive."

"An educated guess," Bolan said with a smile that lacked any warmth. "But the joke's on you, since I had already considered the possibility this was nothing more than a trap. You see, I came prepared for a fight."

As if on cue, the door burst open and a fresh torrent of gunmen—about a half dozen all told—fanned out and trained an assortment of machine pistols on the Executioner's position.

CHAPTER SEVEN

Bolan dropped and rolled behind the desk, which provided cover while also putting hesitancy in the minds of his enemies—they couldn't open up on him without running the risk of hitting their boss. The door guard was actually the first one to make a move, something that Bolan had anticipated might happen if they had planned to ambush him from the start. The guy clawed for hardware beneath his jacket, but Bolan didn't give him an opportunity to bring the weapon to bear. The soldier triggered a short burst from the MP-5 K that stitched the gunman from crotch to sternum. The man's weapon flew from his fingers and he slammed onto the leather couch.

Two more gunners came around in a flanking maneuver, but Bolan easily neutralized them with a near vertical sweep of the subgun's muzzle in minute lead of their movements. The first gunman took multiple slugs to the hip, the impact spinning him into the nearby bookshelf. The second gunner caught three rounds across the chest diagonally and was dead before his body hit the floor.

Bolan rolled out of his position at that point and rose to one knee.

The remaining three gunmen tried to react to this sudden shift in position, but they were unprepared for such a bold move by the enemy. As Bolan fired a salvo in their direction, causing them to scatter, he used his other hand to draw the Beretta 93-R from shoulder leather as backup for his chattering machine pistol. One of the enemy gunners foolishly dived directly into the Executioner's line of fire. He died even as he landed prone on the floor, the bullets cutting through his shoulder, ribs and hip. The man's body twitched in death throes as Bolan took the next gunman with a double-tap to the stomach courtesy of the Beretta.

With more than half their force neutralized, Bolan figured the remaining two would either surrender or turn tail and run. What he didn't expect was the sudden, sharp sensation in the right side of his neck that felt similar to a bee sting. He didn't let it distract him as he held the MP-5 K on the remaining gunner and the Beretta on the man who still remained seated and motionless behind his desk. To Bolan's surprise, the guy still sat there with an almost serene expression and studied him with a level gaze.

Bolan rose to his feet. "Now, where were we?"

"I know it may seem from your perspective right at this moment you are in control," the man at the desk said. "But in reality you were never in control of this situation. You have done exactly as Miguel Veda predicted you would. Including the acquisition of information from a worthless, drunken, whore-mongering idiot."

Bolan's blood ran cold at the mention of Veda. He'd

suspected La Costa's friend of being no friend at all, but a part of him had hoped he could trust the old man. Unfortunately, Bolan knew too well the world was filled with cold, ugly and embittered people who would go to great lengths in the name of an allegedly worthy cause.

But none of that mattered now.

In fact, it was beginning to feel to Bolan as if nothing really mattered at all. For just the briefest moment he thought he saw the man move, but then maybe it was the sudden blur that filled his peripheral vision. He couldn't be exactly sure because he suddenly couldn't seem to comprehend what was happening to him or why.

"I believe before we were interrupted you were asking my name," the man continued. "You may call me Ad-Darr."

Ad-Darr. For a moment that name didn't mean anything to him, it just echoed in Bolan's subconscious as if the man were speaking to him from the edge of a deep well. The soldier realized the reason for that was because the blur surrounding the edges of his vision had turned black and was growing in size. Bolan's knees then went wobbly, and he no longer seemed to have control over his muscles. He didn't have control over anything.

What was it the man said?

His name was Ad-Darr?

Why would that even matter to him?

Bolan knew in those last moments before all went black that the sting in his neck had to have had something to do with his condition. He knew he no longer had control, he thought he knew why and yet it seemed he still couldn't do anything about it. His conscious mind was telling him to pull the trigger, to end it right here by taking some of the bastards with him, but somehow it wouldn't translate to conscious, physical action. And then there was that name that kept reverberating in his head. Ad-Darr. Ad-Darr...

"PULL OVER HERE," La Costa said.

Parmahel brought the van to an easy halt, brakes squeaking slightly from the dampness in the air. After he killed the engine, he looked up the block toward the one building on the entire street with a lit sign. "This is it? This is where he sent this Colonel Stone?"

"Who knows if you can trust anything Frederico says," La Costa replied.

"I'd hope you would, since you gave the guy two hundred bucks."

La Costa flared her eyebrows. "Jealous?"

"Not at all. It's just the next time why not pay *me* the two hundred clams and I'll tell you whatever you want to hear."

La Costa left off the banter to study the exterior of the club. She didn't see anything out of the ordinary about it, and given her Hispanic looks she wouldn't likely even get hassled going inside. The one thing she didn't plan on doing was walking into the place without some sort of backup. She reached forward and opened the glove compartment of the van, moved aside a thick sheaf of papers and withdrew a .38-caliber handgun. She flipped open the cylinder, checked the action, then tucked it in the waistband of her black capris, concealing it under the long-cut, maroon silk blouse.

Parmahel stared at her in amazement. "Is that gun yours?"

"Kind of a dumb question, don't you think?" she challenged.

"Who do you think you are, Dirty Harry?"

"A girl has to take steps to protect herself sometimes," La Costa replied. "There could be a lot of unseemly characters inside a place like that."

"Yeah, and if they catch you walking into that place with a gun, you're going to be classified as one of them."

She patted his shoulder. "Don't worry about me. I'm just going to go poke around, see if maybe I can find Stone."

"I don't like this plan. I don't like it one bit, La Costa."

"Don't get your briefs in a bunch. Just wait here for me and if I'm not out in fifteen minutes you can come in and look for me."

"Oh, no," Parmahel said. "If you aren't back here in *exactly* fifteen minutes, I'm calling the cops is what I'm doing."

La Costa didn't reply as she climbed out of the van, closed the door and headed for the club. She couldn't figure out why she was going to so much trouble. Parmahel had been right in pointing out that it wasn't likely Stone would share information with her. Actually, her presence might just serve to clam him up more. He probably had enough connections to get her reassigned, maybe sent back to America and jailed for interfering with a government operation. Since the war on terror began, the United States government didn't have much of a sense of humor about these things. She knew that if the right people made things difficult for her, the only job she'd be likely to get was as a local newshound in some backwater town.

Well, she didn't much care. This story was too big and too important to her career, and the people had a right to know. It wasn't just her responsibility, it was her duty and she planned to do it. Just like Stone was doing what he thought he had to do, she had the right to an equal amount of respect for what she had to do. And she didn't care if Stone or Julio or her producer liked it or not.

Yes, one way or another, La Costa was going to get her story.

JACK GRIMALDI HAD JUST turned the corner to make his third pass when he noticed the slim, shapely and familiar form that climbed out of a van parked down the street from the club.

Damn it, Grimaldi thought. Bolan had ordered her to stay put for her own safety, but no, she just couldn't get it through her head that her attempt to get a story here might just wind up getting her killed.

Grimaldi could understand that kind of passion—the same passion he and his friends felt about battling terrorism—in someone with a personality like La Costa's. Although he hadn't spent enough time with her to really become acquainted, he knew the type, and it was enough to evoke a little empathy for her. Still, La Costa seemed to be one of those types that needed to exercise more prudence and less sass.

The Stony Man pilot slowed the sedan only enough to confirm her identity, then increased speed until he could turn left at the nearest intersection. He exited the vehicle, dropping the shotgun onto the floor of the backseat where it would be within easy reach, and then proceeded to the trunk. He located the SIG P-226, concealed it in an ankle holster and dropped a spare clip in his pocket. The pilot then turned and angled across the street, heading for the entrance to the club.

As he drew nearer, the two guys in silk suits with long dark hair and beards that Bolan had pointed out earlier emerged from the shadows. Grimaldi could tell the hardmen definitely intended to block his entrance to the club, and he knew they were more than hired bouncers, because they didn't seem the least interested in anyone else coming or going.

So the Stony Man pilot did the unexpected. He dropped his center of gravity—after pretending not to notice the pair approaching his left flank—and performed a reverse leg sweep on the closer of the two. A trained martial artist would likely have responded with a countermove that would have prevented upsetting his balance. Clearly, this guy had no such training, and Grimaldi's sweep not only knocked him off balance, but also caused him to collide with his partner.

As the second man fumbled with the first, Grimaldi pressed the attack with a double punch to his kidneys. The guy howled and danced back while holding his side. Grimaldi used the distraction to deliver an outside karate chop that landed behind his opponent's left ear. The man's eyes rolled upward as he fell prone to the pavement.

Grimaldi turned in time to face off with the first combatant, who had regained his feet. The guy stood taller and broader than the lanky Grimaldi, but this made his movements slower and more awkward. With every punch or kick he tried to throw, Grimaldi simply flitted out of range and landed another blow. This went on for about a minute until Grimaldi delivered the final moves by kicking his opponent in the groin and then delivering a hammer blow to the back of his neck, cracking the guy's spine and driving him to the ground.

Grimaldi spun on his heel, breathing hard with the exertion, and searched frantically for La Costa, but didn't see her. He had to wonder if she spotted him or managed to just miss him. He noticed pedestrians giving him a respectful amount of space on the sidewalk. Drawing that kind of attention hadn't been his intent, but concern for his friend—and the potential trouble La Costa's sudden appearance might bring—overrode all other considerations.

Grimaldi looked in the direction of the van, considered making contact with the driver and asking questions, but he dismissed the idea just as quickly. If Bolan was in trouble, now wasn't the time for idle chitchat. First, they would have to get out of this alive. All of them. Then they could delve into the finer points of exactly why La Costa was here and why she had gone against the big man's instructions.

Without a word to anyone, Grimaldi made his way toward the club's entrance.

JULIO PARMAHEL HAD SPENT his childhood growing up in a pretty rough place.

Nobody could have convinced him that little Havana didn't qualify as one of the most dangerous places of any city in the States. Parmahel had gone to school in places where rape and a vast assortment of other crimes were committed on a regular basis.

Fortunately, Parmahel had come from a fairly large family—eight kids in all—with older siblings who were high-ranking members of some very tough gangs. Because Parmahel had been the second youngest, his brothers and sisters took on very protective roles. Not only did they make sure he wanted for nothing, but they also insisted that he and his younger sister finish school and make something of their lives and careers. Parmahel had never understood it, especially since two brothers ended up dead, another brother and sister were in prison and two others still operated in the gang world. Parmahel, while grateful, had never looked back once he completed his degree in photography.

Seeing those three men fighting on the sidewalk, then, really didn't shock him. La Costa remained his sole concern, and she had managed to get inside the club before the fight even broke out. Parmahel still couldn't understand this almost fanatical devotion La Costa had to getting her story. While he never would've said it directly to her, nothing Parmahel had seen so far had even convinced him there *was* a story to be had here. In one sense he was beginning to wonder if they were wasting their time chasing ghosts. On the other side of the coin, he had to admit that La Costa had repeatedly demonstrated an uncanny sense for newsworthy pieces. It remained one of the reasons he enjoyed working with her; he had shot a lot of great footage in his career while assigned as her partner.

But it wasn't the only reason.

For some time now, Parmahel had been trying to find a way to express his feelings for La Costa. He'd always thought of her as a bright, energetic and astute woman— a young woman with needs—who could look right through him and see what he was thinking. There were times they spent many hours together, like the hours he imagined partners in law enforcement spent; time where the boredom forced people into sharing their hopes and dreams. For Parmahel, it was like a spousal closeness, an intimacy he'd never experienced because such things were foreign to a young kid growing up in a dysfunctional family existing with the hardships of poverty, hunger and crime.

The idea they were from "different sides of the track" also appealed to him. La Costa had been raised in the home of the high-ranking government official, attended all of the best schools and slept every night with a full belly in a dry and warm bed. These were luxuries Parmahel had never known in his youth.

These differences were so opposite that they made up the laws of natural attraction, both physical and intellectual, which scientists claimed played such a critical role in heterosexual relationships. The trouble for Parmahel seemed to be that La Costa didn't understand this in the same way he did. Either that, or she did understand it but the attraction wasn't mutual so she didn't choose to do anything about it. It didn't really matter since he wasn't being fair about it. How could she really know how he felt about her if he didn't tell her? She wasn't a mind reader or clairvoyant, and it seemed almost juvenile now that he'd spent this long with her and remained too gutless to profess his love like some pimple-faced youth admiring the school beauty queen from afar.

Parmahel watched with interest as the smaller guy took out the two heavies like they were nothing more than a couple of punks. Parmahel secretly cheered for the lanky fellow. He'd always been one to support and champion the causes of the less fortunate and oppressed. In some ways he supposed those were attitudes that rubbed off on him in his times with La Costa. He couldn't think of anyone who rooted more for the underdog than she did. It was just one more thing that had made him fall madly in love with her. And come what may, he knew the time would come when he could no longer hide behind their partnership. Very soon he would tell her the truth.

But not yet.

CHAPTER EIGHT

If La Costa could have chosen one word to describe the atmosphere inside the club, it would have been chaotic.

While she couldn't have classified herself as belonging to another generation, there were some things she didn't understand about her own, and one of those was the music. Hundreds of club patrons swayed rhythmically to the rave-style music, a wave of human undulation that made movement all but impossible. La Costa tried to ignore the occasional pawing at her body, some of it definitely not inadvert. The most important thing, she knew, was to protect the pistol tucked in the waistband of her pants.

While the club was dark and smoky, there weren't any strobes or other flashing lights so at least she'd been able to grow accustomed to the environment. A good thing, too, because she might not have spotted the pair of muscular men in T-shirts dragging the inert form of Colonel Brandon Stone along an outer wall of the club and through a narrow door. La Costa had to shove aside several patrons in order to catch up with Stone's little entourage.

La Costa managed to reach the door and insert her arm between it and the doorjamb before it closed, as it would have most likely locked her out. She watched as the two men roughly dragged Stone's body down the hallway and into some sort of alcove at the end. She waited until they had disappeared from view, scanned to her rear one last time to make sure nobody had observed her, then stepped inside the hall and eased the door closed.

With abrupt force the door opened again before it could latch securely.

La Costa opened her mouth to emit a shout of surprise, but a strong hand clamped over it and Stone's pilot friend—a man she knew only as Jack—pushed his way into the hall and forced her against the wall while he closed the door silently. He held his finger to his lips and then released her. He turned his attention to the end of the hall, made sure no one was present, then pinned her with a penetrating gaze.

"You want to explain what you're doing here?" he whispered.

"I might ask you the same—"

"Shush," he interrupted. "Keep it down or you'll get us both killed."

In a strained whisper she said, "I'm here trying to get my story."

"There is no story. There never was a story, at least one that's worth losing your life over. And I don't suppose it ever occurred to you that if whoever's behind these attacks finds out you're a reporter it's curtains for you."

"You're just lucky I showed up when I did," La Costa said. "I just watched two men drag your friend down this hallway."

Grimaldi nodded. "I saw it, too. And you should be leaving this kind of thing to the people who know better."

La Costa smiled and reached under the blouse to retrieve her pistol. She brandished it in front of his face with a smile. "I knew well enough to bring this."

"Yeah," he replied, "and that just might get you killed."

MACK BOLAN COULDN'T be sure how long he'd remained unconscious, but he realized it was long enough for the enemy to secure him in a place where no one was likely to find him for some time. The man who had introduced himself as Ad-Darr stood before him with arms folded. The look of half amusement and half cynicism remained in his eyes, but Bolan could see the wheels turning. Ad-Darr was apparently contemplating what to do with his captive.

The strangest thing to Bolan was that he was lucid, could understand everything and everyone around him, but still didn't seem able to put thoughts into action. Obviously, they had drugged him with some kind of agent that suppressed the psychomotor neuron functions in his brain, thereby effectively removing his ability to act on any thoughts he might have about taking hostile action against them. His eyes took in their surroundings, and he noticed a clock on a nearby workbench in one corner, the digital readout confirming his suspicions that whatever drug they had used on him had only rendered him unconscious for a matter of minutes.

"Well, Colonel Stone," Ad-Darr said. "Welcome back to the land of the living and impotent."

The three or four men in the room with them, some

of whom Bolan could not see, laughed at the comment, and their laughter sounded like tinkling glass in his ears.

"How thoughtless of me," Ad-Darr continued. "I cannot imagine how rude a host you must think me to make a joke at your expense."

Another titter ran through the room.

"Colonel Stone, before we kill you I would like to extend my compliments at your efficiency. You very nearly ruined this entire operation, one for which my client has spent a considerable amount of time and resources. You see, some of the things that Miguel Veda told you were true. He is not a man who believes in violence, neither does he feel that violent actions are a means of achieving political ends. The only trouble is that political ends are not the objectives here."

Although Bolan felt as if he was talking inside a deep, solitary well, he found himself asking a question. "What are your objectives?"

Ad-Darr shrugged. "I see no reason not to tell you. What else do you think the New Revolutionary Justice Organization would want? What do you think is our paramount goal? What would be our highest consideration?"

Bolan thought he knew the answer even before Ad-Darr told him.

"We want the United States of America to die! We want every last infidel Westerner eliminated so that you can no longer spread your poisonous, self-indulgent lifestyles among the children of God. We want you to suffer the indignities that we have suffered. Indignities for our beliefs. Indignities for our convictions of faith. Many times before we have tried to spread the peace and love of Islam so that prosperity might abound to all peoples. Unfortunately, certain members of your government, along with British sympathizers, have attempted to subvert our doctrine.

"Now you must understand that I do not personally care about spreading the Islamic religion. I am more concerned with making sure that men like you do not interfere with the interests of my friends. You see, it is a matter of professionalism for me. I do my job and I do it well, and so I am well compensated for it. I'm sure you will understand then when I tell you I cannot have my reputation sullied. Where would I be then? I will tell you. I would be out of work, utterly ashamed and unable to show my face in any corner of the world without fear of having my head cut off."

Ad-Darr smiled. "This of course brings us to the matter at hand. Shall we begin?"

At that point Ad-Darr brought his hands, which he'd clasped behind him to this point, to his sides. Bolan immediately noticed Ad-Darr held something in his right hand. The man took amused notice and held up the instrument. The long, narrow, wooden handle had a brass cap at one end. A long barbed wire with glittering edges embedded into it protruded from the brass cap and terminated in a large ring surrounded with rubber.

"This device happens to be a particular favorite of mine," Ad Darr said. "This wire, you see, has little diamond chips secured to it, each one honed to a razor-fine edge. The way that it works is I insert my thumb into this loop, and then I begin to draw it across the soft tissue of your throat at the fleshy point just below the angle of your jaw. Then I begin to saw back and forth, back and forth. For about the first minute or so you are able to scream, but after that your vocal cords will be severed and you must suffer great anguish in silence, choking to death on your own blood while I proceed to separate the rest of your head from your body."

The next voice to enter Bolan's consciousness didn't belong to Ad-Darr. This voice, while it had a cold edge to it, sent a blanket of warmth through Bolan's body. Jack Grimaldi said, "I think we'll pass on that."

And then the room became awash in the brutal, raucous sounds of warfare the Executioner knew all too well. And while he couldn't call his own body into action, he could hear the sounds of gunfire, smell the burning cordite of expended gunpowder, sense vibrations of men around him as bullets entered the tender flesh and punctured vital organs. The thunder of battle died in very short order, and then Bolan had the sensation of being lifted from his chair—no longer immobilized by whatever had bound him—followed by forward movement. He realized the hands securing his arms and encircling his waist were strong but gentle, and he relaxed in the knowledge his friends had overcome the enemy.

Bolan willed his legs to work, to put one foot in front of the other and help ease the burden, but he realized that his body still couldn't respond to mental commands no matter how much he might want it to. Every once in a while he could sense getting a foot to move, but mostly they just dragged uselessly beneath him as Grimaldi and La Costa carried him up the stairs, through a hall, across the club and out the door.

"HELP ME GET him into our car!" Grimaldi ordered La Costa.

"But our van is right over there," La Costa said.

"Don't argue!"

La Costa groaned but didn't say anything else as she

and Grimaldi dragged Bolan across the street and to their waiting sedan. It took quite a bit of effort to get the soldier's large frame ensconced into the backseat, but after some maneuvering they managed to stuff his long frame inside. Grimaldi risked a backward glance in time to see a half dozen or so gunmen emerge from the club. He ordered La Costa to take the wheel and she did so, this time without protest. Grimaldi reached inside the backseat to retrieve the shotgun from the floor as he tossed the keys into La Costa's lap.

The Stony Man pilot spun on his heel and worked the pump to bring home the first shell. Grimaldi knelt, brought the stock to his shoulder, took a deep breath and let half out as he squeezed the trigger. The shotgun produced a booming report in the damp night air as the 12-gauge blast of No. 2 shot peppered the oncoming gunners. Grimaldi fired two more successive blasts—just to keep their heads down—before sliding over the trunk of the sedan.

He barely climbed into the front passenger seat before yelling, "Go! Go!"

La Costa dropped the gear lever into Drive and tromped on the accelerator. She swung the nose of the sedan into a 180-degree turn, cleverly putting Grimaldi's side toward the now-regrouping terrorists. Grimaldi had to admire her foresight as this now put him in a position to cover their escape with the shotgun. He leaned out the window as he chambered a shell, leveled the muzzle in the direction of the terrorists and fired off three more shots. One gunner caught an unlucky scattering of pellets to the face that took out both of his eyes and several teeth. The remaining hardmen, who had barely brought their weapons into target acquisition, only managed to get off a few rounds before diving for cover.

Grimaldi watched as a couple of the gunners tried to recover and aimed their machine pistols at the fleeing vehicle. What they hadn't counted on was the driver of the van having the guts to enter the fray. The massive, white equipment van bore down on their flank, but they were too oblivious in their zeal to return fire with Grimaldi. The van caught one of the hardmen dead center, his head smashed by the grille. The second fell beneath the right fender and sent the passenger-side wheels airborne. The van came down steadily enough that the driver managed to regain control quickly.

Grimaldi ducked inside the relative safety of the car and looked at La Costa's taut features. The young woman had a ghostly pallor, her lips tightly pressed together in concentration as she gripped the steering wheel. Other than the obvious stress of what was probably her first true encounter with trained and armed hardmen, she didn't seem any worse for wear.

"You okay?" Grimaldi asked.

She didn't look at him as she answered, "Fine."

The ace pilot turned his attention to his friend in the back, asking Bolan if he was okay. The Executioner nodded slightly. Grimaldi could see just by looking at him that everything was *not* fine. A dull glaze covered the soldier's normally intent, icy-blue gaze, and Bolan's voice sounded hollow. Grimaldi studied him another moment before rendering a smile and a reassuring pat on Bolan's shoulder.

The pilot turned to face forward in his seat and muttered, "Bastards."

"What?" La Costa asked. "What did you say?"

"Tell you later," Grimaldi quietly replied.

"HOW IS HE?" Hal Brognola asked Grimaldi.

The Stony Man pilot sighed into the cell phone as he stood outside the emergency room of the hospital in San Juan. "Doctor says he's going to be fine, should be up on his feet in the next twelve hours."

"All right," Brognola replied, the relief evident in his voice. "Do we know what they did do him?"

"The specialists here said it was some kind of weird mixture of catecholamine and hallucinogens. They said it's similar to pharmacological agents they would use on someone in outpatient surgery where they had to put them under, but not necessarily administer full anesthesia. Apparently it's commonly used for interrogation where torture is employed simultaneously. It's just a good thing we got to him before they could fully employ it."

"Is he lucid now?"

"Yeah, he's doing fine. He's conscious, and I've already talked to him. He says he's aware of everything they did to him."

"And what do you think?"

"What he described to me is pretty much in line with what we witnessed."

"We?"

"I'm afraid there's been a little bit of a complication," Grimaldi replied. "It seems that our lady friend here, that reporter, just couldn't leave well enough alone. She let her curiosity get the better of her and almost got herself and the Sarge killed. She also dragged her partner into it, a cameraman by the name of Julio Parmahel."

"That's it," Brognola interjected. "I'm pulling the plug on this and sending Able Team down there."

"Yeah, the Sarge said you would say that."

"And?"

Grimaldi collected his thoughts before replying. "He wanted me to tell you not to jump the gun quite yet. He also said to tell you he's got the situation under control and you need to let us finish the mission here. Apparently, the story about terrorists being involved in this is completely true. And so is the involvement of Miguel Veda and the Independents in that plot. Sarge is convinced that Veda will get sloppy and try to cover his tracks now that he knows we're on to him."

"And Striker plans to be waiting for him when he makes his move, and doesn't want us overreacting with a battle fleet of marines. That the deal?"

"That's the deal," Grimaldi said.

The silence on the other end of the phone signaled Brognola was considering this request. Grimaldi knew that as head of Stony Man Farm Brognola could pull the plug at any moment on anything and for any reason. Especially if the risk existed that the operation might be exposed, or the mission could fail and result in the loss of life or national security beyond the parameters of acceptable losses. On the other hand, Grimaldi knew that Brognola had tremendous respect for Bolan's judgment and wouldn't counteract that judgment solely for the sake of personal feelings.

"All right," Brognola conceded. "I don't like it, but all right. Tell Striker I'll give him twenty-four hours, no more. But if we don't have results by then I'm going to implement an alternate strategy and I'll want him out of there."

"I'll pass on the message."

"Jack, I want you to be careful. Both of you. And I

want you to put La Costa and this Parmahel on the next plane out of there. I'll make the arrangements through Hernandez's office and their connections with the Associated Press. In the meantime, you and Striker watch each other's backs until the arrangements are made and you can fly them out."

"Me? But I thought—"

"You thought wrong, my friend," Brognola interrupted. "I said I'd give Striker twenty-four hours. But as soon as I get this deal done, your orders are to take La Costa and Parmahel to the airport and fly them straight back to Washington. Do not pass go, do not collect two hundred dollars. Am I clear?"

Grimaldi bit back a stinging reply. He could tell from the tone in Brognola's voice that the subject wasn't open to debate, and as a professional he knew the first rule was to obey orders. On occasion he'd gone against orders, but only in situations where he had no other options. Brognola really didn't have any control over Bolan's actions, but Grimaldi still worked for the head Fed and he had to take that into consideration even over his personal friendship with the Executioner.

"You're clear," Grimaldi said.

After he'd broken the connection, Grimaldi watched the shimmering horizon as the sun rose to signal a brandnew day. He turned at the sound of footsteps and saw La Costa walking down the sidewalk in his direction.

She slowed her pace when she got near him and cocked her head. "I've been in the news business long enough to know just from your expression that phone call didn't go too well."

"I have strict orders to fly you and Julio out of here," Grimaldi said.

La Costa sighed. "When?"

"Pronto. My people are already making the arrangements with the local government and your press offices."

"Well, then, I guess I can look forward to spending some time in a federal penitentiary."

"Not at all," Grimaldi said. "In fact, I wouldn't be surprised if they pinned a medal on you. But the fact of the matter is it's become too dangerous for you to stay here and my friend in there can't afford the liability. No offense."

"None taken," La Costa said. "I probably should have stayed out of this, but I just wanted a story."

Grimaldi smiled. "Maybe you can still have one. But you'll have to get it from a safe distance."

"I suppose it goes without saying, but I forgot to thank you for saving our asses back there."

"Forget about it," Grimaldi replied with a wave. "Besides, you and Julio risked your own necks to help me and the Sarge. And I can promise you that neither he nor I will forget that. We owe *you* one."

"Why do you call him 'Sarge'? I thought he was a colonel."

Grimaldi laughed. "It's a long story."

La Costa arched an eyebrow. "Well, I'm a reporter…I dig long stories."

"Yeah, well that's just it. You're a reporter who deals in facts, and I don't think any serious journalist would believe me if I told him or her the truth."

CHAPTER NINE

Grimaldi and La Costa entered Bolan's private hospital room in time to find the soldier tucking his shirt into his pants. A nurse and doctor stood in the corner looking a bit intimidated. Grimaldi could tell in an instant from the look in Bolan's eyes that he had no intention of sticking around.

"Leaving so soon?" Grimaldi asked.

Bolan muttered something as he continued to dress, oblivious to the stony expressions of the medical staff.

"Colonel Stone," the doctor said, "I cannot stress enough that you reconsider your current course of action. You have suffered some significant trauma that I feel could impair you both physically and mentally. Your body needs time to mend and if you choose to leave, neither I nor this hospital can be held accountable if something happens to you."

"You won't," Bolan replied.

"So you understand it will be charted and recorded that you chose to depart the hospital in the presence of witnesses and against medical advice."

"Hey, Stone," La Costa interjected. "Maybe you should listen to the doc there. You're flesh and blood. Not Superman."

He shrugged into the empty leather shoulder rigging for his pistol and fastened the tie-downs to his belt. "I appreciate you trying to help," he said as he looked in the direction of the doctor and nurse. "All of you. But I'm feeling better now and you can stop worrying. I've gone through a lot worse on less reserves, and I won't hold anyone responsible if something happens to me. You have my word."

The doctor looked as if he was going to open his mouth to protest further, but Grimaldi held up a hand and accompanied it with a warning smile. "He's not going to change his mind, Doctor, so I wouldn't push the issue. Be best to just let it go."

The physician smartly clammed up.

Bolan looked at the doctor. "I'd like you to tell me what I can expect to experience and for how long."

He sighed. "Well, there are a number of potential signs and symptoms with something like this. Nausea is a strong possibility, along with muscle spasms, motion sickness and blurred vision. You may also experience some dizziness, but that would be more likely caused by the counteragents we treated you with. At present, there are still enough drugs in your system that you might have bouts of excessive thirst secondary to dehydration. As the effects of the drugs wear off, you're at risk for pulmonary embolism and cardiac dysrhythmia. Fortunately, you are in excellent physical condition, so that will go a long way toward mitigating some of the signs and symptoms I just described to you."

"Understood," Bolan replied with a nod. "Thanks for pulling me through the worst of it, Doc."

The doctor nodded his acknowledgment.

Bolan turned his attention to Grimaldi and La Costa. "Let's go."

They were joined in the hallway by Parmahel, and the foursome made its way out of the hospital and to the sedan. La Costa and Parmahel acted as if they planned to say their goodbyes and head for their van, but Bolan shook his head and gestured toward the backseat of the sedan. The two journalists exchanged glances, shrugged at each other and then complied. Grimaldi took the wheel as Bolan rode shotgun, and once they were bound for their hotel, Grimaldi turned over the Beretta 93-R to his friend.

Bolan quickly checked the action with the professionalism borne from years of experience and then secured the Beretta in his shoulder holster.

Grimaldi grinned. "Looks like some things are coming back to you right away."

"Just like falling off a horse," Bolan quipped. He turned slightly in his seat as he directed his voice to Parmahel and La Costa. "What I'd like to know from you two is what you thought you were doing down in Las Mareas."

La Costa piped up immediately. "You don't have to put any of this on Julio, it was completely my idea."

"I'm not looking to find fault, but you shouldn't have been there. Period."

"I wouldn't have *had* to go there, Stone, if you had just not tried to cut me out of my story."

"I'm trying to keep you alive," Bolan countered in a frosty voice.

"I didn't ask you to."

"All right, just kill it there and listen up. I have a job

to do and there are a lot of lives at risk, including yours." He looked to Parmahel, adding, "And yours, too."

"From who?" La Costa asked.

"Miguel Veda, for starters. Not to mention his men and whoever is heading up his affiliation with the New Revolutionary Justice Organization."

La Costa opened her mouth in protest, but Bolan wouldn't give her a word edgewise. "No, at the moment your mouth is closed and your ears are open. Now I trusted you once to do the right thing and stay out of this, but apparently that's not going to work. So now you two are going to lay low with my friend Jack here until arrangements can be made to get you safely out of Puerto Rico."

"To where?" Parmahel asked.

Bolan replied, "Anywhere but here."

"Justice is making arrangements for me to take them back to Washington," Grimaldi offered. "Unless you need me here, of course."

Bolan shook his head. "No, let's go with that plan. I'm not sure I would trust anyone else right now to take them where they need to go, and get them there in one piece."

"Aw, Sarge, you say the sweetest things."

Bolan refrained from further discussion until they had La Costa and Parmahel sequestered in a hotel room adjoining theirs. A quick call from Brognola to the governor's office provided a pair of plainclothes security specialists to stand guard over La Costa and Parmahel's room. Bolan made sure they understood nobody was allowed in or out of the room other than him or Grimaldi.

When they were in the room alone, Bolan turned the conversation to a deeper level. "Listen, Jack, I owe you one for coming after me."

"Come on, Sarge," Grimaldi said. "You know you don't owe me anything."

"Yeah, I know, but I thought it needed saying anyway."

"Guess I'll chalk it up to the drugs…but you're welcome." Grimaldi clapped him on the shoulder to signal they were through. "Now, what's next? I figure you'll go after Veda."

Bolan nodded. "You figured right. I owe Miguel Veda quite a lot, and I plan to pay him back in spades. But that isn't what's really bothering me at the moment. I'm way more concerned about this Ad-Darr and what he said relative to the NRJO being involved in the political turmoil here."

"Yeah, I don't quite get that, either. Why would a new cell of a former Lebanese terror group have any interest in Puerto Rico?"

"I figure for the same reason the Russians took an interest in Cuba during JFK's presidency."

"You're thinking Veda solicited the NRJO to help Puerto Rico gain its independence as a country in exchange for rights to conduct clandestine operations against the States."

"Why not?" Bolan shrugged. "Given both its geographic location and influence on American policy, Puerto Rico would be a strategic gold mine for any terrorist group. If Puerto Rico were to become independent, they could expect to receive a considerable amount of time and resources from the United States. Those resources could be put in the hands of any terrorist group operating here, and the puppet government they established would provide the perfect front."

Grimaldi shook his head with disbelief. "That's

pretty ingenious—unthinkable, but ingenious. But wouldn't it make more sense to try to take Veda alive for interrogation?"

"You read my mind," Bolan replied with a grin.

"How?"

"That's the part I still have to work out. One thing I'm certain of, though, is that it wasn't Veda who set me up with Ad-Darr. He only provided the middleman in Las Mareas. No, whoever's pulling Veda strings was controlling Ad-Darr, somebody inside the NRJO and possibly even the top dog."

"You think you might be able to use that information to your advantage?"

"I'm betting on it. I remember Ad-Darr saying some things that led me to believe this cell of the NRJO may be operating *inside* the States."

"Yeah, but with this Ad-Darr guy dead you might never find out where."

"That's why I have to find a way to take Veda alive. I think I can squeeze him hard enough to reveal what he knows about that. And the only way I see of doing that is to draw him into the open. By this time, he's going to assume I'm dead. I think it's time to call the governor's office and test whether they're really on the level."

AD-DARR WINCED a little at the pressure in his back.

The assassin had discovered some time ago the value of wearing a Kevlar vest during those times when he chose not to carry a weapon. Had he not demonstrated such foresight, he would now be lying dead in a pool of congealed blood in the cold, dank basement beneath the club like the four idiots who had been with him.

Ad-Darr didn't mourn their loss. They had given

their lives for the cause they believed in, and Ad-Darr didn't plan to defecate on their sacrifice. Had he died with them, he would've hoped Razzaq would show him the same courtesy. Not that it mattered all that much, since those men belonged to Razzaq; Ad-Darr worked alone, and this was just one of many reasons why.

After the personal physician they kept on staff in the club finished his examination—diagnosing Ad-Darr with nothing more than some simple contusions and a few bruised ribs, and swathing his midsection with a tight bandage—Ad-Darr contacted Razzaq with the news. Razzaq waited politely, not interrupting as Ad-Darr gave his report. After he'd finished, Razzaq said nothing for some time.

"I am not quite sure how to respond to this," he finally said. "I cannot ever recall a time where you have been known to fail. I hired you at considerable expense because you came highly recommended from a good number of close associates. Are you now telling me that I must communicate my regrets to them? Of course, you realize should I have to do that that you will not be able to show your face anywhere in the Western Hemisphere, nor is it likely to some of our brothers back in the Holy Lands."

"There is no need for you to take such a rash action," Ad-Darr assured him. "You can believe me when I say that I have the situation well in hand."

"Is that right?"

"It is. First of all, we now have the advantage of surprise because the Americans believe that I am dead. Second, we know their natural reaction will be to return to San Juan and attempt to extort information from Miguel Veda."

A long silence ensued. "We cannot have that. No, definitely not."

"We are in complete agreement then," Ad-Darr replied.

"You have a suggestion?" Razzaq asked.

"Veda was clearly a liability in this from the beginning. He can no longer be trusted, and therefore it is no longer useful to you for him to go on living. I propose you give me the opportunity to eliminate both him and this Colonel Stone at the same time."

"I would be willing to reconsider my position on your efforts if you could give me your assurances that you will execute this with all of the diligence and professionalism commensurate with your reputation."

"You can consider it done." Ad-Darr paused a moment, then said, "Am I to assume that I may employ whatever methods I see fit to accomplish those ends?"

"How you complete your assignment is none of my affair as long as you don't do anything to bring my name into scrutiny or jeopardize my operations. I will give you twenty-four hours to finish what you have started. If it is not done by then, I would suggest you find another profession."

Ad-Darr considered telling Razzaq he didn't respond well to threats, but the click in his ear signaled Razzaq had already broken the connection. Ad-Darr slowly returned the handset to the cradle and considered his options. Twenty-four hours. That's what he had to get to San Juan, locate Stone and Veda and liquidate the liabilities they posed.

If anyone had asked, Ad-Darr would have to admit that the Americans impressed him. Particularly this military man, Stone. He hadn't been lying when he told the American infidel he imagined they were somewhat alike. Stone had demonstrated a cold and heartless efficiency under fire, as if the eradication of his enemies were a singular objective with no consideration or mercy. Indeed, Ad-Darr had seen many men in combat, but not one of them had carried themselves with the poise and grace of Stone.

Ad-Darr turned to one of the security men standing guard at the entrance to the office and ordered the man to summon his car for departure. One way or another he would need to end this before it got out of control again. His final killing ground had been determined: San Juan.

"THAT'S ABSOLUTELY preposterous!" Alvaro Fonseca protested.

"Now let's everybody calm down," Governor Hernandez said. As Fonseca sat and stewed, Hernandez directed his attention to Bolan. "I'm afraid I'm forced to agree with Mr. Fonseca, Colonel Stone. The very idea of having Miguel Veda or his people come anywhere near this building is a bit terrifying. I'm sure you can understand my reticence in going along with this plan."

"I understand, Governor," Bolan replied. "But the fact remains that Miguel Veda poses a significant danger to this office and to Puerto Rico at large, no matter where he's at. And I don't need to remind you of your promise to the president that I would receive the full cooperation of your office."

Hernandez frowned. "I understand you're trying to help, Colonel. But let me remind you that I am still the governor of Puerto Rico, and I have full discretion in this matter. I will not do anything to jeopardize the citizens of this territory or my staff. And I personally feel that Miguel Veda is a militant and an extremist. His actions in the past border on domestic terrorism in my best estimation."

"And that's exactly why I'm proposing you extend this invitation for discussions, Governor. And with all due respect to your position, I can't stress the criticality of timing here. If word of the NRJO's failure to assassinate me gets back to Veda first, he may escape before I have the chance to stop him. In which case you're going to have one hell of a bloodbath on your hands and that may well force the Oval Office into a full military response."

The governor sighed deeply, sat back in his chair and locked eyes with Bolan.

Bolan met his stare with a level gaze of his own. "Governor, you're running out of time."

"Very well, Colonel."

"Governor," Fonseca said, "I cannot stress to you enough the danger in Colonel Stone's plan."

As Hernandez picked up the phone and punched in an extension, he replied, "Your concerns have been duly noted, Alvaro. But I'm willing to give Colonel Stone the benefit of the doubt for now. He's already put his life at considerable risk a number of times during this mission, and that has to count for something." The governor turned his attention to whomever answered the phone. "This is Governor Hernandez. Get me the diplomatic relations secretary."

Bolan could understand the concerns of these men, but he couldn't help but feel as if he'd won a small victory. He'd also dismissed his suspicions for Fonseca, especially since that information had come from Veda, who had proved himself a liar. When he'd first proposed they coordinate a sit-down with Veda under the pretext of a political quorum, both men had immediately resisted the idea. It had taken some considerable wordplay on the Executioner's part to convince them his plan was sound and presented the least number of risks.

When Hernandez finished his conversation with the DRS, Bolan excused himself and returned by foot to his hotel room. He had some planning to do and very little time left to do it. The numbers were running down now. Hernandez had confirmed that Veda was willing to meet with them about 1300, which left Bolan less than two hours to prepare.

Bolan nodded at the security officer he passed outside La Costa and Parmahel's room. The second man had taken up the detail inside their suite.

As Bolan entered his and Grimaldi's room, he noticed the pilot's flight bag out and packed travel case on a settee. "Ready to go?"

Grimaldi nodded. "Hal called about ten minutes ago. I told him where you were and what you had planned. He says sounds like a winner and update him whenever you get a chance."

"Good deal," Bolan replied. "I'll go retrieve the kids."

Grimaldi chuckled as the Executioner stepped into the hallway and immediately noticed the security guard had disappeared. Where the hell had he gone so quickly? Maybe he'd stepped inside to use the restroom. Bolan rapped on the door and got no response. He was about to knock again when a voice from inside called out, "Who is it?"

That was Parmahel's voice. "It's Stone. Where's the guard?"

Bolan heard the dead bolt and then Parmahel's face appeared in the opening still secured by the chain.

The Executioner tapped it. "Good man."

Parmahel nodded and said, "He stepped out with the other guy. Said something about some lady fell on the stairs and needed help, so they both went to check it out."

"And you let them go?" Bolan asked.

"I'm not a babysitter—"

Movement in his peripheral vision demanded Bolan's attention and he turned in time to see four heavily armed gunners in black leather and gas masks emerge from the stairwell at the far end of the hall.

"Close and bar the door!" Bolan ordered Parmahel.

CHAPTER TEN

Bolan saw the muzzle-flash of the grenade launcher and heard the whip-crack plunk of the weapon as it discharged its ordnance a moment before he dived for cover. There wasn't time to retreat into his room, so the adjoining hallway proved his only saving grace. The Executioner had expected an explosion, but instead the canister rolled to a stop on the crushed-fiber carpet of the hallway a few feet from his position, noxious gas swirling from both ends. Bolan held his breath, but could do nothing about the immediate stinging in his eyes.

Grimaldi opened the door and Bolan waved him back, climbing to his feet and rushing through the building cloud of gray smoke, which served to conceal him from the enemy. He burst through the open door and slammed it shut.

"What the—"

"CS gas," Bolan said as he bolted the door. "Get a towel!"

Grimaldi rushed to the bathroom and returned a

moment later with a towel, which the soldier rolled and used to block the bottom seal of the door. "That should buy us some time. Get La Costa and Parmahel."

As the pilot accessed their room via the adjoining door, Bolan went into the bedroom and retrieved the weapons bag he'd brought earlier from the trunk of the sedan. He withdrew an FN FNC from the bag, slammed home a magazine and dropped two spares into his pocket before grabbing an Uzi SMG for Grimaldi. Bolan considered drawing one or two Diehl DM-51 hand grenades, as well, but dismissed the thought—the hotel was full and it might risk the lives of bystanders if he started using heavy explosives.

Bolan slung the weapons bag and emerged from the bedroom as Grimaldi reappeared with La Costa and Parmahel in tow. He tossed the Uzi to the pilot, who caught it one-handed and put the weapon in battery with a quick working of the charging handle. Bolan never lost stride as he went to the door and pressed his ear to it. He could sense the hiss of the gas as it continued to fill the hallway, but the towel did the trick to prevent seepage.

Bolan turned toward La Costa and Parmahel. "There's tear gas venting just outside this door. On my count, you two are going to hold hands and follow Jack out the door while I provide cover. Keep your eyes closed and hold your breath until you're through it."

Bolan told Grimaldi to make for the back stairwell, and the Stony Man pilot nodded.

The Executioner counted to three, threw open the door and stepped into the hallway. He swung the muzzle of the FNC in every direction, ready to meet their aggressors with deadly force. His eyes immediately began to sting and tear as he sensed the trio rush past him. A salvo of rounds buzzed through the smoke, but none made contact. Bolan held the FNC low and steady, and squeezed the trigger twice to send a pair of short bursts in the direction of the gunfire. In the confusion he couldn't tell if he'd hit anything, but with Grimaldi and crew clear it didn't matter.

Bolan launched into a full sprint down the side hallway that ran along the north-facing exterior of the hotel. The cityscape outside rushed past him through the tall windows, and Bolan triggered some bursts on the run to shatter them. The gas had to be vented so civilians would suffer minimal exposure. Somewhere along the line the fire alarm sounded. Bolan caught up to the others just as they reached the door to the stairwell and Grimaldi looked askance in his direction.

"Right behind you."

Grimaldi tried the door. "It's locked!"

Bolan waved him aside and then triggered a burst from the FNC at the lock. He followed it with a kick and the door gave under the assault. Bolan stepped aside to allow his charges to pass while he covered their flank. As Parmahel passed, several enemy gunners materialized from the smoke at the end of the hallway. Using the edge of the doorway for cover, Bolan crouched and raised the FNC into target acquisition. He steadied his breathing as he squeezed off a short burst. The first gunman in line took three 5.56 mm rounds to the chest, puncturing heart and lungs. A spray of blood erupted from his mouth as he toppled to the ground and rolled to a stop. Bolan followed with another 3-round burst that blew off the top of a second man's head.

Bolan rose and dashed through the stairwell door, descending the steps three at a time. The blood pounded in his ears and he stumbled a couple of times, almost taking a header at one point. Fine time for the dizziness to come on him, he thought. The soldier pushed it from his mind and concentrated on the path ahead. They were only on the third story of the hotel, and he reached the first-floor landing in under a minute.

The soldier continued down the hallway and out the back door that opened onto the two-story parking structure. He spotted the rest of his crew just as they reached the waiting sedan. The Executioner poured on the speed, his legs pumping for all they were worth as he made his way up the ramp. He caught the glimmer of sunlight on metal and spied two men with pistols headed on an intercept course. Bolan recognized them as the pair on Fonseca's staff he'd encountered the day before. At first they didn't seem to pose a threat, but then one of them raised a pistol in Bolan's direction.

The Executioner shoulder-rolled in time to avoid two shots from one of the men. He came out of the roll on his feet, planted and sprayed the charging gunners with a full volley of hot lead. The shooter went down first under a stream of choppers that cut across his midsection and exposed his innards to daylight. The impact spun him, and his body stiffened and performed an odd pirouette before hitting the pavement. As his partner fell, the survivor erred on the side of self-preservation by breaking off and heading for the cover of a nearby car. He didn't make it. Bullets punched through his ribs and hip, and he smacked into the car under his own impetus before falling dead onto his back.

Bolan reached the sedan just as Grimaldi got the engine fired up. The ace flier floored it and reversed out of their parking spot in a noisy, smoky display of burning rubber. He put the car in Drive just as their pursuers from the hotel burst into the parking structure and directed a maelstrom of autofire at them. A couple of bullets slapped into the trunk with a metal-on-metal reverberation inside the vehicle compartment.

"There goes our security deposit," Grimaldi said.

Bolan didn't answer as more trouble loomed ahead. An SUV jounced into the parking garage, not even slowing as it smashed through the entrance gate and bore down on them.

"Steer into them," Bolan said.

Grimaldi gave his friend a momentary look of disbelief even as he complied.

Bolan leaned out the window and leveled the FNC at the enemy troops inside the SUV. He held back on the trigger and swept the muzzle in corkscrew fashion in an attempt to disable the vehicle. Seeing they were under attack, as Grimaldi simultaneously raced toward them in a game of chicken, the driver swerved to avoid death and managed to catch the right fender against a support stanchion. The impact created an array of sparks as the body of the SUV scraped against the concrete pillar.

Bolan noted the fiery display. "That vehicle's armored."

Grimaldi swerved from impact at the last second and redirected the sedan toward the gates. The ticket taker could see they weren't stopping and raised the gate before Grimaldi smashed that one, too. The car bottomed out as the undercarriage hit the low point of the decline and roared into a street full of traffic. Horns blared and drivers swerved to avoid the hard-charging Grimaldi, but the pilot only grinned with adrenaline.

"Yee-haw!" he hollered as he righted the vehicle after nearly putting them on two wheels.

"Been spending time with Iron Man, I see," Bolan said.

Grimaldi winked. "That I have!"

"Who in the hell were those guys?" La Costa asked. "More terrorists?"

Bolan shook his head. "Doubtful. Those two in the garage were the same ones I ran into yesterday morning. The ones Fonseca sent to tail you."

"I thought Fonseca was clean," Grimaldi said.

"So did I."

"Looks like maybe Miguel was telling the truth," La Costa said.

"No dice," Bolan said with a shake of his head. "Fonseca had no idea we'd stashed you and Julio at the hotel. Plus, he didn't have enough time to mount that operation. I think those guys were working for Veda all the time."

La Costa scoffed. "Miguel would never send someone to hurt me, Stone. Never. You hear me?"

"Veda wants you dead," Bolan said simply. "You know too much, and that makes you a liability to him. Whatever he's planning has been orchestrated by the NRJO. They're going to keep coming after you until you're either deceased or they can no longer get to you. That makes you a liability to my mission, too."

"You want me to head for the airport?" Grimaldi asked.

Bolan checked his watch. "Yeah, I'll go with you and make sure you get off all right."

"Hey, I don't have anything with me," Parmahel protested. "All my stuff is at my house."

"Time to get new stuff," Grimaldi replied.

ONCE HE'D SEEN Grimaldi, La Costa and Parmahel safely airborne, the Executioner headed for Veda's coastal estate. He still had about forty-five minutes before the meeting between Hernandez and Veda. That gave him enough time to plan his assault.

As he drove, he did a quick mental inventory of the weapons case. Grimaldi had been able to provide him with some fresh weaponry from the mobile armory aboard Stony Man's Gulfstream C-21. The cache he unloaded included plenty of spare ammunition for the FNC and Beretta, his .44 Magnum Desert Eagle, a new blacksuit and incendiary grenades. Bolan had also procured a stand-alone version of the M-203 grenade-launcher with a bandoleer of assorted 40 mm shells.

All told, Bolan figured it would be enough to get the job done.

He reached his destination in about twenty minutes; he didn't have to fight any real traffic, as Veda's sprawling estate lay on a course northwest of the airport. Bolan drove up the winding road until he estimated he was within a mile of Veda's palatial home. He pulled his sedan off the road, concealed it within a copse of trees and then went EVA. The Executioner quickly stripped out of his civilian clothes and donned the skintight blacksuit. He retrieved the load-bearing harness, also acquired from the Stony Man armory aboard the C-21, and then went about securing his equipment in its rightful places. The Beretta 93-R rode in shoulder leather under his left armpit, the Desert Eagle hung on his right hip in a military-style flap holster and the combat knife was in a special spring-loaded sheath on the left strap of the LBE. Grenades hung from the right strap, and the various spare magazines, a utility tool and a garrote were tucked into pouches lining the web belt.

Bolan slung the M-203 grenade launcher, secured the sedan and then set off toward Veda's estate with the FNC held in the ready position. The verdant, tropical terrain around him provided shade from the blazing afternoon sun but that did nothing to curb the humidity. At one point Bolan experienced a little more dizziness, but stopping a moment and leaning against the tree—along with frequent pulls from a canteen of water—proved adequate to restore him. Before long he knew he would have to rest, but he was determined not to let up until he had dealt with Veda.

Even over the jagged and unpredictable terrain, Bolan reached the perimeter of his objective within thirty minutes. He came out to the edge of the tree line and a slight promontory that overlooked the majority of the estate. Bolan removed a pair of miniature field binoculars from a belt pouch and carefully studied the layout. A three-foot-high decorative wall was all that surrounded Veda's property. Bolan figured that meant there would be an adequate security detail, most likely heavily armed, and a whole array of electronic detection and security countermeasures.

After completing his reconnaissance and forming a plan of action, Bolan unslung the M-203 and loaded a high-explosive grenade. He engaged the quadrant sight, knelt and gathered range on his first target. The small, squat structure appeared to be an outhouse, but the small satellite dish and radio antenna protruding from the top gave away its true purpose. Bolan put the range at just shy of 250 yards—well within the M-203's effective

range for an area target. He took a deep breath, let out
half of it and squeezed the trigger.

The 40 mm grenade arced gracefully through the air
and landed dead-on. The entire structure erupted into a
red-orange fireball of superheated gases, and the PETN
explosives did fine work in sending flaming glass and
wood flying in multiple directions. Even as the grenade
hit its target, Bolan had loaded a second HE round and
sighted on the front-gate area that marked the entrance
to the estate. Bolan squeezed the trigger and this grenade produced very similar effects on the wrought-iron
gate and guard shack.

Bolan followed up his initial assault with a series of
smoke grenades to add to the confusion and provide
concealment along his line of approach. The soldier
broke the cover of the tree line quickly and descended
the promontory, exercising caution so he didn't stumble
or twist an ankle. When he reached level ground, he
crossed the open field of about seventy-five yards in no
time. Bolan vaulted the decorative wall and made a
beeline for the side of the house.

Two of Veda's security men rounded the corner and
were taken completely off guard by Bolan's appearance. The Executioner, however, had prepared for such
an eventuality. He let them know it by triggering several
short bursts from the FNC. Slugs hammered into the
guards' chests and stomachs, and one even caught a
round in the upper lip. The impact at such close range
smashed most of the first guard's upper face bones,
shattered his skull and exited out the back of his head.
The second guard suffered a bit more shock, as he
grasped his stomach and dropped to his knees. For a
moment his body remained there, then his eyes rolled

into the back of his head. He collapsed face-first on the manicured lawn.

Bolan knelt and slammed home another shell, this one another HE. He swung the muzzle of the M-203 toward an upper-story window of Veda's mansion and triggered the launcher. The window shattered under impact, but didn't prove enough to set the grenade off; however, the ceiling proved sufficient to the task and a moment later red-hot gas, black smoke and flaming debris came roiling out the opening created by the blast.

Turning just in time to catch another pair of guards approaching his flank, Bolan dropped the launcher as he went prone and brought the FNC into target acquisition. The two guards had already started to open fire, but the rounds buzzed harmlessly over Bolan's head. The enemy had no time to correct its aim. The soldier took the first of the pair with a 3-round burst to the midsection, and the second died with two rounds to the chest and a third through the throat—the latter of which snapped his spine and nearly decapitated him.

As the reports from the FNC died out, Bolan heard the roar of an engine. He rolled out of his prone position, got to one knee, then turned and leveled his weapon in the direction of the sound. To his surprise, the vehicle that had produced such a ruckus was moving away from him. The soldier flipped out the stock of the FNC, brought it to his shoulder and pressed his cheek against the receiver. He quickly acquired a sight picture and held the trigger back. A steady stream of 5.56 mm high-velocity rounds beat a straight and true path to the vehicle's tires. The driver lost control at the point of blowout, causing the shredded tires to veer off the driveway and catch in a rut. Totally out of control, the vehicle flipped upside down and Bolan followed up with several more well-placed rounds to the gas tank. The car exploded, trapping the would-be escapees inside a fiery tomb.

The Executioner jumped to his feet and sprinted for the front of the house. He made the door unmolested, kicked it down and moved inside. Nobody arrived to challenge him and that gave him pause. Adding together the four he'd taken on the lawn, one in the guard shack and an untold number in the vehicle, the count was about eight. When he and La Costa had visited the day before, he remembered counting at least twice that number of hardmen. Even if Veda had left with a detachment of four, that still left another half-dozen unaccounted for unless some of those they had encountered at the hotel were also part of his crew.

The Executioner quickly made his way to Veda's office, where he removed a couple of incendiary grenades from his LBE harness. Bolan primed them and tossed one into the room adjoining the office—it turned out to be Veda's bedroom and was littered with medical equipment. He closed the door and left the remaining grenade primed on Veda's desk.

Bolan cleared the front of the house before the grenades blew, their sound muffled by the thick exterior walls. The incendiary grenades, coupled with the oxygen tanks in the bedroom, would make short work of the house. By the time anyone could respond to this remote area, or even realized something was wrong, the entire house would likely be engulfed in flames.

Mack Bolan had definitely paid back Miguel Veda in spades.

Now it was time to get back to the governor's headquarters and deliver that message personally.

CHAPTER ELEVEN

Guadalupe La Costa stared out the window of the private jet, lost in her thoughts. She looked across the seat from her now and again to see Julio, his head propped against a pillow, snoring like it was nobody's business. Man, but that boy could sleep. La Costa had to admit she envied his ability to doze off anywhere and anytime. Not that sleep would come easily to her. It hadn't since the events of yesterday morning, when she first opened up to a dark-haired stranger with cold blue eyes and a stubborn streak.

There were moments when Stone really infuriated her, and yet she couldn't stop thinking about him. The guy just had…*something*. Aw, what the hell did it matter now? She wouldn't get her story and it wasn't likely she'd get the guy, either. This was the real world, so she might as well get used to it.

Getting past the idea that Veda had betrayed her had proved to be the hardest obstacle. She'd known Miguel since shortly after her arrival in Puerto Rico, and to think that he had not only lied to her, but had also sent someone to kill her was preposterous. But she couldn't deny the evidence; it was overwhelming and she had this strong feeling that Brandon Stone had been telling her the truth. She'd been there when Veda agreed to meet with her and Stone, heard everything that he heard, and yet when she showed up in Las Mareas where he sent them, all of them almost got wiped out. She couldn't chalk it up to coincidence, and her reporter's intuition told her that there was more to Miguel Veda than met the eye.

But the idea that the U.S. might be forced into sending military troops to Puerto Rico—occupying the island under a blanket of martial law until the situation there was deemed safe—all at once thrilled her and scared her to death. And for anyone to tell her there wasn't a story in that had to be lying through their teeth. Well, she couldn't do anything about it now. Stone had told her that she could still get a story, but would have to do it from a safe distance. He didn't apply any caveat to that, and La Costa assumed they would be free to go once they were in the States.

La Costa laid her head back, closed her eyes and tried to sleep. She'd had a long day and probably a good part of the evening ahead of her, and it wouldn't pay to be exhausted. As she drifted off she dreamed of a tall, dark-haired soldier with cold blue eyes.

MACK BOLAN STRIPPED OFF his gear and traded the blacksuit for his class-B military uniform before returning to downtown San Juan.

He thought Miguel Veda might have a coronary right there when he stepped into the conference room where Governor Hernandez and staff had been stalling for time. Veda's eyes grew wide, standing in stark contrast to his darker skin, but he recovered quickly and nodded a greeting in Bolan's direction.

"Ah, here's Colonel Stone now," Hernandez said. "I believe you two know each other?"

Veda nodded at the governor. "We have met once before, but there is no reason to be coy, gentlemen, as I assume you already know that. Otherwise, why would I be here?"

Bolan smiled, a hard smile solely intended to make Veda uncomfortable. "Yeah, we've met. The funny thing is, I don't recall you mentioning you were involved in a plot to turn Puerto Rico into a haven and base of operations for international terrorists during that little chat."

"What?" Veda rendered an expression like he just gagged on something. "That's absolutely ridiculous. I have no idea what you're talking about. You came to me and asked for information, and although I had absolutely no reason or obligation to cooperate with you, I did."

"No. What you did was sent me on a wild-goose chase to Las Mareas, where you knew an assassin by the name of Ad-Darr was waiting for me. Well, actually, him and about a dozen soldiers of the New Revolutionary Justice Organization."

Bolan saw two of Veda's security personnel—who were standing behind their boss—stiffen at the mention of the NRJO. However, he knew they weren't armed, while he wore his Beretta 93-R at his side. A courtesy clearance had been issued straight from the governor allowing him to carry a firearm for the duration of his stay in Puerto Rico.

"Don't bother denying it, Veda," Bolan continued. "The only reason you're not dead is because we need you alive to answer questions."

Veda looked at Hernandez. "With all due respect, Governor, I am not a prisoner, neither have I been charged with a crime."

"Actually, you are a prisoner," Bolan said. "A prisoner of war."

"That's absurd! We're not at war."

"You're at war, Veda. You were at war the moment you decided to ally yourself with the enemies of America. Well, here's a news flash for you. Ad-Darr is dead, your assassination attempts on both me and Guadalupe La Costa have failed and your plan to subvert democracy in Puerto Rico will never succeed."

Veda stood and clenched his fists. "I came here on good faith and with the intention of reaching a reasonable agreement with this political leadership. I can see my attempts at conciliation have gone unnoticed. Let's go, men, we will return to my estate."

"Sit, Veda," Bolan countered. "You're not going anywhere. I imagine by now your estate as you know it no longer exists."

Veda paled. "What does that mean?"

"It means someone paid a little visit to your home, and I'm afraid there's not much left of either the structure or the goons you left to guard it."

"You had no right!"

"Really? Twice you lied to me and twice you tried to kill me, not to mention the attempts you made at the hotel. I think you should fire whoever's left in this private little army you have. They're amateurs."

"I don't know what you're talking about."

Bolan raised his eyebrows. "Are you really going to deny that you sent a hit team to our hotel? Or that you connected me with one of your peons specifically for the purpose of gaining my trust? And meanwhile, as I'm running down the phantom leads that don't even exist, you're plotting with Lebanese terrorists. It's over, and the only one who doesn't seem to realize that is you. I know that you're fatally ill, Veda, and it's only a matter of time. Frankly, I couldn't care about that. What I do care about is the security of my country, and you have a chance here to make it right. At the very least, you'll likely buy yourself a stay-out-of-prison card and be able to die in peace in your own bed."

Bolan could see his words were having an impact, stinging Veda's ears and seeping into his conscience—if he had one.

It wasn't the first time the Executioner had chosen to give a mortal enemy the benefit of a reprieve, and it probably wasn't the last. He hadn't earned the Sergeant Mercy name because he was an unfeeling war machine; the conservation of human life still ranked at the top for Bolan. It didn't matter how despicable he might find the mere thought of Veda's continued existence, but there were higher considerations here, not the least of them the security of the nation and the lives of many thousands of Puerto Rican citizens.

If Veda could help Bolan keep the bloodbath to the enemy, then he figured he owed it to duty and country to give the guy the opportunity.

"I'm handing you one last chance, Veda," Bolan said. "Are you smart enough to take it?"

Veda collapsed into his chair. For a long time he sat in stony silence, acting as if he had no intention of cooperating, but Bolan could see the wheels turning. Miguel Veda really didn't have any options left. His choice was to keep up the charade and die a lonely, bitter old man who didn't have anything to show for his efforts. Or he could cooperate and retain what little pleasures there were left in his failing life.

Veda finally looked up and met the Executioner's expectant gaze. "You will guarantee me immunity?"

Bolan looked at Hernandez, who mulled it over a moment and then nodded slowly.

"What do you want to know?" Veda asked.

JACK GRIMALDI PUT the Gulfstream C-21 down at Andrews AFB shortly after 1700 hours. As the jet engines whined down and the plane rolled to a stop, the pilot sat back in his seat and removed his headset. He let out a sigh, deeply relieved to finally be back in familiar territory, while simultaneously trying not to wonder about the fate of his friend. If Grimaldi had learned anything, it was that Mack Bolan could take care of himself. Grimaldi eased out of the pilot's chair and made his way into the cabin. La Costa and Parmahel were stretching and yawning, obviously trying to come awake after their long naps.

"Welcome to Washington, D.C., folks," Grimaldi said with a grin. "The captain has turned off the seat-belt sign and you are now free to exit the aircraft."

La Costa glanced out her window, then turned to Grimaldi and arched an eyebrow. "I take it the two men standing outside near that black SUV with the suits, sunglasses and bad haircuts are here for us."

Grimaldi nodded. "Afraid so, ma'am. They were sent straight to you courtesy of the United States government."

"I had assumed that once we got to the States we would be free to go."

"So did I," Parmahel agreed.

"Sorry, guys and dolls, but I don't make the rules here, I just follow them. My boss isn't convinced you two are out of the woods, and until he is this is the way it has to be. Now, you guys are going to be fine. I understand that those men out there are with the U.S. Marshals Service, and they're going to escort you to a secured location."

"How about clothes?" La Costa asked. "Or maybe a hot meal and a shower? Could I at least make a phone call?"

"I'm sure they can provide you with whatever you need," Grimaldi said in as soothing a voice as possible. "I understand that you two are supposed to get the VIP treatment, and if you don't—" Grimaldi reached into his pocket and withdrew a plain white card with a phone number "—you just call this number."

"Your number?" Parmahel asked.

"Nope. Complaint department."

La Costa frowned. "Oh, you're a riot. Just a barrel of laughs."

"Cheer up, La Costa. You won't be detained long. Maybe thirty-six hours, max. And then you'll be free to do whatever you want or go where you want or say whatever you want. Just think how much your people are going to pay you guys for this story. Firsthand eyewitnesses to the rescue of a military special ops agent. Flown in a private jet by a highly trained and ruggedly handsome pilot—that's me—and stashed away in a safe house guarded by nameless federal agents." Grimaldi winked. "Got all the makings of a Pulitzer if you ask me."

La Costa didn't look convinced and neither did Parmahel as the two climbed out of their seats and followed Grimaldi out of the plane. As they started heading in the direction of the waiting agents, the Stony

Man pilot's cell phone rang. He whipped it out and read the number on the digital display. It was a series of alphanumeric characters.

"Yes?"

"I take it you're in Washington," Hal Brognola replied in his usual, gruff manner.

"Well, I'm sure the GPS tracking system Aaron has on us could tell you that much."

"That would be true if I were at the Farm, smart guy."

Brognola tried to sound tough, but in reality Grimaldi knew it was just his way of saying he was glad to hear the Stony Man pilot was safely home. "You're not minding the shop?"

"No, I'm on my way to meet you, but I'm running a little behind. Barb called in on her vacation just to check up, and as soon as I told her about Striker she took the next plane out of Seattle."

Grimaldi nodded, remembering Barbara Price had been taking a rare vacation visiting an old friend who lived in rural Washington State. "Against strict instructions not to, of course."

"Of course."

"Well, we just got on the ground here at Andrews, and I'm about to turn our two newshounds over to your guys."

A moment of silence followed before Brognola said, "What guys?"

"The ones you said you were sending. They were here waiting for us at our private hangar."

"What are you talking about? I'm *with* the two U.S. Marshals who will be taking protective custody of La Costa and Parmahel."

Grimaldi stopped in his tracks and his blood ran cold. He reached out and grabbed hold of La Costa's elbow, turning her back in the direction of the plane and gesturing for Parmahel to do the same. At the same moment he steered them into a reverse course, Grimaldi looked in the direction of the two men, who began to shift nervously.

"Hal, I think we may have trouble."

"Do what you have to," Brognola said. "We'll be there in under five."

"Hurry."

Grimaldi broke the connection, pocketed the phone and then began to hustle La Costa and Parmahel toward the plane. He looked over his shoulder in time to see the two "agents" reach into their jackets and draw pistols. Grimaldi shouted a warning at the two reporters to get it in gear and all three broke into a flat run. They reached the plane and dashed up the stairs just as the enemy opened up. Grimaldi was the last into the plane and got winged in the right shoulder by a round. The bullet tore a neat furrow in his flight suit and left a minor flesh wound in its wake.

Grimaldi glanced at the wound briefly, judged it was nothing and then rushed to the mobile armory in the back. The pilot came away with an M-16 A-3, slapped in a loaded magazine and brought the weapon into battery with a yank of the charging handle. He palmed the forward assist to ensure the bolt was fully forward, then ordered Parmahel and La Costa to get flat on their bellies as he returned to the door.

Grimaldi peered around the edge of the door, raised the M-16 A-3 to his shoulder and squeezed off a 3-round burst. The rounds went high, but the pilot quickly and expertly corrected his aim with the skill of a seasoned pro. His second three rounds were spot-on, splitting open the skull of one of the gunners and spraying blood and gray matter in all directions. Realizing his opponent was now armed, the survivor quickly went for cover.

To Grimaldi's dismay, however, three more enemy gunners bailed from the SUV to follow suit with their cohort.

"This is serious!" Grimaldi said, looking at the two journalists. "What is it with you two?"

Parmahel managed a quick-witted reply as he jerked his head in La Costa's direction. "I think it's her perfume."

Grimaldi returned his attention to the situation at hand. There was no way he could cover all angles of the plane without shooting out some windows, not to mention the thin metal body wouldn't provide much in the way of protection if they all decided to start shooting at once. The best he could hope for was to hold them off long enough for reinforcements to arrive, either Brognola or the military.

He didn't have to wait that long as he suddenly saw the approach of flashing lights from two separate military police vehicles on different approach vectors.

The pilot caught a glimpse of one enemy gunner trying to change positions, and he seized the advantage by triggering off several more controlled bursts and leading the target. He was rewarded with the sudden spinning of the guy's corpse and watched with satisfaction as it eventually landed on the pavement and lay still. The two military cruisers screeched to a halt and disgorged a plethora of air patrol officers, who were armed to the teeth with pistols and automatic rifles.

The trio of enemy shooters tried foolishly to repel the veritable small army of trained military policemen, and although Grimaldi couldn't see the results of that encounter he was pretty sure he could guess as the shooting didn't go on for more than a few seconds. As the sounds of battle died out, Grimaldi laid his M-16 A-3 aside and stepped out of the plane with his hands high in the air. It wouldn't do to have these same cops—now totally pumped on adrenaline—cut him down with similar zeal.

As the officers gathered around Grimaldi, a couple headed to the plane to retrieve La Costa and Parmahel, and Hal Brognola and the two U.S. Marshals pulled up. The Stony Man chief climbed from the front passenger seat, pushed his way through the array of military policemen and clamped his left hand on Grimaldi's shoulder while vigorously shaking the pilot's hand with the other.

"Damn glad to see you in one piece, Jack."

"Glad to be in one piece."

La Costa and Parmahel walked up and Grimaldi said, "Hal, I'd like you to meet Guadalupe La Costa and Julio Parmahel."

"Charmed, I'm sure," La Costa said with an expression that said she was anything but.

"Can't say I blame your skepticism," Brognola replied. "But I have very much been looking forward to meeting you two in person."

"Great," Parmahel said. "Now can we get something to eat?"

CHAPTER TWELVE

"Jack's okay?" Bolan asked Brognola.

"Fine," the Stony Man chief replied. "La Costa and Parmahel were also unharmed. We have them tucked away safely under heavy guard."

"Good. I'd keep them on ice until this is done."

"Understood. What's your status there? You need Jack?"

Bolan thought about it a moment before responding. "Negative. Not right now. I may have you send him to Georgia depending on what I find there."

"Georgia?"

"Yeah, specifically the swamplands."

"Give me the rundown," Brognola said.

Bolan filled him in briefly on the events leading up to the interrogation of Veda. "The main player here is a terrorist named Siraj Razzaq. I'll need a complete dossier as soon as you can get it to me, including whatever photos Bear can dig up."

"Done. What else?"

"Veda says he's never met Razzaq face-to-face, but

his spies confirmed Razzaq's operation is based in the States."

"How he could operate this long without being discovered?"

"Apparently he's established a base somewhere inside the Okefenokee Swamp."

Brognola let out a whistle. "That's a big area."

"Yeah," Bolan said. "About seven hundred square miles if memory serves. I think Bear could help us with this."

Aaron Kurtzman oversaw all data processing and storage. The massive computer systems buried beneath the Annex of Stony Man Farm served as the heart of intelligence for the field work of the Stony Man's fire teams, Able Team and Phoenix Force. Every processed scrap of information ran through the computer systems and was sorted, disseminated and archived by Kurtzman's team, providing valuable intelligence at the push of a button whenever called upon. A dedicated satellite disguised as a weather and news uplink could then send and receive encrypted transmissions by interfacing with personal digital assistants carried by every member of Stony Man.

"You think Bear can narrow the search parameters?"

"Exactly," Bolan replied. "I'm guessing Razzaq couldn't run a decent firebase within those swamps without some kind of electronic connection to the outside world. I think Bear's geo-informational programs could pinpoint such a location for me."

"I'll get him and the team working on it pronto."

"Thanks, Hal."

"So you buy the theory this is, in fact, a terrorist plot to overthrow the established government in Puerto Rico?"

"I do now," Bolan said. "I'm still not optimistic about Veda's trustworthiness, but given what happened at Andrews it seems what he says is plausible."

"How so?"

"Veda's connections appear localized. He didn't even know the hit here at the hotel had failed, and he wasn't prepared for my offensive against his estate. I sincerely doubt he could have orchestrated the attempt at Andrews. That leaves Razzaq."

"What makes you think so?"

"I think Razzaq had a watcher for Veda."

"You have anyone special in mind?"

"The probable candidate is Fonseca. He's the only one with company contacts, which makes him the only one with ears inside DHS."

"So he hears about Jack bringing La Costa and Parmahel to Washington and contacts Razzaq to take them out of the picture."

"Why not? The risk is worth it to him now that he thinks our focus is on Razzaq. The guy didn't twitch a muscle during my entire interrogation."

"No offense, Striker, but that's hardly an indicator of guilt."

"True. But he stayed awfully quiet while Hernandez and I questioned Veda, and he even excused himself a couple of times."

"You think he may have warned Razzaq."

"Right," Bolan replied. "Which is why I think I'm going to have to move fast."

"Okay, we'll make arrangements to get you on the first bird out of there."

"How soon can you have Bear's intelligence to me?"

"I've already paged him. Plus, Barb's on her way

back now and should arrive within the hour. That'll help speed up the dissemination."

"I thought she was on vacation."

Brognola sighed. "She was until she heard about you."

"Well, give her my best when you see her."

"Will do, Striker, and take care."

"Out."

Bolan clicked off the cell phone and tucked it into the breast pocket of his shirt. His eyes danced between the rearview and side mirrors. He'd picked up a tail. The same car—a tan, late-model BMW—had been following him through the evening traffic of downtown San Juan, always two or three cars back. Strange make for a tail car, especially if the observers wanted to remain inconspicuous.

Bolan hated to make a move in the traffic at the risk of endangering bystanders, but he was smack in the middle of the downtown area with no running room. He noticed an intersection ahead and slowed the vehicle, putting on his signal plenty in advance to make sure the tail saw it. He hoped none of the cars between them also wanted to turn. Good fortune prevailed.

Bolan made a right turn but to his surprise the vehicle didn't follow, instead continuing on the straightaway. Could he have been wrong? Bolan wondered until another vehicle, this one a dark nondescript car behind the tan vehicle, turned and maintained an even distance. He slowed even more and the vehicle slowed with him.

The soldier decided to test his theory as potential fact rather than just paranoia stemming from his recent ordeal. He needed sleep, but he figured he would have time for that later. Bolan turned left and caught a red light at the intersection two blocks down. As he rolled to a stop, the tan sedan passed by and slowed as it went through the intersection. No question now, the followers were using multiple vehicles and waiting for an opportunity to pen him.

The Executioner decided to give them one.

Bolan turned right on a red and increased speed to catch the tan BMW. He rolled up on them quickly and saw that the driver kept turning his head just enough that Bolan could tell they were scoping him out. He practically tailgated the sedan for several blocks until they rolled up to a light just turning yellow.

The soldier engaged his left-turn signal and then watched as the BMW driver followed suit. At the last moment, Bolan whipped into the outside lane and passed the sedan to enter the intersection just as the light turned red. The dark vehicle far back couldn't even attempt pursuit without risking an accident with oncoming traffic, which left only the BMW standing even a remote chance if the driver blew the light. He did and that proved to be all the confirmation Bolan needed.

He pretended not to notice the BMW pursuing him and maintained a steady speed. He proceeded another three blocks and turned onto a side street—this one void of traffic—then accelerated quickly to put distance between his rental vehicle and the BMW. The streets were still slick with rain, which made the soldier's next maneuver all the easier. He waited until he'd reached about 50 mph, then stood on the brakes and jerked the steering wheel to the left. A moment later he tromped on the accelerator and then jammed on the brakes again to put the vehicle into a 180-degree power slide. The nose of his vehicle now faced the oncoming BMW. The driver of the pursuit vehicle stood on his own brakes. The back fishtailed but stayed in control.

Bolan had his window down and stuck his left arm through it, .44 Magnum Desert Eagle in hand, before any of the BMW occupants could react. The warrior triggered a round and the weapon boomed into the night as a 240-grain slug smashed through the windshield and pebbled the safety glass. The BMW's tires skidded against the slick pavement as the driver put the car into Reverse to beat a hasty retreat. Bolan loosed three more rounds from the .44 Magnum handcannon before dropping his gearshift into Drive and pressing the offensive. As the BMW driver increased speed, he began to lose control, as often happened with an inexperienced wheelman, and his vehicle eventually vaulted the sidewalk and smashed into the side of a building.

Erring on the side of survival, all occupants but the driver bailed and presented three viable targets for Bolan. The soldier took the one coming out the right, rear passenger side first as he emerged and tried to swing a machine pistol into action. The heavy slug cored through the gunner's chest and slammed him against the building. He slid to the ground and left a gory streak in his wake. Next came the front-seat gunman, who was felled with a clean head shot that blew apart his skull.

The remaining man outside the vehicle had the luxury of using the BMW for cover until the driver, seeing he had nowhere to go, blasted off the sidewalk and left his partner unprotected. No longer covered, the gunman reacted by triggering his weapon at Bolan on the run. The soldier frowned as he ducked to avoid the hasty autofire that shattered the rear passenger window of his car. If the man had simply run away, Bolan would have let him go, but with this act of aggression the Executioner had no choice but to neutralize that threat. He popped off two rounds, the first striking the man's machine pistol. The second ripped through his opponent's midsection and sent him tumbling head over heels along the sidewalk.

Bolan took off in pursuit of the BMW now, undaunted in his determination to verify the identity of his assailants. He knew this couldn't be the work of Veda; the leader of the Independents had been incommunicado since his interrogation.

That left Siraj Razzaq's crew.

But how had the NRJO known where Bolan would be? Fonseca? Bolan couldn't see the guy putting together anything that fast. He might have bought that theory relative to the attack at Andrews AFB. But was it possible Fonseca and Razzaq put together a tail and potential ambush on such short notice? Well, if there was another explanation, then Bolan planned to find out what it was.

As he raced in pursuit of the BMW, the dark sedan rolled past, muzzle-flashes winking from the driver's window. Bolan's windshield turned into a maze of cracks that partially obscured his vision but he didn't slow down—to do so would have cost him his life as the rounds skittered over the roof of his vehicle. Had Bolan decreased speed, the shooter would likely have tagged him.

The soldier watched his side mirror as the black sedan squealed to a halt and performed a turn similar to the one he'd executed just a minute before. This guy was good. Bolan returned his attention to the BMW, reached out the window just as they cleared an inter-section and snapped off a pair of rounds. At these speeds and over the rough, narrow back streets of this San Juan neighborhood the .44 Magnum wasn't par-ticularly effective.

Bolan knew this would end only if he took more extreme measures. The BMW's engine exceeded that of his rental in power and performance, which meant the only way to bring the chase to a halt would be to outdrive his quarry. Bolan increased speed until he was on the BMW's tail. He saw a car parked at the curb and then timed a bump against the left quarter panel of the BMW with the right front fender of the rental. The driver lost control, went into a skid and somehow managed to jump the sidewalk and narrowly avoid the obstacle. As Bolan drove past, he saw the driver look behind him with disbelief and then at Bolan with a smirk of victory. Too bad his attention wasn't ahead, because he missed the concrete stoop of a porch and his right tire smacked it head-on. The impact launched the vehicle into the air and brought it down on the driver's side, skidding for another twenty feet before smashing into a utility pole. The pole groaned, but seemed to hold, although the impact sent showers of sparks from the transformer mounted atop it.

Bolan skidded to a halt, and his eyes flicked toward the rearview mirror as the headlights of the dark sedan drew nearer by the second. The Executioner popped the trunk and went EVA. He accessed the weapons bag, pulled out the FNC and prepared for the other arrival while keeping one eye on the wreckage of the BMW. So far he hadn't seen any movement, but that could mean it might have shaken up the driver or he might be seriously injured. In either case, and as long as he wasn't deceased, Bolan had to view him as a threat until confirmed otherwise.

With one eye on the BMW, he prepared to face the sedan bearing down on him.

IT HADN'T PROVED difficult to track Stone to San Juan.

Within a few hours of Stone's return from Las Mareas, the American CIA man—Alvaro Fonseca—contacted Razzaq and advised him Stone had shown up alive and well at their offices downtown with a crazy plan to get Veda to come to the table under the pretext of talks. Of course, Fonseca had wisely suspected that this mysterious Colonel Stone, a high-ranking military officer attached to the DSS who didn't allegedly exist, planned to set a trap for Veda and his people.

So Fonseca had been bought off by Razzaq, so he did the only thing he could do. He contacted Ad-Darr and advised him where to find Stone. The assassin had arranged a three-car tailing detail and would wait for the best time to strike. Unfortunately, Stone had proved resourceful enough to take out one car and nearly lose Ad-Darr in his midnight-blue Chrysler. The third team had waited up the road, but Stone had picked them up well before that and turned, and with Ad-Darr being unfamiliar with the area he could hardly call them and ask for assistance.

Not that it mattered. Ad-Darr would take care of Stone himself.

His first attempt in Las Mareas had failed, as had his second just a minute ago, but this would be the final conflagration. Here on this backwater street in this backwater city, Ad-Darr would deal with Stone once and for all.

And then he would move on to his next mission. A mission of purpose.

THE SEDAN SQUEALED to a halt and the dome light came on a second later.

Bolan knelt, FNC held at the ready, but a glimpse of the face illuminated in the light froze him in place a moment as he considered the almost spectral sight. Ad-Darr? How was that possible? Jack Grimaldi had confirmed he'd killed him. Had the Stony Man pilot been mistaken? No, highly unlikely and yet there he was—at least someone who looked like Bolan's torturer and captor—emerging from the dark sedan with a machine pistol in hand.

Well, spirit or not, the weapon in the man's hands looked plenty real, and the first volley of rounds he triggered in Bolan's direction that skipped off the pavement or buzzed over Bolan's head were definitely real.

Ad-Darr burst from the cover of his sedan and made for another car parked along the street that would provide better protection. Bolan swung the muzzle of the FNC into target acquisition and led his mark as he moved the selector switch to 3-round-burst mode. His first volley went wide, and the second came much closer, but Ad-Darr gained cover before Bolan could bring him down.

The Executioner considered his options a moment, then snaked his arm over the lip of the open trunk from his cover position and retrieved a pair of the Diehl DM-51 grenades. The versatile, Austrian-made ordnance served a dual purpose. More than two thousand steel balls were compressed within a removable sleeve that fit over the slim, cylindrical body filled with RDX high explosives. Without the sleeve, the weapon provided an offensive role, and if the user locked the sleeve into place it became an effective antipersonnel weapon.

Bolan yanked the pin on the first sleeveless one and tossed it side-handed across the street so it skittered to a halt beneath the vehicle. The soldier followed with a second one toward the rear, risking a fusillade of heavy lead to make the appropriate distance. One of the rounds winged Bolan, but he ignored it, clenching his teeth against the pain as the round burned over his shoulder and cut a furrow through the meaty portion of muscles connecting shoulder and neck. The first grenade exploded just as Ad-Darr dashed from the cover of the vehicle. The HE blew with enough force to shatter the jalopy's gas tank, and a secondary explosion lifted it off the ground with a whoosh.

Ad-Darr crossed directly in the path of the second grenade, apparently believing the grenade that blew was the only one Bolan had tossed. The grenade was far enough away not to kill Ad-Darr instantly, but close enough to send the steel balls flying into his lower extremities and effectively taking him down. His collapse into the rain-soaked ground coupled with his distance from the blast saved his body from being torn apart by the concussion.

Bolan rose and marched toward Ad-Darr, who lay writhing and moaning on the lawn. Porch lights began to wink on and the faces of a few residents peered from windows or doors. The Executioner ignored them as he stopped and stood over Ad-Darr's mangled form. Bloody holes covered the left side of the assassin's body like a series of festering splotches. Bolan leveled the FNC muzzle at the man's head.

"You're supposed to be dead," Bolan said.

"I am invincible," Ad-Darr replied in a hoarse whisper.

Bolan looked him up and down and shook his head. "Doesn't look that way."

"You have been an honorable enemy. You are to be…commended." On that last word, Ad-Darr coughed blood.

"You're finished."

"You would not let an enemy suffer."

"I wouldn't let anyone suffer, friend or foe."

Ad-Darr managed something close to a smile. "You…you are more honorable than I thought, Colonel."

"One question," Bolan said. "Razzaq, Siraj Razzaq. He's behind this?"

Ad-Darr couldn't reply because he'd lost consciousness. Bolan called his name a couple of times, but the assassin failed to respond. The Executioner ended it with a single shot to the head. A confirmed kill, yeah, but another casualty, however guilty he might be, of this never-ending war against terrorism. Then again, he was the only one who knew Ad-Darr was dead at this point. Maybe he could use that to his advantage.

And the Executioner thought he knew exactly where to start.

CHAPTER THIRTEEN

Security Adviser Alvaro Fonseca looked up as Bolan pushed open the doors of his office and stalked into the room like a vengeful wraith.

"You look surprised to see me, Fonseca."

The man frowned. "Not really, I just—"

"What?" Bolan interjected. "Thought I was dead? I had a little run-in with Siraj Razzaq's hired assassin. Ad-Darr's dead and Razzaq's op in Georgia will soon be finished."

"Who?"

"Don't play stupid, Fonseca. You've played that role too long, now. Veda might have had time to sic Razzaq's dogs on my friends back in the States, but he wouldn't have been able to make contact and disclose my where-abouts. That left you, although I didn't want to believe it at first. But you and Hernandez were the only two who knew what happened in Las Mareas, our exact location in the hotel and when I left your office this evening. Razzaq's people were too well-informed to chalk this up to good intelligence sources."

"How dare you come in here and accuse me—"

The sight of the Beretta 93-R in Bolan's fist—muzzle glinting in the fluorescent lights of the office—silenced Fonseca.

"You're the one with guts, Fonseca, smiling in the faces of the leaders here in Puerto Rico while sharpening the knife you planned to run into their backs. Well, I'm shutting you down."

"You won't kill me," Fonseca said. "There'll be too many questions."

"No, there won't," Bolan replied. "I've already told those who need to know."

Fonseca swallowed hard.

"What's the going rate these days for turning your country on its ear?"

"I don't know what the hell you're talking about!" Fonseca said, sputtering now and clearly in fear for his life.

"Sure," Bolan said. "You're like everyone else, totally innocent."

"Nobody's *totally* innocent."

"That what you tell yourself every morning when you look in the mirror?" Bolan demanded.

"You're no one to judge me, Colonel."

"No, you're right. I'm not your judge or jury."

Fonseca nodded. "That's right."

"I'm your judgment," Bolan said coldly.

"Come again?" Fonseca replied with a half laugh.

"You heard me. I have a message from your boss."

"Sure you do." And with that Fonseca dived toward his desk drawer, fumbling with the handle.

"You're fired."

The Executioner squeezed the trigger.

"I CAME BACK AS SOON as I heard," Barbara Price told Bolan, the concern evident in her voice. "You okay?"

"I'm okay," Bolan said. "Although I could use about a full day's sleep."

"Well, I wish we had better accommodations for you, but you wanted something on short notice. You're booked on a military hop leaving out of the army air base there."

"Where to?"

"A supply run going to Fort Stewart."

"Their timing's impeccable."

She laughed. "It's not first-class, but it's something and you're cleared to bring your equipment along, no questions asked."

"Nice work, Barb."

"You better hurry, though, because it leaves in an hour."

"I'm on my way now."

"What's that?" she asked, her voice distant. Then she came back stronger with, "Hal wants to know Fonseca's status."

"Tell him I terminated his position. With prejudice."

"Will do."

"Any updates from Bear yet?"

"Not yet, but we're all burning the midnight oil here to narrow your potential targets. We've also notified local law enforcement and they're on standby. Your contact is a field warden with the Okefenokee Swamp patrol boat unit, a Captain Don Wharton."

"Cover?"

"FBI Special Agent Matt Cooper with VICAP, fugitive retrieval unit."

"That should keep the questions to a minimum."

The FBI's Violent Criminal Apprehension Program

routinely employed special agents to pursue hardened criminals like bank robbers, repeat felons and gun-runners. In fact, any violent crime committed within federal jurisdiction or where the crimes spanned multiple states fell into the auspice of VICAP.

"Okay," Price said. "Have a good flight."

"Wilco," Bolan replied. "And Barb?"

"Yes?"

"Thanks."

"Anytime, big guy."

Bolan disconnected the call and began to consider his tactical options. Once Kurtzman and his team narrowed the search parameters, he'd be better able to formulate an offensive against whatever stronghold in which Razzaq might be operating. He had to admit that one of the largest swampland areas in the country—a wholly inhospitable environment with peril at nearly every turn—would make for a very interesting battle-ground.

This time around, however, he wouldn't have the luxury of operating alone. That area was simply too vast to tackle by himself; he would need the cooperation of this Wharton and his men. He expected he'd get it. He couldn't think of a scenario where a "good ol' boy" from the South wouldn't want to take on a potential terrorist organization. Bolan had already decided that if the situation warranted it, he'd likely tell Wharton and his men the truth. They deserved to know what they were walking into. Or at least what the hell they might be walking into. Trouble was, not even Bolan knew what that was yet. Then again it didn't matter.

Terrorism had reared its ugly head inside America. And Mack Bolan planned to cut it off.

"LUPE, WOULD YOU SIT DOWN already? You're pacing like a caged lion."

La Costa didn't bother to speak. She stopped and glared at Julio Parmahel a moment before resuming her vigil. Their rooms couldn't exactly be called first-class, although they were cozy and clean. The agents had escorted them to an older house, an abandoned structure that looked as if it had been refurbished, at the end of a road deep in the heart of farm country. The last hour of the trip they were asked to wear blindfolds so they couldn't know exactly where they were, but being the daughter of a diplomat La Costa knew enough about the area to know they were somewhere on the fringes of West Virginia.

Truth of it was, her friend's assessment hit real close to the mark. At the moment she *did* feel like a caged animal. What had led her to this point? It all started with wanting to get a story and agreeing to help Stone, and in the end this is what she got for her troubles. La Costa couldn't think back to a time when she'd wanted to be anything but a reporter. Even as a kid her parents had bought her a miniature tape recorder. She would run around the block where she lived and "interview" her friends or neighbors. At one point, she even started a small neighborhood newspaper in her area that was read and enjoyed by everyone.

All her life's pursuits had led to this point. And when she finally landed the position of her dreams with the Associated Press covering politics—a subject matter rarely reserved for the female of the species—in the territory of her birth, La Costa thought she had it all.

La Costa stopped pacing, turned to face Parmahel and put her hands on her hips. "It's Stone."

Parmahel looked up from the game of solitaire he'd been playing. "Come again?"

"It's that damned son of a bitch Colonel Stone."

"That 'damned son of a bitch' saved both of our lives, as did his friend Jack." Parmahel lifted the sweating bottle of beer he'd been nursing and tipped it in her direction. "Now the fact I'm still breathing is something I can drink to."

"Very funny," La Costa shot back.

Parmahel took several long pulls and smacked his lips in an exaggerated fashion. "I'm not trying to be funny," he replied matter-of-factly. "I'm just saying I find it pretty hard to be pissed at either one of those guys. That's all."

"So you're siding with the men."

Parmahel sighed and put down his cards. He crossed his arms and fixed her with a stern expression. "I'm not siding with anybody, Lupe. In fact, I'm on *your* side if you want to know the truth. But that doesn't dismiss the fact that these guys put their necks on the line to help us, and I think we could give them a little latitude."

"A little latitude?" La Costa expressed disbelief. "A little latitude?"

"Yes."

"Hmmph, that's fine sitting there saying that," La Costa said. "Do you realize that by cooping us up like this and preventing us from getting the truth behind this story that these guys are violating our civil rights? Not to mention that conducting military operations inside any sovereign border of the United States is a clear violation of the Constitution?"

"All I know is that they saved our asses."

"Don't you see, Julio?" La Costa insisted. "This has

turned into the story of a lifetime and we're sitting here like a pair of fools and missing all the action."

"Well, what do you think you can do about it?" Parmahel pointed toward the door that led from his room and said, "You don't actually think the two big goons out there are going to let us just walk out of here."

"Why not? Even that guy with the Justice Department said we're not prisoners."

"No, we're not prisoners. But we're still under protective custody and while the Justice guy, Hal, didn't imply we didn't have to stay, he also didn't imply we could leave of our own accord."

Before La Costa could reply there was a knock at the door. It opened a moment later and one of the men from the security attachment strode in followed by none other than the Justice Department guy from Andrews. In their brief encounter with the man, Julio Parmahel had quickly taken to Hal, but La Costa had confided to Parmahel her genuine dislike for him. It wasn't anything in particular. In fact, he'd been pretty decent to them. La Costa simply didn't trust bureaucrats, and so far the guy named Hal had neither said nor done anything to make her think he was anything other than another government lackey.

"Good evening," Hal greeted them. He dismissed the U.S. Marshal with a nod and when the man left the room he asked, "How are you two holding up?"

La Costa arched an eyebrow as she sat on the edge of the bed. "We'd be holding up better if you let us leave."

The Justice man set his briefcase on the floor and gestured to one of the unoccupied chairs at the small table where Parmahel had been playing solitaire. "Do you mind?"

La Costa shook her head and Hal took a seat. The man from Justice leaned forward as he put his elbows on his knees, fingertips pressed together. He brought his hands to his mouth and looked at La Costa intently for some time. She couldn't tell if he was trying to intimidate her or simply size her up, but she met his gaze without flinching. No way would she allow anyone from the government to intimidate her; she still had some connections that dated back to relationships forged by her father while serving as a diplomat abroad.

"I understand how you feel," he began.

"Do you?" La Costa asked.

"Actually I do, whether you believe that or not. I know it hasn't been easy and I can assure you that the president asked me to personally extend his thanks to both of you."

Parmahel stopped playing cards and looked up. "Wait a minute, you talking about *the* president? Of the United States?" When Hal nodded, Parmahel looked at La Costa and said, "That's impressive."

La Costa chuckled. "I suppose you have the direct ear of the Oval Office."

"I do," he said.

"You see, I *knew* there was a lot more going on here than met the eye. I had the story of a lifetime to tell, but because I chose to trust Colonel Stone I ended up getting screwed out of that story. And just to rub salt in the wound, my government shows their gratefulness by packing me and my friend up and shipping us off to some remote area, not letting us do our jobs or talk to our families to let them know we're okay or even giving us the opportunity to take a few of our personal belongings."

Hal shook his head. "You're looking at this all wrong,

Ms. La Costa. First off, a number of very good people nearly lost their lives keeping you safe, Colonel Stone being chief among them. Second, we have repeatedly told you that we're willing to provide any and all of your necessities at no cost to you for the duration of this emergency. And last but not least, part of the reason you're in this situation is because you chose to follow Colonel Stone to Las Mareas instead of staying in San Juan, as you were instructed to do. That's one of the main reasons you're in this situation. So while I understand you're angry and frustrated, I would ask that you not lay the blame for this on someone else. You made a decision and with every decision comes consequences. The only question that remains now is if you're willing to live with that."

"Do I have a choice?"

"If you're asking do you have a choice to accept your situation or not based on your decision, the answer is yes. If you're asking if you have a choice to stay here or go I'm afraid I'd have to tell you no. But as I've already said, you'll only have to be here about another twenty-four hours and then you'll be free to leave."

La Costa looked at Parmahel and started with derision. "So much for not being prisoners."

"You're not prisoners," the Justice Department man countered. "And I told you before you shouldn't look at it that way."

"And how should we look at it?" Parmahel asked.

Hal looked at him. "As far as your current status you might want to view this as an opportunity to stay alive."

"You see, that's the thing I don't understand," La Costa interjected. "Everything was just fine until Colonel Stone showed up in Puerto Rico and started blowing everything to kingdom come. Up to that point, nobody had been trying to kill me and nobody had been trying to kill Julio. So why now?"

The bureaucrat expressed discomfort as he cleared his throat and shifted in his seat. He replied in an even tone, "We don't know yet."

"You don't know yet," La Costa repeated with an expression of skepticism.

"Maybe we can help you there, Hal," Parmahel offered. "Can you tell us what you do know so far?"

"I'm afraid because neither of you possesses a security clearance, I'm able to tell you very little."

La Costa chuckled. "Well, if you are who you claim to be then I'm sure you know my background, and I'm equally sure you know who my father was."

"I know who your father was," Hal replied. "In fact, it might surprise you to know that I met your father on a couple of occasions. He was a good man who was devoted to the security of this nation. I was sorry to hear of his death."

The Justice man's statement took La Costa completely by surprise. More than fifteen years had passed since his death, the result of having had a heart attack while driving to work. His vehicle had swerved out of control and plunged into an inlet of the Potomac. The medical examiner had ruled it an accident, but La Costa's suspicious mind had always postulated otherwise. Over time she had come to accept the circumstances of his death, but she'd never stopped wondering if it had truly been an accident. She knew there were times her father hadn't exactly been a choirboy, and that he had a history of relations with numerous intelligence agencies.

"If you worked with my father in any capacity, then I'd say you've been in this business quite a while."

Hal smiled at her and winked. "You could say that."

La Costa decided right there that maybe she had misjudged the man some. "We know how to keep a secret, Hal. So what this now comes down to is whether or not you trust us."

He sighed deeply, sat back in his chair and folded his arms. "Okay, I'm willing to break the rules here as long as both of you realize the danger of the information I'm about to give you and give me your personal assurances you'll be discreet with what you hear." When both of them had nodded their agreement Hal continued, "Colonel Stone doesn't work for the Diplomatic Security Service. In fact, he isn't even a member of the U.S. Armed Forces."

La Costa shook her head. "Well, that much is obvious, but why don't you tell us what we don't know."

"After the incident at the political rally, we sent Stone to investigate," Hal replied. "You see, we weren't buying the story Alvaro Fonseca of Governor Hernandez's office told us about this being the work of political dissidents. That's why we got you to arrange the meeting with Miguel Veda, and subsequently that led Stone to Las Mareas, where he learned of the New Revolutionary Justice Organization's involvement."

"Yeah," Parmahel said. "He mentioned them before, but we just didn't get the connection."

"Neither did we," Hal said, "until we learned that Fonseca was feeding them information and that Miguel Veda had entered into an agreement to let the NRJO utilize Puerto Rico as a base of operations if they could secure Puerto Rican independence."

"A terrorist organization in Puerto Rico?" La Costa asked with disbelief. "That's…that's unthinkable!"

"That it is," Hal said. "But those are the facts, and right at this moment Stone is on his way to Georgia, where we believe the NRJO has established its headquarters."

"That still doesn't explain why they're trying to kill us," Parmahel said.

La Costa took a sharp intake of breath. "Maybe it does, Julio."

Both men looked at her.

"Do you still have the footage we took at the rally?" she continued.

"I turned it in to production," Parmahel replied. When La Costa's face fell, he added quickly, "But every good cameraman always keeps a copy."

Parmahel rose and left the room, then returned a minute later with a DVD-ROM case in his hand. "I've got a copy of the entire shoot right here."

"Julio, I could just kiss you right now."

Parmahel's face reddened.

"I don't understand," Hal said.

"I didn't, either, until you explained to us what's going on, Hal," La Costa said. "I think you need to watch this."

CHAPTER FOURTEEN

The C-141 cargo plane carrying Mack Bolan landed on the tarmac at Fort Stewart, Georgia, just a few minutes after midnight.

The military police vehicle awaiting him at the airfield rendezvoused with the Executioner and drove him off the military installation and into the neighboring city of Savannah, the headquarters of the Southern patrol division for the Georgia State Police. The Okefenokee Swamp patrol unit was actually part of a federal program enacted in the 1930s when Franklin Roosevelt, during his term as president, had declared the entire area a national wildlife refuge. Because the swamplands spanned several law-enforcement jurisdictions, responsibilities were shared among local, county and state authorities in conjunction with federal officials.

A Georgia state patrolman—a big, muscular black man by the name of Rawlins—drove Bolan southwest to the city of Waycross on the northernmost edge of the Okefenokee. It was here that Bolan finally met Captain Donald Wharton. The wildlife officer was tall and lanky, in his midfifties, with dark hair graying at the temples and dark green eyes. He didn't wear a uniform, at least not exactly. A camouflage ball cap sat rakishly on his head, and he wore a short-sleeve shirt to match. Green-and-khaki waders with suspenders rode up to midchest level. Bolan noted the Glock pistol Wharton carried in a high-mounted shoulder holster beneath his right arm.

Wharton smiled and stuck out his hand. "I'm supposing you would be Special Agent Cooper?"

"That's me," Bolan replied and shook the man's hand.

Wharton's voice had a warm and friendly quality, a Southern drawl common to most natives of the area. "We've been expecting you for a while now. Seems to be a little bit of a mystery about exactly who you were and when you'd get here. I could hardly get my highers in Washington to spill the beans." Wharton delivered a good-natured laugh as he added, "Not that I would've gotten the truth anyway."

Bolan smiled. "I understand, Captain."

Wharton waved away the formalities. "Call me Don, no need to stand on ceremony."

"I go by Cooper."

"So what exactly brings you to this neck of the woods?" Wharton asked, sitting on the edge of his desk and proffering Bolan a nearby chair.

The Executioner sat to give his legs a break. His entire body still ached—likely the aftereffects of the drugs—although he had slept well on the C-141. The trip had provided him with enough time to rest and rejuvenate for the activities ahead. He didn't know how long it would take them to find Razzaq's base or even what perils they might encounter while combing the swamps. Bolan had no misconceptions about the dangers of a place like Okefenokee.

"We don't have a lot of time for lengthy explanations, so I'll get to the point. We believe there are some very dangerous people operating somewhere inside the swamp."

Wharton's eyebrows rose. "Somewhere?"

"I know right now it doesn't sound like much to go on," Bolan replied and splayed his hands. "But I have some of my people back in Washington working on that right now. They're going to try to narrow it down for us some."

"How?"

"I'm not authorized to disclose that. But to show you I'm willing to cooperate with you and your people, I will tell you that we believe these individuals are Lebanese terrorists."

"Terrorists?"

Bolan nodded. "They call themselves the New Revolutionary Justice Organization, and they've been planning a coup inside Puerto Rico for some time. They're well-equipped, well-armed and extremely dangerous. They also have a significant intelligence network established. Up until recently they had contacts inside the U.S. government, but I've since neutralized that pipeline."

Wharton scratched the back of his neck as he said, "I know something about Lebanese terrorists. I served in the Marine Corps in the early eighties, including a tour of duty in Beirut."

"Then I don't have to tell you about the NRJO or what they're capable of."

"What I don't get is how a terrorist organization could operate inside the United States without being detected."

Bolan frowned. "I was kind of hoping you could tell

us, since you know this area a lot better than I do. Is it possible someone could establish a base of operations inside the swamp without anybody knowing about it?"

Wharton was quiet for a time as he considered the Executioner's question. Bolan could see the man still had a lot of questions and doubt, merely by the expression on his face. Even Bolan had to admit the idea of terrorists operating deep in the heart of Georgian swamplands for any period of time without being detected was preposterous at best. Then again, many would have called al Qaeda's plans and activities leading up to 9/11 just as ludicrous. Bolan had learned long ago never to underestimate the enemy, or to make too many assumptions about what they were and were not capable of doing.

"Well," Wharton finally said, "I suppose it's possible. There are some remote areas extremely difficult to access where they could find ground stable enough to build makeshift shelters of some kind. They could use the natural water flow to provide their electricity, and other natural resources to meet their needs. The two biggest factors to consider would be medicine and fresh water."

"What about wildlife?" Bolan asked.

"Not too much to worry about there if you're well-armed. Biggest danger is alligators, but of course they're pretty well-fed right now. This is the rainy season and with that comes an abundant supply of food sources."

"So what I think I hear you telling me is that these terrorists could be operating here after all."

"Yeah," Wharton said with a grim expression and nod. "It's possible."

Bolan contemplated Wharton's forthright answer. It

wasn't what he wanted to hear, but it was what he'd pretty much expected to hear. It left little doubt in Bolan's mind that Miguel Veda had told them the truth. When he had first heard Veda mention the information about Siraj Razzaq's operations in Georgia, Bolan had demanded that Veda flip on the people who brought him that intelligence. Unfortunately, they were the same people Bolan had encountered on the fringes of San Juan just hours after his arrival in Puerto Rico; the people who had been keeping an eye on La Costa.

Before Bolan could reply to Wharton, his cell phone signaled for attention. "Cooper."

"Striker, it's Bear. This a good time?"

"Couldn't be better. What have you got?"

"It looks like you were dead-on about the digital communications," Kurtzman replied. "We managed to track an open cellular link between a European Union satellite and a triangulation point of approximately five square miles in a southeastern part of Georgia, particularly Charlton County."

"Hold on a sec," Bolan said as he looked at Wharton. "Charlton County?"

Wharton nodded. "We are right on the edge. The vast majority of the Okefenokee is in Charlton. The main port of entry is in a town about forty miles southeast of here called Folkston."

"Any public areas there to be concerned about?"

"Folkston provides the main entrance point into Suwanee Canal Recreation Area." Wharton rose and skirted his desk, then settled behind his keyboard and began to type quickly. He ended with a pronounced tap of the enter key and one wall suddenly illuminated. A digital map spanning a 60-inch plasma screen TV was displayed. "The red dot is Folkston. The area surrounded in green marks the boundaries of the recreation area. Due west, about twenty miles, that green line indicates the beginning of Stephen C. Foster State Park."

"You getting all of this, Bear?" Bolan asked.

"Absolutely. In fact, I'm looking at the exact same map you are."

That didn't surprise Bolan in the least. It almost didn't seem fair not to tell Wharton that the Stony Man wizard was deep inside their information and control systems, and had probably been there for several hours now.

"So if I'm looking at this right," Bolan said, "we have two remote areas where they might be operating. Wharton, can you tell me how big those search areas are?"

Wharton didn't bat an eyelash. "The area east of Stephen C. Foster and north of Suwanee Canal is about 150 square miles. The area south of Sewanee Canal, just north of the Florida State border, is another sixty to sixty-five, or thereabouts."

"Can you get the search area any narrower?" Bolan asked Kurtzman.

"Based on the data I see here, I'm about ninety-five percent certain we're dealing with a point south of the Suwanee Canal recreation area."

"Nice job, Bear. I'll be in touch."

"One other thing before you go," Kurtzman said. "Barb needs to talk to you."

"I'm listening."

"Striker, I just got off the phone with Hal and we have some additional information here, but I'm afraid it's not good. You remember we were a bit puzzled about why Razzaq would be concerned about taking La Costa and Parmahel out of the picture, especially after you had already exposed Veda and the attempts by Ad-Darr to assassinate you had failed."

"Right."

"It seems our reporter friends got some footage that night at the political rally, which provides damning evidence Razzaq may not be operating alone."

"In what way?"

"We ran facial recognition on a copy of the footage Julio Parmahel shot the night the political rally was attacked. It wasn't until after we had La Costa and Parmahel in protective custody that La Costa remembered seeing Ad-Darr's face. That's when we put two and two together and figured out the significance. Ad-Darr's real name was Mahmud Hassani, a well-known assassin who was repeatedly hired by al Qaeda."

"You think al Qaeda may be financing Razzaq's plans?"

"No, we think that Hassani was actually in Puerto Rico to commit a political assassination, and Razzaq didn't know about it. The video shows footage of Hassani approaching the podium just seconds before the attack. There's complete pandemonium on the stage at that point, so it's difficult to tell who he might have been targeting but there's no question he was intending to assassinate somebody."

"So Hassani was double-dipping," Bolan replied.

"Exactly," Price said. "And we think that the situation here is completely unrelated. Since Ad-Darr is dead, it stands to reason that al Qaeda will try again, but they can't do that if there is even a remote possibility the information on their target could fall into the hands of U.S. authorities."

"Which is why they'll do anything to erase La Costa

and Parmahel," Bolan concluded. "At the moment it seems like Hal and DHS have their security in hand. I've got my hands full here or I'd attend to the matter personally. For the moment, keep them under wraps."

"Oh, we intend to do that. Although I don't think our friend Ms. La Costa is feeling too cooperative on that point. It seems she's none too happy about the situation, and from what Hal tells me she's blaming it on you."

"She wouldn't be in this situation if she'd stayed put in San Juan like I told her."

"Doesn't sound like she wants to hear that," Price said. "But I think Hal's doing a pretty good job bringing her around. In the meantime, we've contacted Governor Hernandez's office and advised them to be on high alert."

"It's a good precaution," Bolan said. "But I don't think there's any threat to them, at least not now. Al Qaeda won't make a move until La Costa and Parmahel are dead."

"We're keeping an eye on things at this end, and Hal wanted me to assure you personally not to worry about it. He's handling all of the security arrangements himself and he's decided to move them to a more secure location."

Something rumbled in Bolan's guts, something that said moving the two reporters might be more dangerous than keeping them where they were at, but he didn't say anything. Harold Brognola had plenty of experience with this kind of thing and the Executioner trusted him implicitly. Keeping La Costa and Parmahel alive had become Stony Man's charge, and for the moment Mack Bolan was content to leave them to it.

"Pass my best onto him with my thanks," Bolan said. "I'll be in touch as soon as I know something."

"Take care, Striker."

"Out."

Bolan disconnected the call and then rose and stepped closer to the wall map of the Okefenokee swamplands. He pointed to the spot south of the Suwanee Canal Recreation Area. "My people have triangulated a cell to satellite signal in this part of the swamp, and we're convinced this is where the terrorists may be operating."

"It's not a small area or an easy one to negotiate," Wharton said. "But I'm willing to give it a go if you are. Any idea what kind of numbers we might be talking about here?"

Bolan shook his head and looked levelly at Wharton. "None, although from what you've already told me about the topography along with my personal knowledge, I can't imagine it would be many. At most we're probably talking about fifteen to twenty men, none of whom will be clustered together, the majority of them on a continuous roving patrol to maintain security in the area."

Wharton's attention fell to his computer screen, and he lifted his finger to request a moment of silence. Bolan respectfully held his tongue and let Wharton have the time he needed to read whatever had caught his attention. After about a minute, Wharton cursed and sat back in his chair.

"We got a new problem on our hands."

Bolan came around the desk to look at the computer screen. "What is it?"

Wharton pointed to a black spot moving directly toward Georgia, and Bolan immediately recognized the image, this one coming from weather radar. "You remember me telling you this is the rainy season? Well, that spot right there is one hell of a storm and it's headed directly toward us."

"ETA?" Bolan asked.

Wharton sighed and shook his head. "At its current speed I'd say four, maybe five hours."

"It just keeps getting better and better. Options?"

Wharton shrugged and replied, "We can make a try for Folkston about thirty-four miles from here or head to St. George, which is about twelve miles south of that, and follow the trail line up County Road 121. Frankly, it's as good a place as any to start search and if things get too rough we have some shelters built along the road we can access until things blow over."

"If the monsoons could affect our search that much, why wouldn't it affect the terrorists, as well?"

"You said it yourself, Cooper. Those guys have had plenty of time to embed themselves deep in the heart of Georgian swamplands. There are people here who lived in those swamps for a long time and managed to survive. It's a way of life for them, a way of life we're not going to change easily and probably wouldn't if we wanted to."

"Any chance some of those residents might get in the line of fire?"

"It's possible but unlikely," Wharton said. "Something you got to remember is that it's not the people in the swamps that'll kill you fastest. It's the black water and the gators and the quicksand, and myriad other dangers lurking for the unprepared and untrained. You got any experience in places like this?"

"Enough to hold my own," Bolan replied easily. "But I leveled with you about the possibility terrorists are operating inside this area because I don't assume you're ready to take the same kind of risks I am."

"I got no love for terrorists, Cooper. And I especially don't have any love for foreigners who come into my swamps uninvited for the purpose of planning the murders of innocent Americans. We've already lost enough lives to terrorism between worldwide attacks and the war in Iraq. Near as I can tell it's time we start dishing out some of what we've been taking. So if that means I got to guide you through every last square inch of that swamp in the most hellish storm the good Lord can muster, by golly, I figure it's worth it."

Bolan had to admit that he hadn't expected that kind of response from Wharton, but at the same time he couldn't say he wasn't glad to hear it. That was the problem with some people. They talked about wanting change and about the security of the nation against her enemies, but then turned around and complained about all the inconveniences. Everybody wanted security, but nobody wanted the additional hassles that sometimes came along with it.

Captain Donald Wharton wasn't like that. No, Wharton came from a rare breed, a stock of warrior that not only talked the talk, but also walked the walk. Wharton said what he meant, and Bolan knew right at that moment he couldn't have asked for a better ally. First, the guy knew the swamps like the back of his hand. Second, he was willing to do what he had to even against insurmountable odds. Finally, he carried an air of toughness and authority that Bolan knew would carry through no matter how rough the circumstances might get.

And given their current situation, things were about to get real rough.

"Okay," Bolan said. "I'm for heading to St. George

and taking our chances with the storm. How soon can you be ready to go?"

Wharton scratched his chin and smiled. "How's about now strike you?"

CHAPTER FIFTEEN

Harold Brognola stood on the covered porch of the safe-house in rural Virginia, an unlit cigar clenched between his teeth, as two U.S. Marshals escorted La Costa and Parmahel to a waiting black Ford Expedition.

A second crew of marshals stood outside a late-model Crown Victoria, their eyes searching for potential threats. Brognola would have taken greater solace to have Able Team on this detail, but they were currently assigned to a mission across the country and this situation didn't merit pulling them off that. Still, for this kind of situation the U.S. Marshals Service remained the next best option. Brognola's status as a "high-ranking official" with the Department of Justice was the only clout required to get what he needed when he needed it. Having the backing of the Oval Office helped a bit, too.

Within minutes the trio was aboard the SUV and headed toward a new location, this one assuredly more secure. Brognola had thought about simply transferring La Costa and Parmahel to Stony Man Farm, but dismissed it as too risky. In other circumstances it would have been perfect, but terrorists had compromised their security in the past and Brognola refused to expose them again without very good reason; especially when both field teams were absent. Not to mention the fact that Kurtzman and Price had too many other things to worry about right now without adding babysitting duties to the equation.

No, he could handle this one on his own.

Brognola rode in the front seat of the SUV with a third marshal behind the wheel, and a two-man detail watched over Parmahel in the second car. The reporters had protested being separated, but the big Fed insisted they go this route. Having two different targets would make it twice as difficult for a hit team to kill both of them and reduced the chances of total success by fifty percent. It also split responsibilities between the protection detail and that made it easier, as well.

He had also added an additional layer of security. Far above them a helicopter followed the detail with none other than Jack Grimaldi at the stick. For some reason, the pilot had taken a special interest in La Costa and Parmahel. Brognola bet one of the reasons was their willingness to help when Bolan had been captured by the NRJO. Grimaldi related that both of them had risked their lives to help someone they didn't really know, and that spoke volumes as far as Brognola was concerned.

"Where are we going?" La Costa asked from the backseat, wedged between two marshals.

"I can't tell you yet," Brognola said. "But once we're there I'll let you contact any one person of your choosing to let them know you're all right."

"Have you talked with Stone?"

Brognola shook his head. "Not personally, but I passed on our message about Ad-Darr. I'm sure he'll get it."

"Stone really is good, isn't he?"

Brognola glanced at La Costa with an unabashed expression. "The best."

"I guess maybe I was pretty hard on him when I had no right to be. Will you tell him I'm sorry next time you talk to him?"

"Knowing Stone like I do, I can tell you it won't even be necessary," Brognola replied. "But I'll give him the message."

"We're not going to come out of this alive. Are we?"

Brognola shifted in his seat so he could look at La Costa more directly. "Listen, I don't want you to worry. We have everything well in hand."

"But if this is al Qaeda, like you say, they could get to us. They can get anybody. They've been operating right here in the U.S., for god's sake. They found us on a military air base, so what's to stop them from finding us again?"

"Well, for one thing, there was a traitor in Puerto Rico feeding the terrorists information. Stone took care of that little problem."

La Costa's expression soured. "You mean he killed him."

Brognola remained impassive. "I mean he took care of the problem. The other important thing to remember is that up until this point we'd been stumbling around in the dark about who was trying to assassinate you and why. Now when Jack first flew you and Julio here we thought you were out of the woods, and we had no reason to think anyone would be after you. Now that we know, we're better prepared."

"You hope."

"We know," Brognola replied. "So to answer your original question, you are going to come out of this alive. And I'm going to attend to that matter personally."

"And what about my story?" La Costa demanded.

Brognola sighed. He couldn't really tell her she'd be free to report everything that happened to her, yet he also couldn't keep her in protective custody forever. He decided to change tack. "When this is over and you're released from custody, you would naturally be free to report whatever you wanted. Unfortunately, though, neither you nor Parmahel will ever really be out of the woods. The minute you publish your story, you'll have everyone and their dog on your doorstep. Any idea you might have about privacy will disappear, and you'll be a perpetual target of terrorists for the rest of your life. Not to mention you'll become a subject of interest for other journalists and they will hound your every step."

"You trying to dissuade me from reporting the truth?"

Brognola laughed. "Not at all. You're welcome to report whatever you want. But I can guarantee that a larger part of those who read it won't believe you, and the minority that do will make your life a living hell. You'll be famous, sure, and maybe even you'll make some money off it. But you'll always be a target."

La Costa remained silent for a time, the wheels turning, and finally said, "I appreciate everything you've done for us, Hal. But you're a real bastard."

"I know it's not what you wanted to hear, but it's the truth, Ms. La Costa. And you know it."

La Costa fell silent and Brognola returned his attention to the darkened, winding road ahead. He hadn't wanted to sound quite so harsh, but La Costa struck him as a straight shooter who probably expected everyone to deal the cards to her in kind. Brognola had to admit he hadn't expected La Costa to ask him to apologize to Bolan, but it wasn't the first time he'd seen someone get a poor read on the Executioner first time around. To know a man as complex and deep as the one named Mack Bolan took more than a few brief encounters. There had once been a time—long ago, but a time all the same—when Brognola and Bolan had been on opposite sides of the fence. Then the U.S. government wised up and realized if they couldn't contain the man, they should extend a hand of friendship, a pardon and a higher purpose.

Brognola's cell phone rang and he pulled it from inside his coat pocket. He glanced briefly at the digital readout, but he already knew by the ring who was calling. "Yeah, Jack."

"How're things?" Grimaldi asked.

"Couldn't be better. What about from your angle?"

"Looks like the road ahead is pretty clear," the Stony Man ace replied. "I don't see any headlights or approaching vehicles. One oddity I see, though, is on the FLIR. About two miles ahead."

Brognola's neck hairs stood on end. Grimaldi was airborne in one of Stony Man's specially equipped choppers.

"What do you see?" Brognola asked.

"Looks like a single vehicle, two occupants. No lights, but the engine's registering very warm so it's probably been running recently. It's parked just off the road in a stand of trees."

"Maybe kids," Brognola suggested. "Love birds out necking?"

"I don't register much in the way of movement."

"Well, I certainly don't want to look for zebras where there are no stripes. Keep your eyes open and let me know if the status changes."

"And if it does?" Grimaldi asked.

"You're authorized to do whatever you have to."

"Roger, out."

Brognola disconnected the call, took a deep breath and let it out slowly. He could feel his heartbeat quicken in his chest and the sudden rise of bile. The reflux had come with the job so many years back he couldn't recall. Brognola fished a few antacids from the ever-present roll he kept on him and chomped them down. The burning subsided.

But only a little.

AFTER AN UNEVENTFUL ROAD TRIP of about an hour to St. George, Bolan and Wharton made preparations for their departure into the unknown.

Wharton first reported in at the small, two-man station posted at the edge of the swamp, then the Executioner assisted with offloading equipment from the truck and onto the airboat Wharton had towed behind their SUV. Manufactured by Razorback Industries, the airboat was a modern work of genius. It boasted a large flat-bottom frame with a thirty-inch aluminum grass rake. It was capable of seating four passengers—two seats up with a double-front bench—or in this case allowing the carry of extra equipment. A 454hp engine powered a three-blade prop attached to a belt-driven counter rotator and stainless-steel exhaust mufflers. The V-8 engine could achieve speeds up to sixty miles per hour with a range of 100 miles.

"She isn't necessarily the best," Wharton had told Bolan. "But I guarantee she's better than anything the terrorists will have going for them."

"I don't doubt it," Bolan had replied.

As soon as they had the equipment loaded, Bolan disconnected the airboat from the trailer and got it into the water.

Wharton parked the trailer and then joined the Executioner. Bolan noted the pair of waders in Wharton's hand, extended out to him. "You better put these on. They should fit."

Bolan thought about it a moment and then realized Wharton knew a lot more about this than he did. He quickly stripped off his combat boots and stepped into the waders. Once finished, he donned his shoulder holster. Earlier he had treated his weapons with a special antimoisture agent. He double-checked the action of the Beretta 93-R and the other weapons in his waterproof bag. While Bolan checked his weaponry, Wharton had prepared his own gear and now stood in about a foot of water and waited for Bolan to board before following after.

It didn't take more than a minute to get the airboat engine started and in short order they were advancing slowly but steadily into the bowels of the Okefenokee. A little light would have helped, but Lady Fortune didn't smile on them and an overcast, starless night was their lot. The lack of natural lighting also signaled the approach of what Wharton predicted could be the mother of storms this rainy season.

Bolan had one thing going for him. The PDA he carried sported a GPS system, and Kurtzman had downloaded the triangulation data to it. While the signal wasn't presently active, Bolan could use the data to make sure they stayed within the search area. This would facilitate their ability to conduct a grid-by-grid search, ruling out each area and reducing the chance they would retrace their steps.

The soldier waved at Wharton to cut speed, then moved just aft of the grass rake and began to sweep the area with infrared field glasses. One thing the enemy could not totally conceal was their heat. Whether generated by human bodies or simply by their equipment, unless they had a way to completely mask infrared signatures, Bolan would find it. The NVDs he carried not only illuminated the dark, but also rendered strong, white outlines of images wherever Bolan looked at a heat source.

They had proceeded about two miles and the Executioner only spotted some land animals and a pair of alligators. The fauna kept a respectful distance from the boat, giving the machine a wide berth. They had obviously had contact with man before.

Bolan remained diligent, however, and before long it paid off. Directly ahead of them he could make out where the waterway split, an inlet to the right choked with wild rice and tall grass. But it was the outline beyond the overhanging trees that prompted Bolan's attention. The shape looked similar to that of their own boat, and as they drew closer to the split in the waterway Bolan could see the formation of heat signatures through the NVDs that could only have been humans.

He turned to Wharton and waved his hand across his throat several times. Wharton killed the engine and then looked in the direction Bolan pointed. He nodded, a gesture barely perceptible in the dark, as he reached to the gun case and withdrew his rifle. Bolan reached into his own bag and withdrew the FNC. He knelt and put the weapon into battery, then signaled Wharton to engage the powerful twin spotlights mounted to the front of the boat.

Wharton reached down to engage the separate, onboard battery and a moment later the floodlights winked on and bathed the area beyond the overhanging trees in several thousand lumens. Bolan heard the roar of the engine milliseconds before the airboat erupted from its cover and bore down on them, weapons chattering and blowing out both of the forward spots. Bolan raised his FNC just as the airboat swung to the right and glanced off their own. The impact knocked Bolan off balance and he was thankful he'd dropped to one knee; otherwise, he would likely have fallen over the side.

Bolan regained his balance and triggered a 3-round burst at the retreating boat even as Wharton fired the engine. The soldier braced himself by wrapping one hand on a grip attached to the rake as the airboat lurched into a pursuit course. He couldn't make out many details about the airboat ahead of them, but he could tell it wasn't as big or powerful as their own.

The soldier raised the FNC to his cheek, locked the butt against his shoulder and triggered a sustained burst. Sparks whined off the grate and blades of their quarry's airboat, but not enough of a hit to do any sort of real damage. Bolan considered switching out for the M-203 grenade launcher, but eventually ruled out the idea as impractical. At these speeds, he couldn't be sure to land a 40 mm grenade with accuracy. Bolan emptied the magazine and slammed home a fresh one. The only way to slow them would be to see if he could get the airboat to take on water. Bolan adjusted his aim and went for the lower portion of the vessel. This time he was rewarded with significant sparks and he could hear the motor ahead begin to miss. He'd hit a vital part of the engine, and that worked for him.

The airboat began to slow and Bolan waved Wharton to approach on its port side. As they drew nearer, the soldier raised the NVDs and scoped out the occupants. Earlier he'd seen two, but now he could make out three, one in the pilot seat and two more forward of the center block. And Bolan could see they were training weapons toward him. He shouted a warning to Wharton and went prone on the grass rake. The enemy had foolishly failed to use weapons with flash suppressors, and while they triggered their weapons in the dark they also provided a beacon to Bolan's crack marksmanship.

The Executioner triggered a short burst and a moment later he was rewarded with a splash.

Bolan heard the booming fire from the bolt-action rifle he'd seen Wharton store in the protective case of the boat mounted alongside the pilot chair. He'd recognized it as a Savage 7 mm Magnum hunting rifle, a powerful and accurate weapon with an effective result in the right hands. Obviously, Wharton possessed a pair of those hands because it took only two shots before the muzzle-flashes from the second gunman's weapon ceased and then audibly clattered against the deck plating of the airboat.

The motor chugged and chattered as the pilot tried to start it, but to no effect. Bolan watched the shadowy figure dismount from the pilot seat and a moment later the night came alive again with autofire. Bolan heard a shout of pain from Wharton and turned his attention toward him, but the captain was moving and cursing. Just a graze.

Bolan reached across to the weapons bag and brought the M-203 into play. He made his best estimate and triggered the grenade launcher he had loaded with a 40 mm HE shell. The blast followed a moment later and illuminated the night, the force blowing apart the remaining opponent as the high explosive did its work on the airboat. The flaming body parts bounced off several overhanging tree limbs before toppling back to the water.

The soldier rose and made his way to Wharton, who was busily wrapping his upper thigh with a tight elastic bandage. "How bad?"

"Not too, partner," Wharton replied. "I'm good."

"Nice work, guy," Bolan said.

"Not bad yourself, fella. You been at this awhile?"

Bolan smiled. "Yeah, awhile."

CHAPTER SIXTEEN

If Siraj Razzaq, freedom fighter and leader of the New Revolutionary Justice Organization, had expected anything, it wouldn't have been the news that fell upon his ears this early morning.

There had been no communications from Miguel Veda or the infidel Fonseca over the past eight hours. That didn't concern Razzaq nearly as much as the fact he hadn't received confirmation from Ad-Darr that the meddling Stone was dead. So the lack of communication from any of his contacts within Puerto Rico prompted Razzaq to contact his spies, and that's when he got the news. Razzaq felt the heat rise in his neck, and he tried to keep his anger in check even as one of his men reported the current situation.

"Veda is now being held by Puerto Rican officials, and it is possible that he has agreed to barter his knowledge of us for immunity. Fonseca is dead, killed by Stone. We have been unable to find Ad-Darr."

"What do you mean unable to find him?"

"He disappeared. We were assisting him in following this Colonel Stone, but then they never showed up at the contact point. We have searched all the places we know to look and still have not found him."

"Then I would suggest you begin to search all of the places you *don't* know where to look. I want Ad-Darr found and I want the American dead. Do you understand?"

"Yes, sir, we will continue our search."

"That would be a very good idea," Razzaq said, then disconnected the call.

He rose from the makeshift desk. A steady rain had begun and rivulets of water seeped through the cracks of the shelter and streamed down the walls. Being used to hot, dry countries and stuck for the past six months within this foul-smelling swamp in an even fouler country did nothing for Razzaq's disposition. He studied the photo of his wife in a crude frame lying flat on the desk, then slammed his fist against the top of the desk. A heavy vibration rumbled along the floor as the sound from the impact reverberated through the cavernous shelter. The curtain leading from his office whipped aside and Razzaq's adjutant, a dedicated and ruthless youth named Iskander, stepped in with weapon drawn.

Razzaq waved him away. "I'm fine. Get out!"

Iskander hesitated a moment, then ducked out in reverse. Razzaq knew he shouldn't have yelled at his faithful aide, but at the moment he didn't care. Whatever had possessed him to ally himself with the likes of scum such as Veda and Fonseca he couldn't surmise. He'd forged the relationships against his better judgment and, at first, it seemed like the alliances might pay off. But as time transpired he could see the ineptitude of these men. They were like most Americans: soft and undisciplined, cut from an entirely different cloth based on living in luxury and having all they acquired handed to them.

Well, Siraj Razzaq saw things more clearly now, and he wasn't about to let a lapse in judgment ruin his plans. He could still salvage something of the operation if he just focused and channeled the burning anger he felt for his enemies into a constructive plan. At this point, most of what he could do would be a salvage operation—he could expect little chance of completely recovering from the death of Fonseca, and Veda's arrest.

"Iskander!" Razzaq bellowed.

His adjutant appeared just as quickly as he had the first time, although now he had the expression of a cat caught with the bird between its teeth. Razzaq didn't let this one's attempt at expressing meekness fool him; he knew much better than that. Iskander had proved himself to be nothing less than cunning and resourceful, a consummate fighter who operated with a deft hand, and had managed to learn shrewdness was a major trait in getting ahead. Razzaq knew it would take only one call from his superiors and Iskander would cut Razzaq's throat as the NRJO leader slept.

"Yes, sir?"

"I've been informed that both of our contacts in Puerto Rico are out of the picture and that Ad-Darr is dead."

"Ad-Darr? Dead?"

"Do you have some kind of hearing problem?" Razzaq said in a sarcastic tone.

"No, sir," Iskander replied.

"Good. I want you—"

Before he could finish, the field phone on the wall buzzed for attention. Razzaq cursed at the interruption even as he reached to the handle and picked it up. He barked a reply and then listened as one of their field sentries informed him a new crisis had arisen. Razzaq grunted his understanding, advised the sentry to remain where he was until reinforcements arrived and then hung up.

He returned his attention to Iskander, who stood patiently waiting. "That was a guard in perimeter B. He's telling me one of our patrol boats hasn't checked in."

"I just received word that a heavy fog is rolling in and a severe storm is on the way. It could well be some kind of radio interference."

"And then it could be something more," Razzaq cautioned.

"What are your orders?"

"I want you to take a detachment of our men and go check out the area where the boat had its patrol. If you see anything, avoid engagement. I'm not ready to abandon our operation here until I know we can implement our secondary objectives in Puerto Rico. It would be most unfortunate if we're forced to our backup location as it would result in significant exposure. I'm not sure we can afford that right at the moment."

"I understand. But given our present situation, a conflict may be unavoidable."

"What may be, may be," Razzaq said with a short wave. "But I want you to exercise prudence and avoid engaging our enemy if at all possible."

Iskander nodded. "Understood."

"Get moving."

Iskander disappeared and Razzaq dropped tiredly into his straight-back, wooden chair. He wondered if Iskander would really do whatever he could to avoid a confrontation with the Americans. The man was known to have a short temper, not to mention he would have rather implemented a genocidal plan of action than hide and wait. Razzaq had to admit he wasn't overly enthused with such an option, either, but his superiors had been clear.

In some ways, Razzaq felt cheated. He was a native of Lebanon, not like some of his new Middle Eastern masters. Ever since his alliance with al Qaeda—the result of inadequate funds to maintain training and increase recruitment number among the ranks of the New Revolutionary Justice Organization—Razzaq had played second fiddle to the al Qaeda leadership. He could hardly become accustomed to such arrangements since he'd been a high-ranking member of the original RJO.

Ah, another time that had been when they were fighting solely for the right to land and prosperity without Western interference. Or without *any* interference for that matter. But times had changed and as Razzaq matured he realized that a man of battle, a patriot like himself, learned to either be flexible and grow with the times, or wither and die, ending up as little more than a shell of a man, a mere shadow of what had once been.

There were those inside al Qaeda who had actually thought of Razzaq as an anachronism to "modern" terrorism, but he chose to ignore such a characterization. Who else could have thought up a plan to attempt political subversion in Puerto Rico. The situation had been unstable there for a while now, and anyone could have seen that it would be only a matter of time before someone took advantage of the situation. All Razzaq had done was sweeten the pot for those most willing to help him destabilize the situation to the point the locals cried for reform.

Now he had to wonder what went wrong. Ad-Darr missing, Fonseca dead and Veda prisoner. That left little in the way of leverage, where it concerned Razzaq and his team. To make matters worse, their perimeter here might have been compromised, whether intentional or not, and intelligence reports indicated there were American reporters who might pose a liability to his operations in Puerto Rico. His superiors had indicated he should proceed as planned and not worry—they would take care of those details.

Yes, Razzaq thought he knew how they would take care of it. If he failed, they might well tell Iskander to assassinate him and take over, or even send a special team to eliminate him. The thing that infuriated Razzaq most was the plan to use Ad-Darr hadn't even been his idea. His al Qaeda masters had insisted, no...that wasn't the right word, more like *demanded* that he conform to their ideas about this operation.

Well, it didn't make a difference in any respect. Razzaq was now fully committed to the plan, and while many of the details were not his own he knew they held him responsible for its success. Or failure. Razzaq tried not to focus on that, instead deciding what he would do next. He opted not to worry about the airboat patrol that missed their check-in. Iskander was probably right.

Just a glitch from the approaching storm.

WHARTON CURSED as he hung up the portable satellite phone on which he'd been talking to one of the men at the Folkston station.

"What is it?" Bolan asked.

"That storm's picking up speed," he replied, shaking his head. "It's going to be a doozy, Cooper."

"How long?"

"Hour at most."

Bolan didn't have any response other than to ask himself what else was new. The numbers were running down, and they hadn't come any closer to locating the enemy than before their initial encounter. Bolan had searched the debris left by the boat, what little there was, but came up empty for intelligence that might lead them to the NRJO base of operations.

"This isn't going well," Bolan replied.

"Aw, I don't know about that. I mean look on the bright side."

"Which is?" Bolan queried.

"We at least killed three of those sons of bitches, which means we have to be close."

"Not necessarily. We have a sixty-square-mile search perimeter, and that patrol could have been any distance out from the main area of operations."

"What about your computer friends?" Wharton suggested. "Any way they could help us out?"

Bolan shook his head. "They've done all they can, which was a lot. We would have had a much larger problem if they hadn't narrowed it down."

"I think we should keep looking."

The soldier looked at Wharton. Here he was, an older guy—Bolan noticed a wedding ring—probably with a couple kids and he was out here risking his neck to help his country. It didn't seem to faze him that he'd been winged by a bullet, or that a storm was approaching or that they were faced with potentially ugly odds. Bolan's original assessment of Wharton turned out to be correct. He was a hard-nosed go-getter who wasn't about to let a few terrorists scare him away.

"All right," Bolan finally said. "We keep looking."

"Here, put this on."

Bolan turned just in time to catch something Wharton had thrown at him. When he unfolded it he realized it was a hooded poncho designed to match the waders Wharton had loaned him.

"You're gonna need it, friend," Wharton added with a grin.

BROGNOLA BREATHED a sigh of relief when they passed the occupied vehicle without incident. He scolded himself for the paranoia. He knew a lot of it came from the stresses of the job and part of it was simply the by-product of his concern for Bolan. The Executioner had been in plenty of worse scrapes than this one, and the big Fed had to remind himself of that. The other consideration was the dangers posed by terrorist infiltration of the U.S.

While there had been increased pressures to maintain a security vigil across the country, Brognola wasn't naive enough to believe Americans were secure. There had been a large improvement, but al Qaeda and its allies still operated within the borders of America. The current situation in Georgia served as proof enough of that.

The hum of the powerful engine and drone of tires on pavement had lulled Brognola to sleep, which he only realized when the ring of his cell phone startled him awake. It was Grimaldi. "Yeah, Jack."

"Hal, I think you may have a problem."

"Sitrep."

"I've got a ground bogie approaching your position from a connecting highway to the northwest."

Their convoy was headed south on Highway 52,

toward a tiny town in North Carolina called Mount Airy—a small city at the southern fringe of the Blue Ridge Mountains. Due to the large tourism trade there, Stony Man considered it the perfect place. Anyone needing protection could be just another face in the crowd.

"What makes you think it's a threat?"

"For starters, there are four occupants in the vehicle, and I see shapes in the FLIR that look ominously like firearms. I also noticed that they suddenly appeared off an entrance ramp when two other vehicles of identical size and make pulled onto the highway behind you a few miles earlier."

"Sounds like a corral team," Brognola agreed.

"The vehicle coming up on you is not going to be a problem, Hal, but the two behind you are too close for me to handle. Anything I try on them poses too great a risk to your party."

"Acknowledged. Just do what you can to keep them off our back until I come up with a plan."

"Wilco. Out."

Brognola replaced his cell phone in his pocket and told the driver, "Don't take Mount Airy exit. Just maintain speed and direction. We may have followers."

The U.S. Marshal acknowledged Brognola's orders with a "Yessir," then keyed up the shortwave radio headset transmitter and advised the other driver of Brognola's instructions. The big Fed didn't like doing it this way, but he realized they didn't have any other options. If they let their potential pursuers follow them into the small town, they risked not only exposing their plans, but also losing this destination as a safe haven.

Brognola waited until they were several miles past

the exit and then ordered the driver to pick up speed. "Twelve miles to the next town?"

The driver nodded. "About that, sir."

"You'll take the exit there," Brognola said.

He didn't know much about the town, but he was pretty sure it didn't sport a high population. If there was to be a conflagration, and Brognola felt it might very well be unavoidable at this point, he wouldn't risk exposing bystanders to danger if he could avoid it. Their fearsome pursuers didn't trouble him nearly as much as the thought that if violence erupted somebody innocent could get hurt.

Brognola pulled his cell phone and hit the redial button. He glanced behind him and saw La Costa with her head back on the seat, softly snoring away. Good, at least she wouldn't be stressed or worried needlessly if this whole thing turned out to be a bust, although Brognola knew their luck couldn't probably hold out that long.

The pilot answered on the first ring. "Go, Hal."

"Status of that vehicle you spotted to our northwest."

"Closing fast," the pilot replied. "And the two others are just about on your tail now."

"We're going to get off at the next exit," Brognola said. "I want to get clear of bystanders before we make contact."

"Shouldn't be a problem at this time of morning," Grimaldi said. "Whenever you give the word, I have a clear shot from here to eternity."

"What kind of vehicles here?"

"The two following you are SUVs, make unknown although I'm pretty sure they're imports. The one coming on your flank is a large panel van."

"Blast it, how in blazes did they find us so fast?"

"Could you have an informant among the marshals there?"

"Doubtful," Brognola said.

"Maybe they've tagged one of your vehicles," Grimaldi suggested.

"These babies are fresh out of the motor pool, Jack, and only I knew their final destination. There is another possibility we might consider."

"What's that?"

"Al Qaeda's been one step behind us ever since you left Puerto Rico."

"La Costa?"

"Or Parmahel," Brognola said. "Maybe both."

"You think one of the al Qaeda operatives somehow managed to land a bug on one of them?"

"Why not?" Brognola said. "They've done it before."

"Only way to be sure would be split them up," Grimaldi replied.

"I've considered that as one possibility, but for now we'll need to deal with any potential threats. There'll be plenty of time to worry about it later. We're coming up on the exit now, Jack. I'm going to sign off."

"You take care of yourself, boss."

"You, too. When it's time, I'll send the arranged signal."

"Acknowledged. Out."

Less than a minute after they descended the exit ramp and reached the intersection of the road running under the highway, the two SUVs made their move. One came up on the gravel shoulder of the left, the other on the strip of tall, dry grass to the right. Brognola ordered the driver to take evasive action. Years of training took over as the marshal turned unexpectedly into the vehicle on his side and rammed it with the fender of their own SUV, and then slammed down on the accelerator. Brognola heard the *pop-pop-pop* of small-arms fire and looked in his side mirror to see muzzle-flashes coming from the passenger side of the second car.

The sudden impact jolted La Costa from her nap. "What the hell is going on?"

"Stay down!" Brognola ordered her.

And then the back window of their Expedition shattered and glass flew through the interior.

CHAPTER SEVENTEEN

Brognola opened his eyes and did a rapid self-assessment once the glass stopped flying. He ran his hands over his face and came away with a small shard in his palm, flecked with his own blood. Aside from that minor nick, he had miraculously come away from the fierce attack unscathed.

That didn't, however, mean they were out of the woods yet, not by a long shot.

He turned to inspect La Costa. For all her screeching and cursing, the reporter didn't appear any worse for wear. Part of La Costa's ire came from the fact that one of the marshals had her pinned against the other. In the fear and adrenaline of the moment, she obviously hadn't taken notice of his demise. She was berating him, beating on his shoulder as she demanded he stop leaning against her. A safety belt restrained his lifeless body and prevented him from slumping forward, so his corpse had gone the only place it could by sliding sideways into La Costa. Blood ran freely from a large, gaping hole in the back of his skull.

Brognola ordered the second marshal in the backseat

to check status of the other vehicle and then directed the driver to get them the hell out of there. Although the driver seemed a bit dazed, he managed to disentangle their SUV from the enemy vehicle. As they rocketed from the scene, Brognola turned his head and looked expectantly at the marshal in the backseat, who wore an earpiece attached to the VOX system the protection team used to stay in contact with each other. The marshal held up his finger to indicate he was listening to a transmission at that moment. Finally, he keyed the radio to indicate he copied and then turned his attention to the waiting Stony Man chief.

"They're clear, sir," the marshal reported from the backseat. "They kept to the highway and nobody followed them."

That clinched it! The enemy was bent on killing Guadalupe La Costa, or at least that's how they were tracking them. She had a bug planted on her somewhere, somehow, but unfortunately they didn't have time to sweep her at the moment.

"Tell them they're in the clear," Brognola replied. "Their orders are to turn around as soon as they can and get to the safehouse in Mount Airy. Tell them we will join them as soon as we can."

Brognola turned, reached into the glove compartment and retrieved a flare. He rolled down the window, yanked the self-activating striker from the flare and tossed it out the window.

Now all he could do was hope and pray Jack Grimaldi got his signal.

JACK GRIMALDI, ace flier for Stony Man, not only got the signal, but he also knew what it meant.

They had discussed it before ever deciding to make the move from the safehouse in rural West Virginia to North Carolina. While Brognola didn't like the idea of splitting up the parties, making it more difficult to protect them, he had also heard Grimaldi's wisdom and decided to order the split if they made positive contact with the enemy. That moment had arrived and Brognola's arranged signal involved the discharge of a flare from whichever vehicle the enemy converged on. As rotten luck would have it, that happened to be the one with Brognola aboard.

As soon as Grimaldi saw the signal, he swung the chopper around for his second flyover and flipped the switch that activated the chopper's advanced heads-up display. The HUD utilized an electronic imaging system on a wafer-thin plasma screen that provided key targeting capabilities to the weapons systems aboard the chopper. This included the 30 mm, nose-mounted chain gun and 102 mm HE rocket pods on the starboard side.

As the panel van jumped off at the exit and approached where the terrorists had made initial contact with Brognola's SUV, the computer emitted a steady beep that alerted Grimaldi he had lock. The pilot flipped a rocker switch on the stick and pushed a fire button set in the main instrument panel. A pair of 102 mm HE rockets left the pod and bore down on the target with trails of blue-white flame that lit up the night. The rockets exploded on impact and turned the panel van into a fireball. Flaming wreckage erupted in all directions and only a smoking, charred hulk remained to roll through the stop sign at the end of the ramp.

Grimaldi flew in close to verify the hit, then began to search the area for Brognola's flare. He reset the

FLIR to scan a 360-degree area and in less than ten seconds he had acquisition. Grimaldi turned the chopper in that direction and caught up to Brognola's vehicle a moment later. The pair of terrorist SUVs had cleared the fire zone and were in hot pursuit of their lone quarry, completely oblivious to the air cover Grimaldi provided.

The pilot gauged their speed, estimated a safe altitude and then swung in low and tilted the nose of the chopper at an angle designed to facilitate maximum efficiency to the chain gun. Originally designed as part of the Area Weapon System for the AH-64 Apache gunship, the Hughes-designed M-230 utilized an external, electrical power system to reload the linkless ammo. This provided a cyclic fire rate of approximately 650 rounds per minute, which made it an extremely effective offensive weapon for a fast-attack helicopter.

The terrorists learned of the weapon's effectiveness quickly as Grimaldi came in low on their flank and sent the first message by sweeping their tails. The 30 mm rounds chopped up the metal and fiberglass bodies of the SUV imports and immediately diverted the attention of al Qaeda to this new threat, giving Brognola and crew respite. Just exactly as the Stony Man pilot had planned.

Grimaldi buzzed them and continued until he had just passed Brognola's SUV, then spun and took up a defensive posture. As soon as the government vehicle cleared his gunsights, the ace pilot opened with another full salvo, this time chopping the front end of one of the pursuing vehicles to shreds. Steam belched from the wounded SUV and the pilot swerved to avoid further damage, but thoughtlessly maneuvered directly into the path of Grimaldi's strafing run. Another volley of heavy-caliber slugs punched through the vehicle's windshield and transformed the driver and three passengers into mincemeat.

The other driver—obviously seeing the error in judgment made by his partners—swung wide in the opposite direction and nearly vaulted onto the curb of the quiet, country road leading toward the small town a couple of miles ahead. The driver argued with the man riding shotgun, and then after a moment of animated discussion he stood on the brakes and brought the SUV to a screeching halt. One of the passengers in the backseat went EVA.

Grimaldi turned the chopper in time to see the terrorist with something propped upon his shoulder, but he registered what it was a moment too late. A millisecond later a flash followed and the Stony Man pilot felt the abrupt heat of the explosive charge as it connected with the underside of the chopper. Good fortune smiled on him, however, and while the rocket-propelled grenade blew inside and set most of the fuselage ablaze, it didn't take out either the main or tail rotors. This gave Grimaldi enough time to respond to the emergency and get the bird a safe distance away before he had to put it down.

By the time Grimaldi found an open field near the road—muddied by heavy rains the previous week—his cockpit had filled with thick, noxious smoke. He managed to roughly set the chopper down and get clear of the whirlybird before flames consumed the interior. Wheezing, he crawled on hands and knees a safe distance from the inferno. He looked back with amazement once he caught his breath and thanked whatever deity might be listening for sparing him once more.

Grimaldi eventually climbed to his feet, doing a

mental rundown and feeling in the dark for any injuries. Other than a bruised forearm from his rough landing, he seemed okay. The pilot regained his composure and reached to the radio clipped to the waist belt of his flight suit. He brought the radio close to his lips and called for Brognola, but got only static in response. Grimaldi tried several more times with the same effect.

The SUV was probably too far away. Blast it!

Grimaldi replaced the radio and reached for his cell phone. At least he had signal, bless Kurtzman's genius heart. He punched in the special code that would get him hooked up directly with Stony Man Farm.

When Kurtzman answered he said, "Bear, it's Jack. I'm down and I've lost contact with Hal. I need a replacement bird here, and I need it now."

BROGNOLA SAW THE FLASH of light and the flaming wreckage that moved away from them in herky-jerky movements.

"Damn," he muttered under his breath. He turned toward the driver and said, "We lost our air cover. Step on it!"

The marshal nodded as he picked up speed. They passed a sign that announced the town was only two miles ahead. Maybe they could find a place to hide, lay low until the terrorists gave up their search. Brognola was positive Grimaldi had taken out at least one of the pursuit vehicles before they got him with a lucky shot. He also didn't see any explosions after the chopper disappeared from view, so he could only hope Grimaldi had set down intact.

"They're out of range," the marshal finally told Brognola.

"I see headlights behind us," the driver interjected.

Brognola didn't know either of the two Marshals by anything other than last names. The guy behind the wheel was a big, muscular type, broad-shouldered and bald, who went by Tully. Brognola had heard several men call the guy in back Crock, but he couldn't be sure if that was the man's real name or nickname. Not that it really mattered at this point, since none of them might live to see the sun dawn on a new day.

"We need to find someplace to hide," Brognola replied.

"We should consider ditching our ride, sir," Crock suggested.

Brognola shook his head. "No. Not unless it's absolutely necessary. The only thing that's going to keep us alive is our mobility." He looked ahead and saw a bend approaching. "There's a sharp curve ahead. As soon as you get out of sight, I want you to kill the lights and turn around."

"What?" Tully asked. "But, sir—"

"But nothing!" Brognola snapped. "Do it, now!"

The guy fell silent as he rounded the curve, brought the SUV to a stop and killed the lights. He swung the nose onto the shoulder, dropped the gearshift into Reverse and backed onto the road until they were clear of the ditch. As he started forward, Brognola gestured for them to get as far off the road as possible. Once they were in position he ordered Tully to stop there.

It was La Costa who piped up with, "Now what?"

"Now we wait," Brognola said quietly.

La Costa snorted. "I hope you know what you're doing."

The road ahead began to glow steadily in the illumination of approaching headlights. The al Qaeda vehicle would likely come around the corner at a pretty good clip, and Brognola was banking on one of two scenarios: one, they wouldn't see the dark Ford Expedition parked off to the side and completely blow by them; two, they would see it, but the delay of turning around would buy them enough time to get close enough to call for additional support from the other team.

The light grew steadily brighter and then the SUV came around the curve and zipped past them in a whitish blur.

Brognola made a chopping motion with his hand. "Go!"

Without depressing the brake, Tully put the car in gear and accelerated steadily from the shoulder onto the road. As soon as they made the curve and were completely out of view, he turned on his lights and before long had the accelerator to the floor. The heavy V-8 engine rumbled with power as the Expedition exceeded ninety miles per hour.

"Anybody behind us?" La Costa asked.

Brognola, who had been watching their flank over his shoulder, said, "Not so far."

The Stony Man chief realized a moment later he'd spoken too soon as a pair of headlights suddenly flashed into view although they were a considerable distance. Brognola then recalled that they were probably tracking La Costa electronically and such maneuvers, while they might work temporarily, would not have any permanent effectiveness.

"Blast it!" Brognola looked at Tully. "I think they've got her bugged."

"What do we do, sir?"

"Well, we should head for Mount Airy," Brognola

said as he whipped out his cell phone. "I'm going to call my support team and get them working on sending some additional help."

"Why the hell do they keep coming after us?" La Costa asked.

"They're not after you and Julio, they're only after you," Brognola replied as he listened to the connection made at Stony Man and the short, fast ring of the secured line. "I don't know why, yet. Maybe they don't know anything about Julio."

"Let's hope not," La Costa said, not without feeling.

"Bear," Brognola said when Kurtzman answered, "have you heard from Jack?"

"Just hung up from him. He said to tell you he's okay, just banged up a little. I'm sending another bird to him right now."

Brognola couldn't find words to describe the feeling of relief that washed over him. He tuned it out and got down to business. "Listen carefully. We still have one of the terrorist vehicles pursuing us. We're going to head for the safehouse in Mount Airy. I want you to contact the men there and tell them to meet us at the exit ramp for that turnoff. Tell them the pursuers are in an SUV." He gave Kurtzman a description.

"Understood."

"Also, I need you to start running a trace on our position from the satellite fix," Brognola said.

"Okay."

Each member of Stony Man had a special locating beacon on his person. This particular chip emitted a radio frequency signal that sent telemetric information to Stony Man's dedicated global satellite. With this information, Kurtzman's cybernetic team at the Farm could track the location of any field member and send additional assistance or reinforcements at a moment's notice.

"I then want you to scan for any other homing signals proximal to my own. I think they have La Costa bugged and, if so, I need to figure out how to disable it or have you jam it."

"Acknowledged, but just FYI even if I can find the signal most bugs can't be jammed remotely by satellite. You would have to destroy it at the source."

"Understood," Brognola replied. "Just do what you can. Any word from Striker?"

"Nothing so far, although I did monitor some communications between the U.S. wildlife station in Folkston and this Captain Wharton who was assisting him. There's a pretty bad storm moving into their area and it's picking up speed. I imagine they're going to get dumped within the hour."

"That'll certainly slow down the search."

"Maybe not," Kurtzman replied. "I also got wind they encountered some of the NRJO terrorists."

"Striker's getting close," Brognola observed.

"Don't you know it."

"I wish to hell I had him here right at the moment."

"You want me to raise him?"

"No, absolutely under no circumstances. He's got enough on his plate. We'll handle this for now. Just get back to me with that intel as soon as you can, Bear."

"Will do, Hal."

CHAPTER EIGHTEEN

Thunder in the nearby sky signaled a deluge was imminent.

Whatever stars had been visible earlier were now gone and a dense fog settled above the eerily calm waters of the Okefenokee Swamp. Only a single object disturbed that water, creating easy ripples from where its bow cut through the water barely visible except immediately around it: the airboat piloted by Captain Donald Wharton with Mack Bolan acting as forward spotter. The fog lights, the ones that had survived their encounter, had little effect in penetrating the murk ahead of them.

Not that such obscurity didn't provide some benefits. The enemy wouldn't fare any better in this soup.

When the fog set in, Bolan and Wharton had donned small lights with red lenses that flashed, reducing the risk of accidentally shooting each other in the event of another encounter with the NRJO terrorists. Bolan couldn't suppress his frustration at their unfortunate turn of luck. He knew foraging through miles of swampland in the dark wouldn't necessarily yield immediate results, but he'd found cause to be hopeful after their initial battle with the NRJO. The approach of inclement weather had also interfered with the communications equipment and cellular communications, so Bolan no longer had contact with Stony Man. Well, if he couldn't talk to Stony Man with the advanced equipment in his possession that meant the enemy likely couldn't get out a signal, either. At least they couldn't call for reinforcements and might not even have a mechanism to communicate with each other, and if that were true the Executioner would work their disadvantage to his favor. A communications breakdown among units created chaos.

"You see anything out there?" Wharton asked in a low voice.

Bolan shook his head, then realized the man might not be able to see the gesture and replied, "Nothing so far."

They were powering along on a second motor that propelled them through tubes of compressed air. Wharton had put the engine into compression mode, effectively muffling their progress except for the small gurgle created by the bubbles from air jets breaking the surface. If they needed to revert to high gear, Bolan knew Wharton could engage the motor at the push of a button and pour on the speed. Right now, stealth was the order of the day.

Bolan looked toward the pitch-dark sky and heard the reverberation of more thunder, close enough to send vibrations through the deck plates of the airboat. He looked at his watch. "Based on your estimates, we have maybe fifteen minutes before the rain hits."

"If that," Wharton agreed. "Do you think—?"

The soldier cut him off with a hiss and raised his

hand. He'd heard something and now reached out with every combat sense, breathing steadily, ears attuned and eyes darting in all directions. At first he wasn't sure exactly *what* he'd heard, but after listening another minute he caught just a whisper of something.

But what?

And then Bolan heard it again and this time he cocked one ear toward the suspected source of the sound. Finally, he threw the cut signal and Wharton immediately powered down. Bolan knelt on the aft portion of the grass rake and brought up the muzzle of the FNC, steadying the weapon on his thigh so as not to make noise. The boat proceeded another few yards under its own power, and it was enough for Bolan to finally make out the sound clearly. This time he knew it.

Voices.

Bolan listened long enough until he confirmed by the pitch and rhythm that the voices belong to three distinct individuals, and they were speaking a foreign language. Sloppy, at the very least, but the Executioner wasn't hasty to make contact. He needed to think on his decision a moment. There were two possibilities here. The trio was either another airboat crew on patrol, or they had reached the perimeter of the NRJO encampment. In order for Bolan to launch the most successful offensive, he needed to confirm which.

The Executioner moved back to a point where he could speak directly in Wharton's ear.

"Company ahead," he said as he held up three fingers close enough for the boat patrol captain to make out. "Twenty, maybe thirty yards that way."

Wharton nodded. "What's the plan?"

"I need to recon," Bolan said. "Stay here while I take a look."

"Are you crazy?" Wharton asked with a wild stare.

Bolan put his finger to his lips, although he already knew why Wharton protested. Never mind the inherent risks involved with trudging unprotected through the slimy, murky waters of the swamp in complete darkness—the alligators and black water notwithstanding—but the rains could hit at any time and make it next to impossible for Bolan to relocate the airboat or for Wharton to find him. Their little red lights wouldn't be visible in a torrential downpour, and if they were separated by any distance and the rains started before Bolan could return safely the odds against Wharton finding him went way up.

Bolan considered it worth the risk.

Wharton opened his mouth as if to protest, but then clamped it shut and acknowledged Bolan's plan with a barely perceptible nod.

The Executioner clapped his newfound ally on the shoulder, gave it a reassuring squeeze, then slipped easily out of the boat and into the water. To his surprise the water came only to his waist. Bolan had already shucked the Desert Eagle .44 Magnum and retained only his Colt Combat Commander Knife and Beretta 93-R. The Executioner held the FNC in position directly over his head, not only to keep the weapon clear of the muck, but also to assist his balance.

Bolan began to move silently through the water, firmly planting each foot before putting full weight on it to take the next step. Intermittently Bolan would stop and listen for the voices. The trio of men continued their unprofessional chatter. Bolan knew that many terrorist organizations demanded unheralded discipline from their trainees while others were lackadaisical to the point of ineptitude, if they conducted any regular training at all. Bolan had already fought the NRJO, and the performance of their troops hadn't impressed him so far. Still, the warrior refused to take anything for granted.

Bolan continued his arduous course—he avoided a couple of suck holes and froze once when a water snake slithered past him—but otherwise maintained an even and steady pace until the water line began to drop. Bolan had to slow his advance to prevent making noise as he cleared the water for solid footing. Eventually, he emerged from the grass and his eyes had adjusted enough to the darkness such that he could make out the shapes of three people. The buzz of the voices was clear now, and the language they spoke confirmed Bolan's earliest suspicions that they weren't speaking English.

One of the men stopped talking and looked in Bolan's direction at one point, and the Executioner stood in place and closed his eyes. After a few seconds, the conversation continued, but this time with a little more intensity. Bolan opened his eyes again just in time to see one of the men light a cigarette, the match illuminating his face. The Executioner closed his right eye to avoid total loss of his night vision. Moving slowly and purposefully, he slung the FNC and unholstered the Beretta he currently had chambered to fire 118-grain subsonic rounds.

He drew a bead on the first enemy, steadied his pistol in a two-handed grip and squeezed the trigger. The pistol report made less noise than the ratchet of the extractor spitting the first shell clear of the chamber. Bolan already had the second target and was firing again before the first heated shell hit the water with a hiss. The figure crumpled to the ground, disappearing from view with a splash.

The survivor ducked just in time to avoid Bolan's third shot.

The Executioner cursed himself for not being a little quicker on the draw, but he had just lowered the odds by two-thirds. He leaped as best he could and landed on the berm where the men had congregated, but lost his footing on the slippery grass and mud. Bolan wrenched his knee, but managed to keep his balance somewhat and break his fall with an outstretched arm.

The remaining man tried to seize the advantage of Bolan's misstep and jumped on him. He began to hammer his adversary with his fists, but the blows were low and he caught the soldier in the chest rather than in the head, as he originally intended. The Executioner caught the man's left arm as a fist glanced off his chest, wrapping it in the crook of his arm just above the elbow. He bucked his hips while snaking his left arm between him and the enemy terrorist, then twisted down and outward with the arm, trapping his opponent's elbow. The tactic caught the terrorist unaware and he flipped back, losing his position of superiority.

The Executioner followed through with the move, using the impetus of the terrorist's backward motion coupled with his own body weight until he had the upper hand. Bolan brought up the left forearm he'd inserted between them earlier and slammed it hard into the enemy's throat, effectively choking off his ability to speak or breathe. Bolan now had his right arm free after dislocating the terrorist's elbow and cleared his knife from its sheath. He buried the blade in the man's spleen and followed with a second jab to a point between the fifth and sixth ribs of the anterior chest wall. The blade sliced through the man's descending aorta, and within a few moments his struggling ceased as the lack of oxygen rendered him unconscious.

Bolan withdrew the knife and climbed to his feet.

The sky thundered again, but this time Bolan felt the rain drops as the storm moved in. He gathered his strength and headed quickly for the boat. He needed more time to recon the area, but he also knew the weather wouldn't hold out any longer. Bolan got about halfway there when he heard the sudden chatter of a machine gun. The rain fell steadily now and with increasing intensity. By the time the soldier reached the airboat, Wharton had the engine powered and was firing from an area behind the pilot's seat with a civilian law-enforcement variant of an M-16 A-2.

Bolan climbed into the boat and shouted it was him when Wharton turned around with surprise, shotgun in his fist, and held steadily on the Executioner.

"No fair to sneak up on an old guy like me," Wharton said.

"You seem to be holding your own just fine," Bolan replied.

The rounds from the unseen machine gun being fired drew nearer, the buzz of their closeness resounding in Bolan's ears. Whatever the Executioner had discovered, patrol or perimeter of the terrorist camp, they were now committed to join the battle here and now. The soldier didn't really want to keep at the mission this way, a small skirmish here and there, but if it proved the only way to clear the NRJO threat, then he was prepared for the long haul.

Every third round from the machine gun was a tracer,

and Bolan could see it was only a matter of time before the odds were against them. Only the rain and the noise it brought concealed them effectively enough to mask their position and keep the enemy from pinpointing them by the reports of their weapons or the muzzle-flashes.

"Wharton!" Bolan said over a lull in the firing. "Get us clear!"

The captain nodded and got into the pilot's seat. He engaged the engine as Bolan laid down a fresh volley of covering fire. Within a minute they had moved out of effective range of the firing by rounding several turns along the winding, black water. Wharton's path was made visible only by the dispersing fog and the lights reflecting off the water.

"Cooper!" Wharton shouted to be heard above the steadily hardening rain. When Bolan looked at him he said, "We need to get off the water and find shelter!"

Bolan shook his head, certain that would put them off course, as well as increase the risks the enemy could pin them down. "We have to keep moving! Otherwise they'll pin us down."

"If we don't beach this thing soon, we'll start taking on so much water we'll sink right where we are!"

Just in that minute, the rain had started falling so hard it began to hurt. He looked at Wharton and nodded, and the federal officer began to head toward a tall stand of swamp grass just ahead beyond a secondary outlet.

Bolan remembered Wharton saying there were plenty of shelters along the shorelines where wildlife managers had established long, wooden walkways that sometimes spanned lengths of a half mile. The platforms supported wooden structures no larger than twenty-five square feet that weren't much in the way of

providing significant creature comforts, but they were
sufficient enough to provide temporary protection from
the elements. By the time they reached the closest
shelter, the water was nearly overflowing the stern just
aft of the grass rake.

The soldier jumped from the boat onto the wooden
walkway and lay on his belly to retrieve the equipment
case and weapons bag Wharton handed to him. The
man then folded the pilot's seat, disengaged a lock on
the airfoil and folded that onto the boat. He then used a
winch-and-pulley system mounted to the side of the
walkway to drag the boat beneath the walkway and
shelter it from the elements. Once secured, he engaged
the bilge pump to start pumping the water from the boat
before securing Bolan's assistance in making the top of
the walkway.

Within minutes the two men were secured inside the
small shelter. Bolan went about stripping down his
weapons one by one under the illumination of a small,
propane-powered lantern Wharton retrieved from a
lockbox beneath a floor panel inside the shelter. He
couldn't afford to have the weapons jam on him.

As he worked, Bolan spared Wharton an occasional
glance. "You look uncomfortable."

Wharton shifted uncomfortably in the canvas seat
and rubbed at his graze wound. "I'm feeling that way.
This son of a bitch is really starting to hurt."

"You want some pain meds?" Bolan asked.

Wharton shook his head. "No, I need to keep alert."

The Executioner nodded in understanding, unable to
keep from respecting this man. He inclined his head at
the propane lantern. "You like to be prepared, I see."

"You know it," Wharton said. "We don't use battery-powered equipment out here because batteries corrode faster than all get-out in this climate."

"Makes sense."

"So, what do you have in mind for our next move?"

"I hadn't planned on a layover," Bolan said. He shrugged and added quickly, "But I understand your reasons for suggesting it."

"Yeah, it's a little hard to hunt these bastards if you're drowning in dark, muddy water or getting overrun by a passel of gators."

"Never mind the other dangerous wildlife."

Wharton nodded. "You haven't seen nothing, Cooper, until you've seen a guy who accidentally got caught in a den of water moccasins. The Indians didn't call this place the Land of the Trembling Earth for nothing."

"I'd take the water moccasins over the terrorists anytime," Bolan replied as he reassembled the Beretta.

When Bolan finished cleaning the weapons, he fished into the waterproof pocket built into the waders and withdrew his cellular phone. He engaged the GPS switch and tried to acquire a signal, but didn't have any luck. If he didn't check in soon, he knew Stony Man might get nervous enough to send in a backup team and locate him. He checked his watch and realized he still had time. Brognola had agreed not to take any action for at least twenty-four hours, but if Bolan didn't report in by then he'd send the cavalry, in the form of Able Team.

The thought of watching the trio of Stony Man's urban commandos dredging their way through the swamp in search of the Executioner brought a grin to his face.

"Want to share that joke?" Wharton asked.

Bolan shook his head. "Just thinking about some friends of mine."

"Good for a man to have friends."

"Yeah," the Executioner replied a bit wistfully. "It sure is."

Bolan then thought of Brognola and Grimaldi and wondered how they were faring along with that little pistol named Guadalupe La Costa. He had to admit he was glad he had her out of his hair. She'd stepped up to help Grimaldi save his neck, but she could turn around in that same moment and become a first-class pain.

Yeah, Bolan thought with some amusement, Brognola probably has his hands full.

CHAPTER NINETEEN

Hal Brognola felt the situation couldn't get much worse.

The terrorists were rapidly gaining on them in spite of the Expedition's powerful engine, not to mention that as they came within a mile of the exit for Mount Airy their reinforcements were nowhere to be found. The situation couldn't get more precarious than this, and Brognola began to second-guess his decision to move La Costa and Parmahel. At least from the structure of the last safehouse they would have had the advantage of mounting some defense. Out here they were exposed and therefore vulnerable.

"Where the hell are they?" Brognola muttered.

"What, sir?" Tully asked.

Brognola shook off the question. He finally reached inside his coat, removed his semiautomatic pistol and checked the action. The .45-caliber Colt pistol was an antique, but still wholly reliable, especially given what they were up against. It might not be much against terrorists armed with rocket launchers and automatic weapons, but the big Fed intended to make sure he used it to take some of those bastards with him.

Eyeing him skeptically from the backseat, La Costa said, "I take it that gun means our chances aren't great."

"They've been better," Brognola replied.

"No alternatives?"

"I don't *want* a fight, Miss La Costa. None of us do. But I won't run away from one, either. And the fact is we need to find out how these guys are tracking you. They didn't follow the other car, which means somehow they're homing in on you. Most likely they're using a bug."

"A bug? On me?" La Costa did nothing to hide the disbelief in her voice. "And how do you propose they did that?"

"There's no time to discuss that now, and until we can find out and neutralize whatever they're using to track you, there's nowhere we can go for you to be safe. We need to neutralize the threat first."

La Costa was silent for a time and then asked, "What about Jack? Is he going to be okay?"

"According to my people, he's fine."

Brognola didn't have more to say on that subject. He would have preferred to impart better news for La Costa's benefit, but right that moment he didn't feel too consoling.

"Try to raise the other team again," the big Fed ordered Crock.

The marshal gave it another go over his headset, but after several hails and only silence from him Brognola knew they weren't in contact. Damn it to hell, where was that second team? He knew Kurtzman would have passed on the message that they needed support, but it shouldn't have taken that long. If they didn't get help soon, they would be forced to either abandon the run for the safehouse or turn and fight. The latter course of action seemed more like suicide than a well-executed plan, but Brognola didn't see they had any other choice.

As they got off the Mount Airy exit, the Justice man searched the road ahead for any sign of the sedan or another government SUV. Nothing—and the terrorists were gaining on them.

Brognola considered his remaining options, but quickly realized he didn't have any. They couldn't very well lead the terrorists to the safehouse; that would only put Parmahel in danger, as well. The big Fed had his hands full enough with trying to protect La Costa, but if he had to defend both of them, and failed, they'd die together and the U.S. government would lose a pair of valuable assets. Whether La Costa and Parmahel knew it or not, they were the only two who could translate the footage and identify Ad-Darr.

In an earlier conversation, Barb Price had told him that it wasn't likely al Qaeda would have relied solely on Ad-Darr.

"They would've had some type of backup plan," Price had told him. "And until we can perform a complete analysis of the footage on that disk, there are still potential targets in Puerto Rico and that means there's still a threat to national security."

Brognola had admitted he agreed with her and that, in turn, prompted this move to a more secure location. What he couldn't have possibly foreseen was that al Qaeda already knew the danger the two reporters posed to their plans and would stop at nothing to kill them. They might even try to retrieve the damaging evidence of their intended plot. After all, the president couldn't put Governor Hernandez and the entire election on hold while Stony Man took the time to investigate. That's why they'd sent Mack Bolan in the first place. The political process had to move forward because it was a fundamental working of government under the U.S. Constitution. The citizens of Puerto Rico might well view any attempt by the government to stall the election for "security reasons" as a threat, and who knew where that might lead.

Brognola breathed a sudden sigh of relief as two vehicles emerged from nowhere, one a sedan and the other an Expedition that matched their own. The two vehicles converged on the intersection at the off-ramp and approximately a half-dozen federal agents armed with MP-5s leaped from their respective vehicles and set up firing positions.

Brognola heard Crock speak something excitedly into his headset and then say, "Sir, the cavalry has arrived!"

Brognola smiled and slammed his fist on the dash. "God *bless* you, Bear!"

"Who's Bear?" La Costa asked.

"Later," Brognola said.

Under Brognola's instructions, Tully maneuvered between the two vehicles that had formed a sort of blockade, their noses pointed at an angle and facing the off-ramp. When Tully had the vehicle stopped, he and Crock bailed while Brognola instructed La Costa to get into the front seat. Then he stepped out and walked around to climb behind the wheel. La Costa did as instructed, and in less than fifteen seconds they were moving and headed down the quiet, darkened main thoroughfare of Mount Airy.

As they drove through the town, two local police cars raced past them with lights flashing.

"They going to the little soiree back there?" La Costa asked.

Brognola nodded. "Probably. I'm sure either the U.S. Marshals Service or my people called them for backup."

"Will they be okay?"

"I don't know," Brognola replied honestly. "But I'm sure that many marshals can hold their own in a fight. For now, you and Mr. Parmahel are safe and that's the important thing."

They rode in silence for a time, and then Brognola turned to notice a glisten on her left cheek, reflected from the streetlights. He opened his mouth to say something, couldn't think of anything, then clammed up again. He wished there was something he might say that would abate her fear and anguish. But the clock couldn't be turned.

After a time he didn't have to worry about it because La Costa spoke. "I still don't get it. Why do they want to kill me? I don't know anything."

"I know this is hard to understand," Brognola said. "I'm not always sure I understand it. But the fact is that terrorists don't care about your political affiliations or your religion, or even your lifestyle. They're only interested in one thing, and it's the same thing they've always been interested in."

"Which is?"

"Terror. The spreading of wanton violence and bloodshed against anyone who might oppose them. They see the American way of life as little more than sacrilegious indulgence and waste. We're not like them, so they want to kill us, and they're not discriminating to those ends."

"It just seems so unfair."

"No offense, but you sound pretty naive for an experienced journalist and especially for someone who grew up the way you did."

"Oh, I'm not naive, Hal, believe me. By unfair I just mean the injustice of it all. I never did any foreign reporting or correspondence, and I've never looked that deeply into terrorist groups. When all this was over I was planning on ratting out all of you to the American public, because I think we have a right to know what the United States government is doing in our name."

"And now?"

La Costa sighed and looked into the darkness outside her window. "Now? Now I'm not so sure. I'm not sure about anything anymore. And after what I've seen you and your people go up against, the bravery of men like you and Jack and Stone, I begin to think I was wrong from the beginning."

"About what?"

"About a lot of things," she replied with a good-natured laugh. "No, I don't consider myself naive, but if I have been it's only due to my own ignorance."

"Whatever the case," Brognola said as he swung the Expedition onto a side road, "I'm glad we've managed to keep you alive this long."

"For what it's worth, so am I. Thanks, Hal."

The Stony Man chief glanced at her, saw the smile and nodded in response before returning his attention to the dirt road. A solid wall of corn bordered one side and there was a field of tall grass along the other. They continued for about a half mile and then the safehouse came into view. Brognola had been here once before, but that had been many years ago, and he hadn't really remembered what it looked like. It was actually a farmhouse the government had bought from some poor farmer who had been forced during the farm crisis of the 1980s to parcel off one piece of land after another until he got down to nothing. To save what was left, he sold the property to the government and moved away to who knew where. Mostly, this property was used for temporary housing of new inductees into the Witness Protection Program, but on occasion other agencies would "borrow" it.

The exterior really didn't look all that different from the house at Stony Man Farm, with the exception this one was ranch-style. Dark, vertical wood panels made up the upper half of the exterior and shared the facade with a brick underlay about three feet high. A large front porch sprawled across the front, taking up about half of the eighty-foot length of the house. If Brognola recalled correctly, the government had paid a pretty hefty sum for this place, which was just over twenty-five hundred square feet.

"Here we are," he announced.

La Costa's eyes scanned the exterior and a tiny smile played at the corner of her lips. "Looks nice."

"Not what you were expecting?"

"Not at all. I figured you'd cram us into some stuffy, one-bedroom condo or a broken-down shack in the middle of nowhere."

"Give a man a break. We're not all bad, you know."

"I know."

Brognola followed the road that became a driveway and followed it to a carport behind the house. They barely had the doors open when a shadow filled the screen door on the back porch, and then the door swung open and Julio Parmahel rushed outside. A pair of marshals emerged on his heels with their hands inside their coats. Parmahel jumped over the stairs of the porch deck and rushed to meet La Costa, who waited at the back with Brognola as he retrieved her overnight bag. Parmahel threw his arms around her without restraint and squeezed her tightly as if he might never let go, and the look on her face made it evident that Parmahel had taken her by surprise.

"Julio," she finally wheezed, "I can't breathe."

Parmahel broke away and composed himself. "Sorry…sorry. I'm just very glad to see you alive is all!"

La Costa managed a smile and replied, "You, too."

Brognola passed her bag to her and then Parmahel abruptly reached out and pumped his hand. "I want to thank you, Hal. Really thank you!"

"For what?"

"For everything, I suppose." Parmahel looked sheepish as he said, "For helping us to overcome our fear and do the right thing. For saving our lives, especially for keeping Lupe alive here. If something happened to her, well…well, I don't know what I'd do."

Ah, so that was it. It looked like Julio Parmahel had a thing for La Costa, and either she didn't know anything about it or she didn't want to know.

Brognola turned to La Costa as he removed his cell phone from the breast pocket of his coat. "Now, let's get both of you inside and see if we can figure out how the terrorists are tracking you."

Brognola hit the redial button and Kurtzman's voice answered halfway through the first ring. "Were your ears burning?"

"Nope," Brognola said, "but I assume you have something for me."

"I do. You were dead-on about that bug. It's an RF-based transmitter somewhere on La Costa's person. Took a little time at first because the thing is transmitting on an extremely high frequency band, also known as millimeter band, at a signal of about 60 gigahertz."

"And this is unusual why?"

"Well, for one thing such as a signal is ineffective over long distances," Kurtzman said. "Due in part to the fact that it's a terahertz classification, EM radiation is extremely low on the infrared scale. This makes it subject to considerable attenuation and signals are easily distorted by atmospheric changes, particularly rain and wind."

"You're right, that does seem like a strange technology to use for homing on someone. GPS would be more effective."

"Well, I'm guessing that they use this because it can be implemented on the microelectronic level quite easily, and whoever planted it on her wasn't expecting to have to track her from any great distances or over any long period of time."

"But this would definitely have to be an externally placed device."

"Right."

"Okay, hold on a minute," Brognola said.

They had all gathered inside in the kitchen area of the safehouse. Brognola looked La Costa up and down a minute, and she studied him with the same cursory inspection. The Stony Man chief didn't see any jewelry on her, no ring or necklace. She wore a pair of stud earrings, but they weren't big enough. And then his eyes caught the flash of light on metal and he noticed a watch on her right wrist. He reached down and held it up for closer inspection.

"What are you doing?" she asked.

Brognola shushed her and then put the cell phone back to his ear. "Bear, how big would this transmitter have to be?"

"Hardly anything," he said. "Like I said before it could be a microtransmitter. The main thing would be supplying power to it for an ample period of time."

"How about a watch battery as the power source?"

"Easily. The signal I found was configured to emit a pulse every five minutes. Now most designers would probably have a backup cell, particularly if they were hiding the circuitry inside a device that needed to function like a cell phone or watch or PDA, something like that."

"So that the user wouldn't become suspicious and go digging around only to discover they were bugged."

"Exactly," Kurtzman replied.

Brognola looked at La Costa, who was still holding her wrist up. "Where did you get this?"

"The watch? Well, it was a gift from—" Her body froze and her mouth opened with a sharp inward breath of surprise. "Oh…my…God."

"What?" Brognola asked. "A gift from whom?"

She looked at the watch now as if it were a manacle clamped around her wrist. "Miguel Veda gave this to me for my birthday."

"How long ago?" Brognola asked. When La Costa didn't answer him he shook her wrist and repeated, "How long ago?"

La Costa looked him in the eyes. "A few days. Right before the political rally and the—"

"Take it off, right now!" Brognola ordered.

La Costa immediately stripped off the watch and held it out to him as if she were holding a dead animal. Brognola snatched it from her and went to the table, phone still cradled to his ear. The Stony Man chief sat, removed a penknife from his pocket and popped off the back cover. Inside he found two batteries and, sure enough, a green chip board of microcircuitry that looked all out of place on a watch.

"What do I do?" he asked Kurtzman.

"Just remove both battery cells. Cutting the power source should be sufficient to neutralize the device."

Brognola did as Kurtzman instructed him and then put the pieces in a paper bag one of the marshals got from the kitchen pantry. He would have destroyed it, but then another thought came to him. "We're still not yet completely sure that al Qaeda are the ones who are actually after La Costa, are we?"

"No, it's still only a theory. Barb's been working on it, but she hasn't had much luck making everything fit into a fully plausible explanation. With Ad-Darr and Razzaq, plus Fonseca and Veda and all the other players here, it's become much more difficult to piece it together into anything that makes sense."

"Agreed," Brognola replied. "Not to mention that we know Veda had an arrangement with the NRJO, but there's no known connection between him and al Qaeda or Ad-Darr. Okay, give me a location on Jack and I'll start heading his way. I want the Gulfstream fueled and waiting for us at Andrews. I'm going to accompany Jack when he picks up Striker. And tell Barb I want her to make arrangements to have Veda brought up here for additional interrogation ASAP."

"Can do, but do you mind if I ask why? I thought he already told Striker where to find the NRJO?"

"He did," Brognola said. "I just don't think he told him everything."

CHAPTER TWENTY

Nearly two hours elapsed before Bolan and Wharton could emerge from their shelter. The rains had abated, and sunlight began to peek through the clouds.

Bolan had shed the waders and donned a spare black-suit from the waterproof bag. He also checked and cleaned his weapons, and all were now loaded and ready for what the Executioner hoped was the second and final round of this operation. Exhaustion had nearly overwhelmed him, and while he'd thought about taking a catnap in the shelter he opted to let Wharton do the sleeping since the wildlife officer had the task of piloting the airboat.

Not that the job ahead didn't require a rested and alert Mack Bolan. It seemed evident to him they weren't far from the NRJO firebase. In fact, he considered it more than possible the three men he'd engaged were likely perimeter sentries. That meant Siraj Razzaq and his entourage weren't far from their present location, and by now the remaining terrorists would be alerted to the fact Bolan was hunting them and ready for any assault.

The terrain and environment added another level of complexity to his situation. Bolan knew he couldn't avoid taking Wharton into consideration. While the guy had shown himself plenty capable enough, the soldier had always considered it important to set boundaries in any situation like this regardless of the participant's willingness or aptitude. Wharton would present a half dozen arguments, most of them probably good, when the Executioner finally identified the line Wharton couldn't cross.

Well, not to worry because the guy was already wounded, and Bolan could use that argument alone when the time came. For now, Wharton had proved a competent and capable comrade-in-arms, and Bolan didn't want to do anything to ruin the bond of respect and cooperation that had seemed to form between them.

Once they had the gear loaded and set off in the airboat, Bolan contacted Stony Man via the highly secured phone that doubled as a PDA.

Price answered. "Striker, thank goodness you're okay."

"Tired, hungry and waterlogged, but otherwise I'm functioning okay on reserves. How are things there?"

"Definitely busy," she said. "We have some updated information on our al Qaeda theory."

"What's that?"

Price chuckled. "Seems I'm a little off my game this week. It turns out maybe Veda didn't tell you everything."

"That doesn't come as any great surprise," Bolan interjected. "I figured he'd hold back on one or two things, maybe information he thought he could use down the line if we reneged on our end of the deal or he thought he could work it to his advantage."

"Well, your suspicions were correct. Apparently he

laid a little gift on La Costa that actually turned out to be a homing bug. That's how they've been able to find her so easily."

"Do we know when Veda did this?"

"A couple of days before you even arrived in Puerto Rico."

"Okay, so this development doesn't mitigate our theories about al Qaeda."

"Right," Price said. "In fact, if anything it disproves them entirely. Veda has no known connections to al Qaeda that we know of. He's never been in contact with any of their operatives. There's no evidence he's ever received anything from them in either financial or material supports. Moreover, we don't have any solid intelligence that points us to al Qaeda ever operating in Puerto Rico. There have never been any incidents there that couldn't be attributed to local problems, be they criminal, political or otherwise, and no record of arrests of individuals fitting the Arab terrorist profile."

Bolan considered that and had to admit Price had made some good points. Up until now they had assumed the evidence in the video of Ad-Darr at the political rally signaled the assassin had other masters who put him in Puerto Rico to do their bidding. If that were the case, though, it would mean Siraj Razzaq didn't know anything about it and neither, therefore, did Miguel Veda. And it didn't make sense that Veda would put a homing bug on La Costa strictly out of self-interest. Veda had already pretty much proved he didn't look out for anybody but himself. He couldn't believe the guy had gone all soft on La Costa just because she was a beautiful woman, even if he thought he could get something out of it. That left one of two explanations: he either wanted to keep tabs on her because of her press connections or Razzaq had ordered him to do so.

"There is one other possibility that might fit the facts we have on hand," Bolan offered.

"I'm all ears."

"Well, have we considered the possibility it's actually Razzaq being financed directly by al Qaeda?"

"For what purpose? Their goals are fundamentally different."

"From a political standpoint, yes, but they're united in their views about the United States. Think about it. Ever since 9/11 the U.S. government has thrown every major military and intelligence resource at al Qaeda and its operatives, giving many other terrorist organizations secondary consideration."

"Okay, I think I'm beginning to see what you're driving at," Price said. "We've turned up the heat so high that al Qaeda can't so much as twitch without us breathing down their necks."

"Right," Bolan said. "So they cook up this little plan and fund the development of the New Revolutionary Justice Organization and the alleged rebirth of a Lebanese terrorist cell."

"But in reality," Price concluded, "they're the ones who are actually looking to get the base of operations into Puerto Rico."

"Bingo."

"So if this thing falls apart, they just let Razzaq take the fall and nobody even suspects they had any part in it. That allows them to try again once the heat is off. Okay, I can buy that, but what happens if Razzaq finds out?"

"He wouldn't find out anything unless he failed, by which time it would be too late because the termination order would be out. Al Qaeda operates that way in situations like this. If one of their own becomes a liability, then they'll do whatever they can to terminate the liability. In most cases, it's someone inside the organization, either an aide or someone the target wouldn't suspect."

"How close are you to wrapping things up in Georgia?"

"Real close."

"Good. Hal's champing at the bit and wants you back here as soon as possible."

"What's up?"

"I'm not sure, but it has something to do with Veda. After he discovered the bug, he told Bear to arrange to get him and Jack on a plane to pick you up as quickly as possible, and arrange for Veda to be released from Puerto Rico and brought stateside for further interrogation."

"Well, I have to believe Hal knows what he's doing. Just tell him to be careful. Veda's a snake and not to be trusted. If he sees an opportunity to break away or deceive us, he'll take it. Make no mistake about that."

"I'll let him know."

"This will probably be my last communication until I have this wrapped up."

"We'll be standing by for your extraction signal. I understand Hal and Jack are already on their way to Andrews, so they'll be there by the time you're ready for pickup."

"Understood. Out."

Bolan disconnected the call and then inspected the area ahead of them. The airboat motor made a lot of noise and would announce their approach to the firebase long before they actually arrived. Still, Bolan wouldn't let that fact intimidate him. By this time Razzaq would already be aware the soldier was coming for him and no amount of stealth would make a difference at this point. The battle with Razzaq was about to reach the boiling point.

And the Executioner planned to make sure he was the only one left standing when it was all over.

A NEW FURY HAD TAKEN hold of Siraj Razzaq's heart, and were it not for the fact he needed Iskander he would have reached across his desk and strangled his aide with his bare hands.

Iskander's report had been anything but promising. He had recruited some men to accompany him as they investigated the reason one of their patrol boats hadn't reported in. It had taken them more than an hour to locate the charred remains of the boat because they had been running in blackout, and only after Iskander's frustration reached the melting point did he authorize them to use lights. That's when they found the charred remains of the airboat and the bodies, or what was left of them, concealed within the weeds where the natural currents had stowed them.

"I do not suppose you have an explanation for this," Razzaq demanded.

"I only wish that I did," Iskander said. "I don't know how they were discovered, but I'm guessing they met with a considerable force based on what little was left."

Razzaq shook his head and slammed his fist onto his desk. "Phah! First, there is no evidence we are up against any official law enforcement or paramilitary unit. And if they are, why didn't they just storm in and finish us off?"

"Probably for the same reason that we lost them

when we discovered they were near the perimeter of the camp," Iskander replied. "The storm was so bad we couldn't give chase without risking additional loss of personnel and equipment. I knew based on our limited resources that it wasn't worth the risk of pursuit when the chances weren't excellent we would succeed in locating and destroying them."

"A prudent thought," Razzaq said, "if not a bit arrogant."

"I don't understand, sir. I thought you'd be pleased with my judgment."

"I'm very pleased with your judgment, Iskander. It's your assumptions that disturb me. Only a pitiless, arrogant fool would assume that official government or law-enforcement units are the only ones operating within these swamps. It could have been pirates you encountered, maybe residents of the region who are protecting their territory. There is no question these parts are filled with crazy militants and other outcasts of this accursed country who have a personal stake in protecting these swamps. Only in here can they hope to maintain their anonymity. Naturally, they would view any outsiders as a threat."

"What threat could they possibly hope to think we pose?"

"None at all," Razzaq said as he took a seat behind the portable field desk. "Except that I have been led to understand that you engaged them first. You attacked when unprovoked."

Iskander swallowed hard and his expression went icy. He gave his commander a brief but chilling gaze as he replied, "I felt their proximity to our perimeter and the demise of one of our patrol units was provocation enough."

"Without evidence this unknown party was actually responsible for that? That seems a little…hasty. Wouldn't you say?"

Razzaq took great delight in seeing Iskander squirm. He still didn't trust the man not to slit his throat the moment the orders came down from his al Qaeda masters. Razzaq knew how things worked. The difference here was, *he* knew how it worked and he believed Iskander didn't. While extremely talented in the art of killing and military operations, Iskander was young and insolent; he didn't understand the inner workings of the jihad network. He would make his move at some point if they failed in their mission.

And Siraj Razzaq would be ready for him.

"I'm waiting for an answer to my question, Iskander!" Razzaq demanded.

"Sir, I don't think we were hasty. There was no other reason for an airboat to be in that vicinity at such an early hour and especially not in that weather."

"This is exactly my point. I believe that a military or police unit would have known about the weather and wouldn't have decided to take a risk."

"Maybe not," Iskander said. "But I was more thinking that it might be…"

When his voice trailed off, Razzaq said, "Might be what? Speak up, man!"

"The American… Colonel Stone."

A taut silence followed that announcement, but it turned out to be short-lived as there was a rap on the frame just outside the canvas curtain that led into Razzaq's makeshift office and living quarters. The man who stepped through the curtain unbidden looked as white as a sheet. At first, Razzaq had planned to berate him for entering without first getting approval, but before either he or Iskander could speak the man addressed them in a voice filled with mounting panic.

"I ask forgiveness for the interruption, sirs, but we have a situation. Three of our perimeter guards have been murdered."

"What?" Razzaq said, upsetting his chair and desk as he came to his feet. "What do you mean? Report!"

"We found them during change to morning shift. Two have been shot at close range. The last one, Fahoud, was taken by a knife wound to the chest combined with strangulation marks on his neck."

Razzaq quickly looked at Iskander askance. "What do you make of that?"

"I believe it is as I just said, sir. I think that Colonel Stone is nearby, perhaps closer than even we would have expected, and that before long he'll make his move."

"Recommendations?"

"I think we should consider conducting the final phases of our operation in a more secure location."

"Evacuate?" The tone Razzaq put in his voice intimated he thought the idea was utterly preposterous. "And to where exactly could we relocate, Iskander? We have no other base in which to operate and to move this many men and equipment into Puerto Rico would certainly fail."

"As would any attempt to remain here and defend what little we have left, sir," Iskander protested.

"How dare you—" Razzaq began.

"Sir, I mean no disrespect. I would ask you give me a minute to speak freely with you." He looked at the waiting sentry and added, "Get out!"

The man nodded, then turned on his heel and left.

Razzaq thought about what he'd just heard and witnessed, but decided not to say anything further on the matter. Iskander was the head of the force and could deal with his men in any way he saw fit. Razzaq had always tried to inspire confidence and loyalty in his men, except for this sniveling backstabber who now stood before him and insolently suggested he be allowed to confer privately with Razzaq, as if they were somehow equals.

"All right, Iskander. Say what you feel you must. And when you are finished, it is my turn."

Iskander nodded in acknowledgment. "Sir, there is little question that whether this is Stone or the American police or even a private party only interested in privacy, that our position here is no longer strong. We have been allowed to operate with relative privacy here, and grown used to the luxury we could work inside the boundaries of this country without being molested. But now the situation has changed, and I feel with it so must our strategy."

"And why is that?"

"It makes sense if you consider it. Miguel Veda is no longer able to help us. Ad-Darr and that Fonseca scum are dead, so we no longer have any support within Puerto Rico. The enemy out there is likely searching for us now that daylight has broken, and given their closeness just a few hours earlier, they are likely to start their search in the same area. It's only a matter of time before they locate our operation."

"So let me see if I hear you correctly," Razzaq said. "You are proposing that we abandon this location so that this mysterious party that may or may not *actually* be searching for us will only discover the remains of the encampment."

"Yes, I believe that is what I'm proposing."

"And where would you have us go, Iskander, eh? Even if we take the minimal equipment we will need, we would have to reduce our forces considerably and scatter in every direction. That sounds more like scared rats than soldiers of the New Revolutionary Justice Organization. We would appear to our enemies as if we were running away like frightened children, with more concern for our own lives than for the greater cause."

"But if we stay here, sir, there is no guarantee we can defend this position."

"And there is no guarantee we will succeed if we split up and evacuate at the last moment. At least we have the advantage of being dug in where we are, no? We have mined the area and we have a full complement of arms and men. We know the terrain and we have a number of resources at our disposal. We are even practically invulnerable to an air assault of any kind.

"No Iskander," Razzaq concluded. "We will make our stand here and defend this position as long as possible. And if it *is* this Stone behind the harassment of our forces, then he will have to come in and get us if he wants us out of here. He must come after us in all his bravado and arrogance and infidel ways, and then I will personally see to it that he pays the price for what he has done. Is that understood?"

"Yes, sir," Iskander replied, quietly staring daggers at Razzaq.

"Now get out of here and go do what you're paid to do," Razzaq said. "See to the defense of our camp. I don't want anything or anyone to get through our perimeter. I'm holding you personally responsible."

Without a word, Iskander bowed and left to obey his

orders. If nothing else, Razzaq had to credit his chief military tactician for knowing when and when not to push an issue. Of one thing he was certain, and that was Iskander would make his move very soon. At some point he would try to make contact with their superiors, spin a tale of how Razzaq had failed the mission and transformed into a raving lunatic. And then he would get his clearance to eliminate Razzaq as a liability. No matter. Siraj Razzaq would be ready when Iskander made his move.

In fact, he very much looked forward to it.

CHAPTER TWENTY-ONE

The first movement of Mack Bolan's fanfare opened with a chorus of well-placed 40 mm grenades.

The HE shells triggered from his standalone M-203 proved to be an arsenal for which the NRJO terrorists had no defense. Even those entrenched in fighting positions dug out of the soft, swampy earth and reinforced with wood cross supports were no match against the explosive ferocity of the grenade blasts. The covered positions on the perimeter of the base camp provided adequate concealment such that Bolan wasn't able to pinpoint each machine-gun emplacement, but he had enough mobility and concealment that he could go in and remove them one by one like a surgeon removing cancer with a scalpel and laser.

First things first, though. The plan called for an opening salvo of grenades to crumble structures within the encampment along with the morale of its defenders.

Wharton and the Executioner had stumbled across the base by accident. They had run into a landmass that, following the previous rains, shouldn't have still been above water. That's until they got close enough for Bolan to discover that the rains had washed away mud and left waterproof sandbags in its wake. He knew he'd found the perimeter.

After offloading the equipment, Bolan had told Wharton, "I imagine we're closer to Folkston now than St. George."

Wharton considered it and nodded. "Yeah, probably."

"I need you to get there and alert your people. Tell them to bring everything and everyone they have down on this location. Get me any air support you can, as well."

"I'm not sure I can leave you here by yourself in good conscience, friend," Wharton had protested.

"I'm not asking, Captain," Bolan replied, using Wharton's title to reinforce the fact he was acting in an official capacity. "Now we agreed before ever setting off on this little excursion that you would do things my way. I expect you to stick to that agreement and do as I say. Understand?"

Wharton had grumbled and complained, but once Bolan was clear he started the airboat and made his way back the direction they'd come. The Executioner estimated it would take the wildlife officer at least two hours to make his way out of the swamplands and get to Folkston. By that time, Bolan would either be dead or the backup forces would act only as a cleanup crew for whatever remained of the NRJO forces. If Bolan had his way, not a single one of the terrorists would make their way out of the Okefenokee Swamp alive.

So he began to send them that message by raining a hail of 40 mm HE grenades on their positions. At one point, a bunch of machine-gun fire came close to Bolan, but not close enough to worry him. He still had concealment behind the tall grasses to his advantage, which allowed him to move among the reeds without being seen. Sure, maybe a stray shot could hit him, but Bolan wasn't worried about it. The uneven terrain of the swamplands had made it relatively difficult for the terrorists to establish interlocking fields of fire between their machine-gun positions.

Once Bolan had delivered approximately a half dozen grenades, he made his way through the high grasses until he came upon the first machine-gun position. The terrorists weren't even facing him when he emerged from the grass, instead firing in a completely different direction. Their bursts were short and far between; at least they were prudent enough to conserve their ammunition without a confirmed target. Still, it wouldn't do them a bit of good in this case, since they had let the enemy sneak up behind them. Even covered beneath a reinforced roof, the pair of sentries was no match for Bolan's FNC. He triggered a pair of 3-round bursts that neatly dispatched both men before they could even bring the machine gun to bear.

Bolan dropped inside the emplacement and did a quick study of the weapon. To his surprise, it was a Heckler & Koch 13E, an expensive weapon and one not easy to export to countries other than the few select with military units actually using it. Capable of firing either a 20- or 30-round magazine, the HK13E chambered 5.56 mm ammunition and sported a longer receiver than its 13A1 predecessor.

The soldier quickly stripped the terrorist corpses of their magazines, put them in a bandolier that he slung across his body and extracted himself and the weapon from the emplacement. The machine gun would not only provide confusion to the enemy, but Bolan could also make good use of it, even in close quarters battle. His original tactic hadn't changed. Create as much confusion and mayhem as possible, rain down as much destruction as he could in as short a time as possible, and he knew his assault might well succeed. The enemy most likely hadn't planned for a small-unit strike, instead designing their defenses around the idea they would be hit by heavy military or police units.

That would make the Executioner's assault all the more effective.

HK13E cradled in his arms, Bolan moved along the perimeter with swift assuredness amid a cacophony of autofire from the remaining machine guns. It took him less than a minute to locate the second one, but he came up on it much sooner than expected. This time, the muzzle of the machine gun pointed straight toward him, and the terrorists behind it showed they weren't afraid to use it to their advantage as they opened up with a full salvo.

Bolan danced clear of their fire just in time to avoid being ventilated by a maelstrom of hot lead, but lost his footing and slipped into calf-high mud. The warrior braced the buttstock of the machine gun against the muddy slope to brace himself and removed his foot with a wet, sucking sound. The terrorists seemed confused about which direction he'd gone and were now shooting in a direction perpendicular to his position. Bolan reached to his LBE harness and unclipped a Diehl DM51 grenade. Sleeve in place, the Executioner yanked the pin and made an easy underhand toss with enough force to clear the green-gray grasses. The grenade exploded seconds later and sent thousands of

2 mm steel balls propelled by superheated gas through the emplacement. Momentarily, the machine gun fell silent.

"WE MUST LEAVE, sir," Iskander said as he burst into Siraj Razzaq's quarters unannounced.

"What's this you say? Leave, leave why?" Razzaq demanded. "And what in the infernal blazes is going on out there? I thought I told you to get this under control."

"We have no control, not here," Iskander said. "That's what I've been trying to tell you! We're under attack. We've lost both our anonymity and our ability to operate effectively. This location has been compromised and we must go. *Now!*"

"You cannot—"

"Yes, I can, sir!" Iskander said. "I wish to see our mission here succeed."

Razzaq had heard enough. He reached into the drawer of the field desk and withdrew a 9 mm Makarov short semiautomatic. "Is that before or after you follow the order to kill me?"

Iskander didn't react in the normal fashion, raising his hands in surprised protest and begging for his life. Razzaq would likely have shot him dead right then. Instead, Razzaq noticed Iskander kept his hands visible—not coming near any one of the many weapons hanging from his equipment harness—while maintaining a mask like cold, chiseled stone.

"You don't look surprised by my accusation."

"That is because it's correct," Iskander said. "I was ordered to kill you."

"Ha, as I suspected! I'm glad you don't deny it."

"I don't deny it," Iskander said. "But I was ordered

several weeks ago to kill you. I ignored the order and instead told them that it was done. As far as the leadership in Afghanistan knows, you have been dead for some weeks and I am currently in charge of this operation."

This was something Razzaq had not foreseen, but he kept his expression impassive as he asked, "And why did you do this?"

"Because I am loyal and I am a professional. This may not be something to which you are accustomed, because most of my colleagues would have already cut your throat while you slept. I do not believe that turning on my superiors is the way to build a reputation among my peers."

Iskander had been correct—Razzaq was *completely* unaccustomed to working with anyone who would show such loyalty. To have perpetrated such a charade in defiance of those above him put his aide's own life in jeopardy, and yet Iskander had done it in spite of that fact. Razzaq could think of the many opportunities Iskander had to kill him these past weeks and he hadn't. Unless, of course, this was all simply an elaborate deception. Razzaq couldn't see that, though. Iskander could have elected to say nothing of this and yet he had been forthright. Honesty was the first and greatest asset in a subordinate and today Razzaq saw Iskander in an entirely new light.

Razzaq lowered his pistol. "I am ashamed for having suspected you, Iskander."

Before the man could reply the ground shook around them with the nearness of an explosion. The attack force had started raining explosives down on them a few minutes earlier and maintained a continuous assault. Another explosion resounded, this one closer, and then a third that resulted in secondary explosions followed by a wash of heat that emanated from the northern wall of their command post.

"The enemy has hit the fuel cans for the boats. I have an airboat on the back side of the perimeter, well away from the fighting," Iskander said. "We *must* go, sir. I have had your belongings already transferred there."

Razzaq responded with an absent nod and immediately rifled through the drawer of his desk to ensure he didn't leave anything behind. He looked for the picture of his wife, didn't see it and decided Iskander had to have already packed it. He slid into the waterproof boots and leggings, secured his pistol in a waterproof pouch and then accompanied his aide out of the command post.

The explosions had stopped, and now Razzaq could hear a considerable amount of small-arms fire. "Obviously they have stopped shelling us."

"That is because I do not think their force is large enough to cover all areas at once," Iskander replied as they picked their way toward the waiting airboat. "As I said before, the force we encountered last night was negligible, and given the way they killed several of our sentries without drawing attention leads me to think we're dealing with only one or two men, three at most."

"I'm beginning to think you are correct." As they reached the airboat and Razzaq climbed in, the NRJO leader continued, "That is why I do not understand why we're abandoning this camp."

"I will be happy to explain to you once we are safely away from here."

"And where are we going?"

"I have a vehicle awaiting us not far from here."

Razzaq decided not to press with further questions

and instead let Iskander focus on getting the airboat started. Four additional men accompanied them. As they prepared to evacuate, several men came and reported to Iskander, advising that a number of their machine-gun emplacements had been destroyed on the southern perimeter and the enemy had penetrated the encampment.

"Hold them at any costs," Iskander ordered one of his unit commanders.

"But, sir, we're being overrun. We must withdraw!"

"You will *not* withdraw, you sniveling coward!" Iskander replied violently. "You will hold this position for as long as possible. You will hold to the last man, and give me the chance to get our leader away from here. Once we have reached our rendezvous point, I will send an extraction team back to get you."

The commander started to open his mouth as if he were going to argue and then nodded and called his aide to accompany him back into combat.

Razzaq shook his head with disgust. These men of his had not received nearly enough training. They didn't understand the importance of their mission here, never mind the fact they were obviously so green that they would run in panic at the slightest hint of possible defeat. And if this attacking force was as small as Iskander hypothesized, they were cowering under an enemy force with inferior numbers. Disgusting!

The engine of the airboat coughed to life, and within a few seconds they were powering from the bank and headed out of the hellish battle zone. They had lost this fight, but they still had a chance to complete their mission. Siraj Razzaq had never failed to execute his plans with success, and he wasn't about to let anything mar that record. From now on he would lead this operation himself, personally oversee every detail.

And soon, very soon, the New Revolutionary Justice Organization would know the taste of victory.

BOLAN ROSE TO HIS FEET, stepped through the grass to inspect the damage and then advanced in search of more terrorists. Much of the indiscriminate firing had stopped, making it more difficult to locate the emplacements and other points where opponents might be hiding. So, the enemy had wised up and realized the more noise they made the harder it would be to find their enemy.

He caught the glimmer of movement in his peripheral vision and took up position behind a curved tree. The area was darker under the canopy of trees, and Bolan became little more than another shadow within the shadows.

A quartet of terrorists stepped into view, hardly visible at first, but quickly taking form as they drew closer to Bolan's position. The soldier waited until they were nearly on top of him before cutting loose the HK13E. The first terrorist caught a burst across the chest that decimated his heart and lungs. Blood sprayed from the wide, flesh-tearing holes left by the heavy-caliber ammunition fired at close range, and the impact lifted the terrorist off his feet. The second hardman met an identical fate with the exception he toppled forward and down the slight rise. Despite the fact the terrorists held the high ground, they were obviously unprepared for an assault of such ferocity.

Bolan dropped the other two with a rising sweep of the HK13E that cut a path of destruction across the terrorists even as they dived for cover. One gunner caught several rounds that split open the top of his skull. One round traveled the length of his spine and exited out his lower back. The remaining terrorist fell when Bolan's shots opened his stomach and caused his intestines to protrude through the holes like cased sausage. Blood and stomach fluids erupted from the man's mouth as he crumpled under the merciless force.

Bolan let several minutes elapse before he scrambled to his feet and made his way up the slope he'd been using for cover. The terrain became more treacherous to negotiate here, so he abandoned the HK13E in favor of the lighter and more rugged FNC. As he skirted the encampment, he noticed something on a distant bank with far too regular outlines to be part of the jungle. The Executioner brought the M-203 into target acquisition, sighted on the structure and triggered a high-explosive shell. He had a second loaded before the first hit and fired a follow-up round just for good measure.

Target destroyed, the Executioner pressed on in search of more terrorist combatants, intent on eradicating them once and for all.

CHAPTER TWENTY-TWO

Guadalupe La Costa decided to take a little time out for hygiene, so she ran a hot bath, dropped into a tub full of suds and had herself a good cry.

It felt good to let it out, relieve some of the stress in her body and mind. The past thirty hours or so had been nothing short of grueling. If she had her druthers, La Costa would have been anywhere else right now—maybe even getting the latest scoop on the political scene in Puerto Rico—except that she was now virtually a prisoner of the United States government. Not that she minded their little retreat here, which was much cozier and more private than the previous safehouse.

She couldn't say much for her latest protectors. One replied to her question in grunts and other strange noises as if he were somehow incapable of forming a coherent sentence. The third man just leered at her most of the time. Not that she hadn't grown accustomed to that reaction by some men. Her father had told the story on more than one occasion that the first thing he said when laying eyes on his newborn baby girl in the hospital was,

"Mama, she's gonna be a heartbreaker." His words turned out to be nearly prophetic because she had the boys after her from about the time she entered puberty until this very day.

She had made sure to lock the door to both her bedroom and bathroom before climbing in the tub, though, albeit she probably had nothing to worry about. These guys were pros. That's why the soft rap on her door so early in the morning surprised her. It wasn't even seven o'clock for pity's sake. Why would they be waking her this early? Unless maybe they were serving breakfast already. As she toweled her hair dry, dressed in a lavender terry-cloth robe, she padded to the door, slippers soundless on the carpeting, and opened it.

Julio Parmahel stood there, and the sudden intake of breath betrayed his surprise at seeing her in such a casual mode of dress. He tried to hide the up-and-down double take, but the reddening visible through the dark complexion immediately betrayed his initial thoughts.

"Take it easy, tiger," La Costa teased him as she turned and went back to the vanity table where she'd been seated. At her request, Hal had been nice enough to get her a few sundries and cosmetics. At least she could put on some makeup to help hide the circles under her eyes.

Parmahel followed her into the room, closed the door behind them and sat on the bed at such an angle she could see him in the mirror. "How are you feeling?"

"Tired and sore," she said as she began to apply eyeliner.

"I felt bad about waking you up so early, but…" His voice trailed off.

"But what?"

"I was concerned about you, that's all."

"Very sweet, Julio," she replied.

La Costa watched him for a reaction, but she didn't get much from him. She had the sense he'd wanted to tell her something ever since they left Puerto Rico, even before then, but anytime she gave him the opening it seemed like he either turned to more casual conversation or didn't pick up the hint. She wondered if she was just imagining things, but something in her gut told her otherwise.

"How about you?" she prompted.

"How about me?"

She sighed. "Are you doing okay?"

"Yeah, just fine," he said.

His tone didn't convince her. Well, could she really blame him—even herself for that matter? They had both been through quite a bit over the past two days, traipsing across Puerto Rico on the heels of the mysterious Colonel Stone who, as it turned out, wasn't really a military officer at all yet fought like a demon soldier from hell. And then there was the cute but all-business pilot Jack, and Hal, the Justice man, a poster boy for McGruff the Crime Dog if there ever was one. She decided to continue busying herself with her makeup rather than put Parmahel on the spot again. He'd come around to whatever was bothering him in his own time.

"You ever wonder what's going to happen to us when all this is over?" Parmahel inquired.

Between lipstick applications she asked, "What do you mean?"

"Well…I mean, I don't know. Just what we're going to do when all of this is done?"

La Costa shrugged. "I don't really know yet, Julio. I guess I haven't really given it much thought. From what

Hal says, we'll never be able to go back to Puerto Rico. At least not for quite a while."

"Well, I can't say I'm exactly disappointed." Parmahel chuckled and added, "All of that humidity was starting to get to me."

"Yeah, imagine what I had to do to keep my hair nice."

"Your hair always looks nice."

Okay, she couldn't take it any longer. La Costa rubbed her lips together gently as she snapped the lipstick applicator in place and then whirled on the padded chair to face him. Parmahel looked surprised when she fixed him with a level gaze and waited for some explanation. When it didn't come, she decided to venture into as yet uncharted territory.

"Honestly, Julio, what's going on with you?"

"What do you mean?"

"You've been moping or lurking around me for the past few weeks, and every time I've given you an opening to tell me what's on your mind you clam up like a company man at an oversight committee hearing." At first it looked like he planned to just brush her off, but after opening his mouth a couple of times and nothing coming out, she made a furious sound and ordered him to speak. "What *is* it?"

"I thought...well, I was just...I just wondered if maybe you'd like to go out some time."

"Go out?"

"Yeah, you know, like not on a job, but more informally."

"You mean a date?"

"Yeah, I mean a date."

La Costa arched an eyebrow. "You're asking me on a date."

"Yes," he replied and swallowed hard.

"Here and now."

"Right."

"After all we've been through these past few days and you're asking me out."

"Goddammit, Lupe!" he snarled. "You ask me what I'm thinking, practically drag and beat it out of me, and then when I speak up you ridicule me."

"I'm not ridiculing you!" she replied, genuinely surprised at his sudden defensiveness. "It's just that I don't understand your timing here, I guess."

"Well, I'm sorry if this isn't convenient for you and all, but I happen to be fresh out of answers right at the moment. I mean, first you drag me around chasing Stone, and then you get me involved with whatever pile of shit you stepped in, so now I'm marked by some terrorists I don't even know who are interested only in killing me!"

La Costa narrowed her eyes. "Don't forget I'm in the same boat as you are, pal."

"I know, I know." He waved it away and sighed heavily. His voice got quiet. "I'm sorry, Lupe. I'm really sorry about all of this. If I could take any of it back I would, but I can't and I'm kind of sick of holding back how I feel."

"How you feel about what?" she asked.

"Well, if you—"

Her exploding window cut him off, and both of them jumped at the loud popping sound that followed. Fortunately, neither of them had been looking in the direction of the object in a desire to avoid some of the flying glass, so the full effects of the flash-bang grenade didn't completely render them helpless. While La Costa's ears rang the flashing light hadn't blinded her. The room took on a dizzying effect as she tried to stand and immediately she collapsed to the floor, her legs wobbly beneath her.

La Costa didn't have time to regain her senses, though, because she realized Parmahel had hold of her wrist and yanked her to her feet. She knew he was saying something, but couldn't make it out through the fog of neurological shock.

"Before this is over I'm going to need a therapist," she said, but couldn't tell exactly how loud she was speaking. Not that Parmahel acknowledged her anyway. His focus appeared to be elsewhere as they ran hand-in-hand down the hall and descended the stairs. As they reached the bottom landing, La Costa's tinnitus had begun to fade and she could distinctly make out the shouting of the marshal, the one who had been leering at her before.

"Get back upstairs!" he said. "We've been compromised, repeat, compromised!"

La Costa thought that was a strange thing for him to say to them, but then she realized he'd directed that latter into his wrist microphone. Parmahel didn't need to be told twice. He skidded to a halt, turned and waved La Costa to get up the steps. She cursed at the sudden change in plan, but then realized the genius of it. Their assassins wouldn't try to come through the upper-floor window—the flash-bang had intended to drive them downstairs where they were more vulnerable, and that's exactly what they did.

La Costa turned to look behind her once and noticed the marshal following them up the stairwell. He said something, but she couldn't hear. She felt a sharp stab in her ear, now, as the shock began to wear off and when she put her hand to it she came away with some watery blood. Obviously she had suffered a ruptured eardrum.

At a prompting from the marshal, a large black guy named Eady, the pair rushed down the hall and into the bedroom assigned to Parmahel. He ordered them into the bathroom, and advised they should climb in the tub and not come out until one of them gave the all-clear signal. Parmahel did as ordered, but La Costa wasn't giving up quite so easily. She started to argue with Eady, but the guy just wagged his fingers and thumb together in the "you talk too much" gesture and then shoved her through the bathroom doorway and slammed the door behind her. He then beat on it a couple of times and ordered them to lock it.

La Costa did and then climbed into the bathtub alongside Parmahel. They crouched, and Parmahel drew the shower curtain to conceal them. When he noticed La Costa looking at him with a puzzled expression he shrugged and sheepishly replied, "What? I thought maybe they won't look for us if the curtain was drawn."

"Maybe not," she said. "But it won't stop bullets."

"No, that's apparently what *we're* for."

The comment took La Costa by such surprise she wanted to burst out in laughter, but somehow it seemed inappropriate in the present circumstances. As they sat there in the shadowy enclosure, their bodies close together, her thoughts returned to Parmahel earlier asking her on a date. She couldn't believe it, and in some sense it repelled her. Not out of anything personal against Parmahel. He was a handsome and stable guy, and had a personality she found comfortable and compatible to her own.

No, what she feared most was a loss of friendship. They had developed such a good working relationship that she couldn't bear the thought of losing it. Not now…not right at this moment when it seemed like her whole world was crumbling around her.

"You know, Julio," she said, putting a hand on his forearm and giving it a gentle squeeze. "I just wanted to tell you that no matter what happens, you've been the one thing I could count on in this whole sordid mess. I just thought you should know that."

Parmahel had a funny expression on his face, but replied, "Lupe, I—"

The sound of gunfire interrupted him this time. The journalists could hear the shooting, and it sounded like a ferocious gun battle was going on directly below them. How the terrorists had found them remained a complete mystery to her. She had thought after Hal destroyed the bug that they wouldn't have to worry about it anymore; she thought it was over and they would be safe. But instead it seemed like this had turned into an endless marathon to save their lives, and apparently it wouldn't end until they were dead.

The sound of gunfire intensified as the terrorists, whoever they were, advanced up the steps. They heard thuds and crashes and La Costa could tell they came from men kicking in doors, making a room-by-room sweep. Eventually they would get to Parmahel's room, and if they had already overcome the three marshals downstairs who had been protecting them, the guy named Eady didn't stand a chance going up against some unknown number of well-armed terrorists. If La Costa had learned anything from Stone, it was that the best defense was a good offense.

La Costa rose to her feet, ripped aside the shower curtain and jumped out of the bathtub before it even registered on Parmahel.

"Where are you going?" he demanded as La Costa ripped open the bathroom door and ran out. "Lupe, get back here!"

Eady, who had taken cover on one knee behind the bed, rose and rushed toward her. "What the hell are you doing? Get back in there!"

"No!" La Costa said, shaking her head adamantly. "Your people downstairs are most likely dead. This place is overrun, and I don't see any reason for you to throw your life away. We should run."

Eady pointed toward the door and said, "No, we shouldn't. You should do what you're told and get back into the tub."

"Yeah, Lupe, come on!" Parmahel protested from the bathroom doorway.

The door to the room thumped once, twice and then someone jiggled the handle. Eady roughly shoved La Costa toward Parmahel just as the door flew open and three men entered. They looked Arabic, but the submachine guns in their hands were the most telling features. Eady managed to get off only two shots—his rounds struck the first terrorist in the chest—before the remaining two gunned him down with sustained bursts. The terrorists wheeled toward La Costa, and she stumbled backward into Parmahel just as they sprayed the place she'd been standing. The wooden doorways and drywall were no match for the high-velocity rounds that chewed them up.

The terrorists strutted to the bathroom doorway, confident their trapped and unarmed targets would provide no resistance. That's why the sudden flash and crackle of mint-green plastic took them by surprise as it suddenly flew through the air and landed directly over them. The two men struggled to get disentangled from the plastic, but in the meantime Julio Parmahel grabbed a heavy wooden chair at a small desk against the wall just outside the bathroom and began to beat the terrorists with it. The blows weren't debilitating, but Parmahel did manage to knock the weapons from their hands.

La Costa watched with complete shock as Parmahel hit the men until the chair broke in his hands. One side of the shower curtain, the one closer to Parmahel, was much lower than the other and something dark and gelatinous could be seen covering certain areas. Parmahel had obviously hit one of them hard enough to cause bleeding. Probably a head wound. La Costa shook off the moment and charged the man who was still standing, throwing her small and petite body hard enough to knock the terrorist off his feet.

In the fray, one of the machine pistols skittered from under the shower curtain. Parmahel scooped it up and screamed at La Costa to move. She didn't hesitate as he swung the weapon onto the struggling forms and squeezed the trigger. The reports were deafening inside the room and Parmahel looked a little surprised, even frightened, as he triggered a sustained burst into the lumpy shower curtain. This time there was no mistaking the blood, and within just a few moments the struggling and writhing ceased. Parmahel kept his finger on the trigger until the bolt locked back on an empty breach.

Parmahel looked at the weapon a moment, then tossed it aside. He then located Eady's pistol, fished through the marshal's pockets until he found a car key and then grabbed La Costa's hand.

"You're really beginning to surprise me!" she exclaimed.

"You kidding me?" he shot back. "I grew up around gangbangers."

He had a point; La Costa hadn't considered until now that Parmahel hadn't exactly grown up with the silver spoon in his mouth. Just like her he had some hidden talents, and just like her he wasn't afraid to use them if pushed to the limits. If nothing else, La Costa knew she had a brand-new story to tell. She only wondered if anybody would believe it.

The pair raced down the stairs and out the back door. As they reached the car, a terrorist stepped around the side of the house and began to fire at them with a pistol. La Costa didn't see him but Parmahel did, and he managed to shove La Costa out of the way just in time to take one of the bullets. He screamed in pain as the round cut through his thigh and ripped out a chunk of flesh.

La Costa cursed as she scraped her hands and knees, bare below the terry-cloth robe, on the rough pavement of the drive. Parmahel managed to get to the door of the SUV and get the key into it. To her surprise it opened the vehicle—somehow he'd picked the right one—not realizing that the government keys were designed to fit into all SUVs on a single detail in case of emergency. La Costa turned to see the terrorist grinning and charging. What he didn't know was that La Costa was familiar with firearms. She snatched the pistol out of Parmahel's hand and kept it out of sight until the terrorist got close. When he drew near, she brought it into view and blew him away with four rounds at point-blank range.

"Take that, you bastard," she cried. She heard a groan and turned her attention toward Parmahel. A quick inspection of the wound revealed it was bad. "Come on, Julio, we need to get you to a hospital."

"No!" he said. "Just leave me here and get out of here. It's you they're interested in. If you take the time—"

"Don't be stupid," she countered. "You just saved my life, and I'm not going to turn around and leave you here to die. Now shut up and let me help you in the car."

CHAPTER TWENTY-THREE

The enemy had Mack Bolan pinned down.

High-velocity rounds buzzed the air over his head or chewed into the ground around him. A natural obstacle separated him from his objective: a single airboat moored approximately twenty yards from what remained of the only physical structure. The NRJO hadn't set up much of a firebase after all, but Bolan would be shocked if the terrorists hadn't left him a surprise or two. It took only one tripwire attached to a claymore or some other booby trap to bring his mission to a close real quick.

At the moment, however, that didn't worry Bolan nearly as much as the autofire from enemy weapons cutting him to shreds. The soldier kept the return fire short and precise to conserve ammunition and make it more difficult for the terrorists to pinpoint his location. One advantage he had was good cover in tall grass on slightly higher ground. Some of the terrorists were firing from positions in the water anywhere from knee to waist deep. Coupled with the fact they were firing upward at an invisible enemy worked to Bolan's advantage.

The Executioner ceased firing to check his grenade satchel. Three HE grenades remained and one smoker— hardly enough to take out the remaining terrorist force with ease, especially given the terrain. A 40 mm grenade wasn't very effective if it landed in five or six feet of swamp water. Bolan also had two Diehl DM51s attached to his LBE harness, but the same story held true for their effectiveness. That left the warrior with one option.

He would have to commence a surgical strike: search and destroy.

Bolan left his position and began to crawl slowly through the tall grasses. His arm, shoulder, thigh and calf muscles burned in protest as he made an arduous trek into the enemy fire zone. He took comfort in the small fact his journey could be made on a downhill slope rather than uphill. As he drew nearer to the first enemy position, he noted that most of the firing had stopped.

And then a fresh salvo opened up from a machine-gun emplacement, but the rounds weren't anywhere near Bolan. The terrorists didn't know his exact location, so all they could do was lay down suppressing fire in the hope they might just hit something.

As soon as the soldier reached the bottom of the shallow slope and came level with the water line, he reverted to a crouched position and unslung the M-203. Quickly and quietly, he loaded a high-explosive charge, slowly closed the breach until it clicked in place, then triggered the grenade. He jumped to his feet as soon as the charge was away and waded into the water, crossing as quickly as his legs would carry him. Although the water came only to just below his knees it remained difficult to move efficiently without making enough noise that the enemy could pinpoint his position.

As soon as he stepped onto another embankment, he crouched and loaded a second shell just as the first one came down in an area slightly to the rear of the base perimeter. Bolan immediately triggered the round, which detonated about ten yards closer than the location where the last one had exploded. The enemy began to direct small-arms fire toward the area of the explosion a heart-beat later, just as Bolan had planned. The sustained autofire would mask his approach. He continued through a small stand of young trees and emerged on the enemy firing line. Directly ahead a pair of terrorists lay in the mud, one triggering a machine gun on a bipod while the second monitored the belt feed. Quick shots to the head took them out of play.

Bolan moved from their position in a perpendicular direction and came upon the second group of terrorist gunners concealed behind a small, aboveground fighting position constructed from sandbags. Bolan snagged a DM51 grenade from his LBE, pulled the pin and tossed the bomb into the midst of the trio taking turns firing at nothing. He didn't lose stride as he pressed on in search of other terrorists, not even looking back when the grenade exploded. The screams of agony were enough to let him know he'd eliminated the threat to the rear.

While the Executioner could be ruthless he wasn't psychotic, and he took no pleasure in taking human lives. He would have lived a life of peace and domestic tranquility given a choice, but he saw his duty as a higher calling to secure that kind of life for those who could not secure it for themselves.

Bolan's encounter with the next group required a bit more effort as the three terrorists had obviously realized they'd been duped. One of them began firing at Bolan as soon as he saw him, giving his comrades time to reposition their machine gun. The soldier knew based on the surrounding topography and the lack of cover here that taking down the heavier weapon had to be the priority if he were to survive. Bolan threw himself onto his belly and brought the sights of the FNC into target acquisition, sighting on the machine gun itself, and squeezed the trigger. A trio of 3-round bursts did the trick, the 5.56 mm NATO rounds turning the M-60 knockoff into scrap metal.

Bolan rolled from his position in time to avoid being ventilated by salvo of rounds from the first terrorist who had finally zeroed his firing zone. The two machine gunners scrambled for their autorifles while their comrade continued to provide cover fire. The soldier put his cheek to the stock of the FNC once more, took a deep breath and let half out, then squeezed the trigger. The first round struck the terrorist in the chest, the second in the jaw and the final slug blew the top of his head off.

Bolan then turned to the task of the surviving duo. One appeared to be experiencing a weapon jam as he floundered with the charging handle; the delay cost him his life. Bolan put a burst through his neck that severed both carotid arteries and ripped out the better part of his upper esophagus and airway. The final gunman managed to get off a short burst before Bolan's 3-round package stitched him diagonally across the upper chest. The man dropped to his knees and tumbled forward into the mud with a splat.

Scrambling to his feet, the soldier realized he was now within reaching distance of the final airboat. The only thing that stood between him and retreat were six armed terrorists who looked determined to protect the boat at any costs. Given that there was no more indiscriminate firing, Bolan considered it safe to assume these half dozen terrorists were all that remained of the New Revolutionary Justice Organization, or at least the force defending the base. He still hadn't seen any evidence of Siraj Razzaq, but he knew the possibility existed that Razzaq had either been inside the makeshift structure or already abandoned the base.

But now wasn't the time to worry about that. Bolan had more pressing concerns, such as how to take out the terrorists without destroying the boat in the process. He hadn't expected to cut through the enemy forces so quickly. If he could take out these guards and escape with the airboat intact, he could touch base with Wharton and nix wasting manpower to send reinforcements. Bolan finally opted to implement the prime tradecraft that had earned him his title in Southeast Asia.

The soldier shed his equipment except for the Beretta 93-R.

He found a tree with a low protruding branch that met him at about chest height and provided a perfect resting place for his arm. The tritium, three-dot sights weren't exactly top-of-the-line, but then Bolan would have preferred a sniper rifle in this kind of situation versus the pistol. Still, the Beretta had always proved itself an accurate and reliable weapon if shown proper maintenance—it would do.

Bolan took steady aim with the Beretta, positioned his arm between the trunk and branch of the tree and tested the muzzle sweep to make sure he could take all six targets unhindered. Once confirmed, Bolan did one more assessment of the group to predict possible avenues of escape. The terrorists wouldn't have many places to go without either running into one another or simply jumping into the water. The place where they had moored the airboat naturally opened onto the main water lane that snaked its way through the swamps like a great river.

He acquired his first target, controlling his breathing and relaxing his stance, and then squeezed the trigger twice. The first terrorist caught both rounds center mass, and the impact flipped him backward into the water.

At just under two seconds after he fired the first round, Bolan had the second in his sights and squeezed the trigger twice more. This time the Beretta awarded him with head shots, one ripping away the lower jaw as the other skull-buster scrambled the terrorist's brains.

Three seconds. The third terrorist had turned in Bolan's general direction and started to raise the SMG, but he wasn't nearly fast enough and Bolan's first round punched through his stomach. The impact spun him into his partner, who tried to bring his own weapon to bear. Bolan's fifth and sixth rounds struck that terrorist in the spine and sent both men collapsing into the mud.

Bolan was halfway into second four before the remaining two terrorists even realized they were under attack. One smartly dived to the ground, but his partner wasn't as agile. The hesitation cost him as the Executioner put him down with two shots to the chest and a third to the head.

The soldier flipped the selector to 3-round-burst mode and took the extra time to settle the Beretta's

sights on the final target. The terrorist began to spray the
area with rounds in hope of keeping Bolan's head down.
Unfortunately, he couldn't tell exactly where his adversary was positioned and his salvos went high over
Bolan's head. The soldier took a deep breath and let half
out before squeezing the Beretta's trigger one final time.
The 9 mm Parabellum rounds followed a natural course
with the rise of the muzzle, the first drilling through the
top of the terrorist's head and the remaining pair
entering his back on very flat trajectories.

As the reports of the Beretta died out, Bolan stood
still and watched for further movement. He wasn't
taking anything for granted at this point. The enemy had
been diligent in leaving behind such a large number to
guard the only remaining transportation out of this
green, damp hell. Only when he was convinced additional enemy terrorists weren't waiting in the wings to
shoot him down on sight did Bolan break cover and trot
to the airboat.

Dropping his weapons bag into the boat, he then retrieved a couple of the submachine guns from their
deceased owners. Ammunition was low, and he didn't
want to risk an encounter with any more terrorists only
to find himself outgunned. Once he had completed his
task, Bolan double-checked the fuel and nodded with
satisfaction. The gauge indicated he had a full tank.
Bolan considered his next move. He could attempt to negotiate his way down the main lane until he found the
point where he'd reached the camp and then backtrack
to St. George.

Unfortunately, that would take too long and he had
another consideration. Looking at the makeshift dock
made him realize that spaces had been made for a total

of three airboats. They had destroyed one the night before and he had another. That meant one was missing, probably the same one he and Wharton had encountered just before the storm moved in. Since he hadn't seen Razzaq's body, Bolan had to assume the terrorist leader had escaped. He couldn't take it for granted Razzaq had been inside the encampment headquarters when he leveled it.

No, the NRJO wouldn't have let its prize commander die unnecessarily. Razzaq and an unknown number of his group had evacuated early during Bolan's primary assault. He could feel it. Something in his gut told him this wasn't over yet. Well, all he could do was follow the only remaining path out of there and hope he could catch up with Razzaq before the terrorist got away.

He had to. The security of America depended on it.

BROGNOLA HAD NEVER been happier to see someone alive than Jack Grimaldi.

The pilot seemed no worse for the wear, although the smell of burned combustibles wafted off his flight suit. There were also soot stains running down the back of his right sleeve where the smoke had entered the cockpit. Still, he wasn't injured, and he didn't seem traumatized by his brush with death. In fact, quite the opposite—he looked more determined and ready for action than ever.

And Brognola remarked so.

Grimaldi laughed. "It's going to take a lot more than that to keep me down. I've had too many close calls in too many birds to let it start worrying me now."

"I don't doubt it," Brognola replied.

The two men had then proceeded to Andrews Air

Force base and boarded Stony Man's spare C-21 Gulfstream, which had been fueled and serviced per Brognola's orders. The other plane Grimaldi, La Costa and Parmahel had arrived in the previous day would be out of service for a while.

The pilot got immediate and priority clearance for takeoff and soon the pair was airborne, bound for Fort Stewart, Georgia.

Brognola had barely settled in for the flight when the computer console in front of him signaled for attention. The incoming link could only be from one place: Stony Man Farm. Brognola wished and hoped that the news would be good even as he reached forward and tapped in a sixteen-character alphanumeric code that would establish the secure connection via satellite uplink. After a slight pause the face of Barbara Price filled the high-definition TFT screen.

"Good morning, Barb," Brognola greeted her.

"I see you guys got off okay."

"Yeah, we're on our way to Georgia now. Jack says our flight time is less than ninety minutes, so we should be there before noon. Any word from Striker?"

Price shook her head. "I'm afraid not, but I do have some news on him. There's a U.S. Fish and Wildlife Service captain by the name of Donald Wharton on your line here."

"Wharton must have contacted his higher-ups. They had my Farm contact number," Brognola replied. "Have Bear put him through."

There was a brief burst of static over the audio speakers and then the screen split into two distinct panels. Price's image remained intact on the left and the new face of an older, weathered-looking man materialized next to her. Brognola could see the man he assumed to be Wharton, and Wharton could see him, but Price would remain visible only to Brognola.

"Captain Wharton, I assume?" Brognola began.

"That's me," the man replied pleasantly enough. "And you are?"

"My name is Hal Brognola. I'm a ranking official with the DOJ, and while I'd like to be more specific about that we don't have the time. Suffice it to say that there are certain parties at 1600 Pennsylvania Avenue who pay me to advise them on situations such as we have there in Georgia."

"I understand," Wharton said with a nod. "I'm contacting you in regard to Matt Cooper. I assume you know him."

Brognola knew from that last statement it wasn't a question, so there was no point in denying it. Although he tried to be diligent and make sure his affiliation with Mack Bolan was kept as private as possible, this particular situation had reached a critical point. It wasn't time to play ignorant just because somebody might not have the same security clearances as he did.

"I do. Is he with you?"

Wharton shook his head. "I'm afraid not, and that's why I'm calling you guys. My boss figured I'd better get in touch."

"What's your status there?"

"Well, Coop sent me back here to pull together all the reinforcements I could find. He's out there in the middle of the Okefenokee right now taking on some Lebanese terrorist group all by himself. If I didn't know better and had seen him in action myself, I'd say the guy had gone plum crazy."

"So would I," Brognola replied. "I don't want you to send out those men until we've arrived. We'll be landing at Fort Stewart, and from there we'll take a chopper to your location. Where are you right now?"

"I'm at the U.S. Wildlife station in Folkston. I've got the men together, but I'll defer to your authority and wait until you arrive. I'd hurry though, Mr. Brognola. There are an awful lot of men here who are getting antsy to take the fight to these bastards."

"I'm sure there are, Captain. But for now you stand them down and advise them that while I appreciate their dedication, this situation falls directly under the jurisdiction of the Justice Department and Homeland Security. Understood?"

Wharton nodded and then Brognola said goodbye before killing the uplink.

"You get all that, Barb?" he asked.

"I did. What you need from me?"

"I need you to get a fix on Striker, if possible, and get that information to me pronto. It's time to lend a helping hand."

CHAPTER TWENTY-FOUR

After a thorough search, Mack Bolan found a map of the region stowed aboard the airboat. A water lane—the one he happened to be traversing at present—was highlighted in grease marker and terminated at a section of dry land about fifteen nautical miles from the base camp. From this point it looked as if a wildlife service road led from the Okefenokee. Bolan was guessing this was his enemy's escape route and he further believed it had been utilized by Siraj Razzaq. That meant only one thing. The terrorist lived and would likely execute some contingency option.

The Executioner had other plans.

His satellite cellular phone vibrated against his chest. He reached into the waterproof lining of his concealed pocket and brought it into the light. Signal at last! Bolan could see it was Stony Man calling and answered before it got halfway through the third buzz.

"Striker here."

Barbara Price's voice sounded immediately relieved. "Glad to hear your voice."

"You, too."

"You okay?"

"Tired, but in one piece. The terrorist compound inside the swamp has been destroyed and the majority of their force neutralized. There may be one or two stragglers, but regular law enforcement will have plenty of time to pick them up. I got out on the last airboat, and I don't think there are any other transports out of there."

"I'll let the locals know."

"Where's Hal?"

"On his way with Jack," Price said. "He wanted us to get a location on you, and the GPS tracker inside your cellular phone finally started transmitting again."

"Was it blocked by the storm?"

"Bear doesn't think so," she replied. "We believe the terrorists were jamming all incoming or outgoing RF signals but their own frequencies as the most plausible explanation. After everything that's happened with La Costa and Parmahel, we think they have at least one highly technical person attached to them and possibly more."

"Makes sense. Are they okay now?"

"Yes. Hal got them to the safehouse in North Carolina, although not without a bit of trouble."

"Is he okay?"

"Yes," she replied. "Jack crashed a chopper, but he's fine. He's not letting it get in his way. So what's next on your plate?"

"I think Razzaq may still be alive. In fact, I'm betting on it. I have a map I think will take me wherever he's headed, although what he's up to is still a mystery."

"Well, certainly he or someone in the NRJO has been intent on eliminating La Costa and Parmahel. We still don't have a motive, but we managed to find a homing bug on her. It was a watch given to her by Miguel Veda as a gift. We thought maybe he was just keeping an eye on her, but now we're convinced this wasn't really his doing. We think the NRJO is actually behind it."

"But you don't know why they would still be interested in her if Ad-Darr's dead," Bolan concluded.

"Right. There's something else going on here, Striker."

"Well, I think we'll find the answers once I've latched on to Razzaq. Is there any way you can put me through to Hal?"

"Absolutely," she replied. "Stand by."

As he waited, Bolan piloted the airboat along the water lane per the map. He kept one eye on places where the terrorists could have turned off or concealed their airboat—searching for things like grasses recently flattened or regularly shaped openings in mud builds—though no evidence pointed to that. The terrorists were definitely running, and Bolan believed Siraj Razzaq was with them. He also figured he couldn't be too far behind.

"Striker, what's your status?"

"I'm okay," Bolan said, knowing what Brognola was really asking.

Brognola emitted a deep, audible sigh. "We were beginning to wonder there after we heard the storm went through and lost the GPS signal link. It was good to hear from Captain Wharton he left you alive and well."

"You talked to Wharton?"

"Yes."

"Okay, so you know what's going on."

"We do," Brognola replied. "In fact, I've instructed him to wait until we get there. He's got a small army down there champing at the bit and looking for some action."

"They might just get their wish. I've neutralized the main body, but I still think Razzaq has a small contingency force and other plans. I've found a map, and I'd say they're headed for a little town on the edge of the swamp called Silver Hill. I don't know what they have planned there."

"Could be a rendezvous point."

"That's the most probable explanation," the Executioner replied. "I don't know anything about this Silver Hill, but I don't imagine it's heavily populated. If the NRJO was planning some kind of an attack there, they would want it to be spectacular if nothing else. Razzaq wants to make his point on the eleven o'clock news and not confine it to a local newspaper."

"Agreed. So how do you want to handle this?"

"That depends. What's your ETA to Silver Hill?"

"Well, we're less than thirty minutes from touchdown at Fort Stewart and I've arranged to have a fully equipped Black Hawk waiting for us. I don't imagine it would take us more than an hour."

"That'll do. Go ahead and contact Wharton. Tell him I'll need a pickup at Station Four." Bolan gave the Stony Man chief the exact map coordinates and name of the access road that led to the station. "And if I were you I'd advise the rest of the men he's gathered to shag their butts up to Silver Hill."

"You sure that's a good idea? Having a posse of armed federal officers go crash the party in a small tourist town may draw a lot more attention than we'd like."

"There's nothing I can do about that now. Unfortunately, Razzaq has chosen the battlefield, and in this case I may need the extra hands to get the bystanders clear. If I get my way, Hal, I'll be able to end this once and for all in Silver Hill and contain any potential threats Razzaq and his people may pose. Shutting them down there and then will draw a lot less attention than if they're able to complete whatever plans they might have, whether it be here in the States, Puerto Rico or otherwise."

"Okay, you know I trust you, Striker. I'll make sure Wharton's people are there to plow the road. Do you need anything else?"

"I'll need some fresh equipment, weapons and supplies…and a fresh change of clothes would be good."

"We didn't bring a spare blacksuit, but I will see what we can do about some urban camouflage fatigues."

"Beggars can't be choosers," Bolan replied with a chuckle. "Out."

He disconnected the call, then focused on his map. If he had oriented himself correctly and was reading the map right, he would make Station Four right about the time Brognola and Grimaldi reached Silver Hill. He'd forgotten to tell Brognola to pass the message that Wharton should be careful as a remote possibility existed he might encounter the terrorists. He thought about calling him back, but dismissed the idea; Wharton could take care of himself and he surely didn't need Bolan to babysit him.

As he traversed the water lane, Bolan considered the situation with La Costa and Parmahel. Stony Man had a mystery on their hands, no doubt about it. Since Veda had been working for the NRJO and the snoopy reporter had befriended him looking for political insights, it only made sense that a radical like that would want to keep tabs on her. What didn't make sense was that the NRJO's plans for Puerto Rico had been foiled by Bolan's intervention, and Ad-Darr was dead. That basically meant La Costa and Parmahel no longer posed any threat to Razzaq or the NRJO. So why assassinate her?

There had to be more to it and Bolan was betting that only Razzaq had the answer. Yeah, Razzaq was the key to it all: find the terrorist leader and in turn find the answers.

THE SERVICES AND STAFF at Hoffman Medical Center were impressive for a county hospital, to say the least.

Of course, La Costa had seen medical facilities in the most economically deprived areas throughout the country, places that it made her shudder to recall. But not this place. Within moments of pulling up to the emergency room in the Ford Expedition and running inside to alert staff, two nurses, two orderlies and a trauma doctor had wheeled a gurney outside. They gently extricated Julio Parmahel from the Expedition, being careful under the watchful eye and strong coaxing from La Costa, and soon had him in the trauma room, where they began a full assessment.

Being the small town it was and in the middle of the day, it didn't take long for the medical staff to notify the police they had a victim of a gunshot wound. The man who showed up in a tan deputy sheriff's uniform was tall with sandy-colored hair and sideburns that look like they'd come straight out of the 1970s. The deputy had a clean and clear complexion, with a young face on the exterior, but La Costa could tell from years of experience that the faint lines at the corners of his eyes and mouth spoke volumes. No, this was an experienced police officer, and La Costa felt a little uncomfortable as he scrutinized her in the surgical waiting room.

Fortunately, they were alone in the room so La Costa felt she could speak a bit more freely. Actually she didn't even know why this was making her uncomfortable. She hadn't done anything, other than maybe killing a terrorist, but then again that had been self-defense. La Costa had been through too much in the past couple of days that she would now let this man intimidate her. And while she wouldn't have admitted openly, she wished Julio were there by her side right now holding her hand and consoling her.

No, what she really wished for was the commanding presence of Colonel Brandon Stone.

"Okay, ma'am," Deputy Holcombe said politely and evenly, "let's try this again."

"I've already gone over this four times," La Costa replied. She made no attempt to hide the disdain in her voice. "I don't know what part of this you don't understand."

"Listen here, Ms. La Costa, I understand you're upset."

La Costa decided to play the role of bitch. "Do you now? For the past two days I've been chased by men with guns, penned up in *Hee Haw* hell, and watched one of my closest friends get shot up trying to save me from a group of terrorist fanatics. And for all of that, for all my troubles, what do I get? I get you standing here, grilling me without offering me so much as a cup of coffee, and without advising me of my rights to an attorney by the way, while my friend is in there fighting for his life. Now why should I be upset by all of that?"

Deputy Holcombe sighed and finally took a chair

across from her. "I'm sorry I haven't been a little more accommodating here, ma'am, but we have a pretty serious situation on our hands. Last night there was a major shoot-out between unknown parties just off the highway a few miles south of here. And then we get called to back up a posse of U.S. Marshals who are up against a local gang armed with automatic weapons.

"Now I don't know about you or your friend on the table in there, but I do know something as strange as hell is going on here and somehow you're involved. So maybe if you just come forward and get straight with me, I can get this issue settled here and now. All I'm asking you for is a little cooperation."

La Costa looked Holcombe in the eyes now, staring daggers at him. "You know, this may come as a bit of surprise to you, but I've been showing a whole lot of people a whole lot of cooperation for the past seventy-two hours. And all it's bought me to this point is a bunch of trouble. I'm starting to get real tired of being the one who does all the giving here."

Holcombe tried a different tack. "You said before that the people who were shooting at you and—" he referred quickly to his notebook "—this Julio Parmahel were terrorists…fanatics. Where exactly did this happen again?"

"I've told you before and I'm going to repeat it one last time, and if you don't get it after that it's your tough luck. We were at a U.S. government safehouse. I don't remember where it's at. All I know is that it's somewhere here in Mount Airy. I guess it used to be some sort of farmhouse that some guy sold off a long time ago. And even if I did remember where it was I'm not sure that I would tell you, because they stash protected witnesses there. If everybody knows about the place, then that would kind of then defeat the purpose of it being a safehouse. Don't you think?"

"Okay, so let's say that I buy the story that you and Parmahel are protected federal witnesses. Give me the name of your case agent so that I can at least verify your story."

"The only thing I can tell you is that the man who was in charge of our case is not with the U.S. Marshals Service. He's with the Department of Justice and his name is Hal. I knew the marshals only by their last names."

"Okay, what else can you tell me? Can you discuss the case with me?"

"We don't have a case, per se. All we were doing was reporting a story and all of a sudden we're involved in some big, international conspiracy involving terrorists. That's all I know. Or at least all I know I can tell you. I would suggest if you want any other information that you contact Hal at the Department of Justice in Washington. And if you don't like my answers, take it up with him because as I understand it he works directly with the Oval Office."

La Costa knew she probably had crossed a line tacking on that last part, but she was frustrated by the treatment she had to endure at the hands of this hick deputy sheriff. At the moment, Julio was her main concern and she really didn't give a tinker's damn about some backwoods cop trying to make a name for himself. She hadn't asked for any of this. It all started trying to get a story, trying to be a patriot and help Stone get to the bottom of whatever had spurned violence in Puerto Rico. She had been trying to demonstrate her dedication to her job while simultaneously her loyalty to her country. That's the way her father had taught her to be and all she had gotten in return was grief.

"Okay, Ms. La Costa, I'm going to check into this." Holcombe stood now in an attempt to pose a more intimidating presence. "I'll see if I can track down this Hal character. But I'm warning you now that if you're sending me on a wild-goose chase, you're going to regret it. Because I will come back here and slap you in handcuffs and take you to jail. Do you understand?"

La Costa simply stared at him, refusing to answer.

"Don't go anywhere and don't leave this building," Holcombe said as he turned and left the waiting room.

La Costa experienced a sudden chill. An aide at the hospital had been kind enough to provide her with a pair of surgical scrubs and some clean slippers, over which she had donned the terry-cloth robe. Although she had just taken a shower a few hours earlier she felt dirty. La Costa knew most of it was insecurity, but she couldn't help herself; she felt like she felt, and she wasn't about to apologize for that to anyone.

The thing that worried her most right now was Julio's condition. She felt guilty for not having settled anything between them following his advances. Then again, how could she have when the terrorists hadn't given her time? She knew one thing and that was if Julio died she wasn't sure how she could live with the fact some things would remain unsaid between them. The emergency-room doctor hadn't given her much cause to be hopeful.

"His condition is serious, even critical in certain ways," the physician had told her once Parmahel had been stabilized. "He lost a lot of blood from that gunshot wound. There was major soft-tissue damage to his thigh, and some significant surgical repair to the bone and blood vessels will be required. There's also the chance of moderate to severe nerve damage, which could to some degree impair his ability to walk. Only the trauma surgeon's findings will give us a better idea as to the extent of the damage and any final prognosis. I'm sorry the news isn't better, but I want you to take comfort in the fact that your quick thinking to get him here in a timely fashion very likely saved his life."

While the doctor's statements made her feel better, La Costa couldn't take a whole lot of credit. It was her single-mindedness and drive to get her story that had put their lives at risk to begin with. If she had just backed off, none of this would have happened and Julio wouldn't be lying on a surgical table fighting for his life.

She felt alone, as if the world she'd known was collapsing on her, and there was no one to save her. She couldn't rely on Hal, she couldn't rely on Jack the pilot, and she definitely couldn't rely on Stone, because at the moment she didn't even know where the hell he was. She could only wish that he, or someone like him, was with her now. Someone to put their arms around her and tell her it was going to be okay.

Overcome with emotion, La Costa wrapped her arms tighter about herself, bowed her head and softly cried.

CHAPTER TWENTY-FIVE

Per Iskander's arrangements, a vehicle awaited their arrival at a vacant wildlife station.

Iskander had taken a considerable risk having the NRJO reserve attachment rendezvous with them close to where there may be law enforcement operating, in Razzaq's opinion, but in this case it had worked out. Once more, his aide had demonstrated his competence and skill as a warrior for the cause of the New Revolutionary Justice Organization. Razzaq made a note that he would publicly honor him in front of his colleagues once they had escaped the country.

After Iskander had ordered his men to return to the camp and extract any survivors, he joined Razzaq and the terrorist leader's two bodyguards in the sedan. Then Iskander ordered the driver to head straight for their rendezvous point in a little town northwest of the Okefenokee Swamp the Americans called Silver Hill.

"You are certain that they will not be able to track us there," Razzaq said.

"Absolutely certain," Iskander replied.

"And how do we know that the Americans who attacked our encampment are not pursuing us even as we speak?"

"It is highly unlikely that they would have been able to track us without my knowing about it. Secondly, if anyone did follow us, then the extraction team that I have sent back will most likely encounter them and slow them down."

Razzaq snorted in derision. "An entire operational force of our best men could not repel a small group of American policemen. What makes you think that an ill-equipped, poorly armed team of four men will be able to stop that same group now?"

"With all due respect, sir, you will recall that I said they would slow them down. It is a stalling action, nothing more, until we can get away. And we cannot do that until we have at least completed part of our mission."

"I was not aware that we still had a mission to complete. Our plans in Puerto Rico have fallen through, and it is likely that upon our return to Afghanistan the leaders and financiers of our cause will demand my head. This is my reality, now, and I'm afraid there's little more that I will be able to offer the New Revolutionary Justice Organization beyond posing as an example of intolerance to failure."

"The mission we have does not originate from within our plans to establish operations in Puerto Rico," Iskander replied. He turned in his seat so he could look Razzaq in the eyes. "There is still a matter of the woman reporter and her friend."

"You're talking about Miguel Veda's personal pet project? That woman— What was her name…oh, yes, Guadalupe La Costa."

"That is exactly who I am talking about. You see, sending Ad-Darr to Puerto Rico wasn't solely for the purpose of assassinating the governor. Neither did our masters approve your using him as an insurance policy just in the event that Fonseca or Veda chose to betray us. There was a very specific reason they chose to use Ad-Darr."

"What in the blazes are you talking about, Iskander?" Razzaq queried.

"It goes back to the lineage of the La Costa woman, sir. Specifically, her father, who while operating as a diplomatic attaché to Puerto Rico, as well as a number of foreign countries, actually served in a capacity for the American CIA. It was during this time when our brothers in Hezbollah were conducting operations against the Soviet KGB. The Americans became very interested in those operations, and so they arranged for the La Costa woman's father to broker a deal that would supply arms and vital equipment to the cause."

"You must be mad! Do you mean to tell me that a part of our efforts was dedicated to some ambiguous arms deal that was supposed to have taken place during the Cold War? You are talking more than twenty years ago, Iskander. That is ancient history!"

"It would be history except for one thing," Iskander replied. "The deal was not ambiguous. It just simply did not happen. For reasons that are still unknown to our brothers, Ambassador La Costa reneged on the deal. A deal that included a weapons cache unlike any you could imagine, of such a size and magnitude that nothing like it has ever been brokered between an intelligence agency and a radical group before, neither will ever be brokered again."

"And why is this important now?"

"Because the CIA supplied the weapons, La Costa's father just never delivered them. We believe that he planned to take the weapons and sell them for personal profit, but he was killed in a car accident before it could happen. We think that the weapons cache is still hidden somewhere in San Juan, Puerto Rico."

"And you think the La Costa woman may know the location of this cache?"

"It is a distinct possibility, and one that our brothers feel we must exploit."

"Why didn't you tell me about this before, Iskander?"

"I did not feel it was important enough to add to your burdens at the time, sir. And I do not think it was worth troubling you for what at this time remains only a theory. Had our plans succeeded in Puerto Rico, I knew that I could tell you about it then and we would have had plenty of time and opportunity to search for the cache at our leisure."

Razzaq's anger manifested itself in the flush of his face. "You should have told me about this! Did you not think that this information would have been helpful for me to have at this time? It might have provided us with additional incentives, given the leadership and al Qaeda a reason to grant us more time. Not to mention the fact this weapons cache may have proved extremely useful in accelerating and fortifying our operations in Puerto Rico. But now I suppose we will never know."

"There is still a chance to extract the information," Iskander protested. "So far my attempts to secure the intelligence have been unsuccessful. It would seem that our mysterious Colonel Stone has friends, and those friends have become aware of our interests in the La Costa woman. The homing device that I convinced Miguel Veda to put on her is no longer transmitting."

"A malfunction?" Razzaq asked.

"Unlikely. It is more probable that the Americans have discovered the device. However, the last report I received from the teams I sent to seize her advised me that the marshals moved her to a safehouse location they have in the state of North Carolina. Our detachment there has been eliminated, whittled down slowly by the cowardly infidels serving with various law agencies of the American government. This means that your contingency force awaiting us in Silver Hill remains our final solution. A delaying action that I will lead personally while you take two men via private plane I have waiting and find the La Costa bitch."

"And what makes you think that I am going to risk what remains of our force on a single woman who may or may not actually possess knowledge of the location of this weapons cache?"

"Because it is the only way that we can go back with the claim of victory, a greater claim than we might have if our operations in Puerto Rico had succeeded. My brother, my loyalty and service are to you and our cause. This comes before any secondary considerations I might have to our brothers in al Qaeda and Hezbollah. The fact remains that if you return empty-handed to Afghanistan your life will most surely be forfeit, and such forfeiture will not be honorable. You will be beheaded, and your body will likely be hung and burned in public for all to see and to know your disgrace."

Razzaq had no answer for that; Iskander was right, of course, but he couldn't openly admit that. Not in

front of his men. This was the time of leaders, the
chance Razzaq had to show that he was not a coward
and that he was not going to return in dishonor. They
were taking a risk, most certainly, especially since deep
down Razzaq had the sense that the hounds of hell were
nipping at his heels. If now in the face of adversity he
chose to betray their cause, he would lose not only the
respect of his men, but most likely his life.

And he would not run—that was totally dishonorable.

No, he had no choice and he knew it. "Very well. We
have a new mission and I am making it official. I will
lead my men into the very den of the infidels and we
will find this La Costa woman. We shall see if, in fact,
she knows the location of the traitor's treasure. And
then we will establish a brand-new order and strike fear
into the hearts of this Western Satan."

THE SUDDEN appearance of the airboat from around a far
bend took the Executioner by surprise.

But that's not to imply it took him off guard.

As soon as he spotted the boat, Bolan cut the speed
of his airboat by two-thirds and then brought one of the
AKM-S assault rifles into play. A variant of the Soviet
Kalashnikov, the AKM-S had a folding skeleton butt
and was a favorite among parachutist soldiers of the
Eastern Bloc during the 1980s.

Keeping one hand on the steering guide, Bolan held
the AKM-S tight and low as he triggered his first sustained burst at the oncoming boat. His goal wasn't ini-
tially to take out the terrorists aboard; frankly, he hoped
to nab at least one of them alive. The more important
step at this point was to neutralize their transportation.
Taking away their mobility in this kind of environment

had proved to be a greater asset than stacking up the body count.

Rounds from the AKM-S chopped through the grating that protected the blades and shredded the thin metal. Bolan's second salvo punched holes in the fuselage and began to dump fuel into the murky water, dispersing the green top layer with an oily sheen. One of the terrorists swung the muzzle of his submachine gun toward Bolan and triggered a burst that burned the air around the warrior's head. Undaunted, the Executioner returned the fire with a burst of his own, but with a bit more accuracy. Several rounds struck the terrorist in the chest. The impact drove him backward until he tripped over something inside the airboat and fell out the far side with a dull splash.

Bolan opened the throttle and gave the engine a full dose of air-fuel mixture. The airboat jumped into motion, and the soldier triggered the AKM-S as he passed the enemy narrowly on one side. He waited until he was clear before cutting the engine in, turning the boat hard, causing it to swing around and point the bow astern of the enemy boat. The terrorist who had been in the pilot seat was crouched behind the fan, partially obscured by smoke that was pouring from the engine compartment.

Two remaining terrorists attempted to fire on Bolan, but the large grate protecting what remained of the fan blades prevented their gaining target acquisition. Bolan engaged the starter of his airboat and the engine coughed to life, the fans immediately beginning to turn. He gave it enough fuel to put the airboat in forward motion, then cut the engines again so that when he impacted the rear of the enemy boat it was with just enough force to knock the terrorist gunners off balance.

The Executioner delivered a swathing, flash-shredding volley of 7.62 mm rounds. One terrorist caught several across the belly that opened his stomach as effectively as a scalpel. The second terrorist avoided death at first, Bolan's rounds striking the receiver of the gunman's submachine gun and ripping it from his hands. The second pass, however, didn't deliver the same reprieve and the terrorist staggered backward and crumpled in a heap. A moment later he slipped overboard and disappeared below the dark water, weighted by his equipment.

Bolan turned the rudder so that his boat scraped alongside the other. The remaining terrorist hunkered down between the fan guard and the pilot seats. The soldier noticed blood running freely from a wound in the terrorist's shoulder, and more from his right hand where two fingers were missing—undoubtedly severed by either flying metal or Bolan's marksmanship. He stared at Bolan with dark eyes that burned with hatred and vengeance.

"You speak English?" Bolan asked.

The terrorist didn't answer.

Bolan leveled the muzzle of the AKM-S at the terrorist's chest, careful to keep it just out of reach. "I'm not going to ask again."

Something glinted in the terrorist's eyes as he replied, "I speak English."

"That's good. In fact, that just may save your life today."

"I will tell you nothing," the terrorist said. "No matter what you do to me, no matter if you torture me or beat me or whatever you do to me. Still, I will remain silent. I will tell you nothing."

Bolan shrugged. "Suit yourself, but it makes no difference to me whether you talk or not. I already have all the information I need. I already know about Silver Hill and about the woman, so there's probably little more you can tell me."

The slight glimmer of recognition in the terrorist's eyes, coupled with the twitch of his cheek at the mention of La Costa, was all Bolan needed to confirm he was right about Razzaq's plans involving Silver Hill and La Costa. His enemy's reaction also confirmed that Silver Hill was likely their rendezvous point just as Brognola had suspected. That meant whatever plans Razzaq had for La Costa, he would eventually have to go where she was. That meant Washington or North Carolina, or wherever she happened to be at that moment.

And Bolan knew the numbers were running down.

"I SEE YOU BROUGHT along a friend," Captain Donald Wharton said to Bolan as he nodded toward the Executioner's prisoner.

"Yeah," Bolan replied. "We've spent a bit of quality time together."

"It surprises me."

"Why?"

Wharton arched an eyebrow and delivered a cocksure smile. "You never struck me as the kind of guy who takes prisoners."

"Generally speaking I don't, but in this case I decided to make an exception. Just don't let my secret get out."

"It's safe with me," Wharton replied as he helped Bolan secure the terrorist in back of his pickup.

Using some thick, steel cable from the spare roll designed for use by the front-mounted winch, Bolan and

Wharton tied the terrorist flat on his stomach in the bed of the pickup by attaching it to tie-down eyelets mounted in the rails of the truck bed and running the cable through handcuffs secured the terrorist's wrists and ankles. It was a crude but effective way of keeping their prisoner from mischief until he could be turned over to the custody of federal agents.

Once the job was complete, the pair climbed into the cab and headed across Chesser Island Road, which would lead them out of the Okefenokee Wildlife Refuge.

"I see you got my message," Bolan said.

"Yeah, when I got back to Folkston I touched base with my boss, and I got in contact with that Brognola guy. Nice feller, but he's no-nonsense, straight to the point. Kind of reminds me of somebody else I know."

"I appreciate the support you've provided us, Don," Bolan said. "When all this is done I imagine you'll be given an assignment just about anywhere you'd like. Might even be able to retire early."

"Are you kidding me?" Wharton asked with genuine surprise in his voice. "I haven't had this much excitement since that honeymoon couple disappeared about six years ago. We thought for sure they'd been eaten by gators until we found them in the wee hours of the morning. They stumbled into an old moonshiner's shack, which sheltered them from the weather and the beasts until we were able to locate them. Ended up confiscating about sixty bottles of prime quality hooch, as well."

"Sounds like you have no shortage of interesting situations," Bolan said with a chuckle.

"That we don't. And for the record I wouldn't trade this location for any other in the whole blessed country.

In the meantime, I went ahead and sent our team up to Silver Hill like you requested. I also talked to that Brognola feller again and he said he was going to meet us there."

"Good. With any luck we'll be able to end it there. What can you tell me about Silver Hill?"

Wharton scratched the side of his neck thoughtfully before replying, "Afraid there's not much to tell. It's not really a big place, maybe two hundred people and three-quarters of them tourists. Biggest attraction in the entire area is the Silver Hill Inn, one of those big bed-and-breakfasts that's big on Southern hospitality but short on modern amenities."

"Will there be a lot of bystanders close by?"

Wharton shook his head. "Nope, not this time of year. This is the off-season for tourists, and since there isn't much of a downtown to speak of there aren't any crowds. Plus the fact most people live far enough off the main thoroughfare they shouldn't pose a liability."

"That's good, that's very good. It looks like this private little war between me and the NRJO will stay that way."

"Looks like," Wharton replied. "You got a plan?"

"I would imagine this Silver Hill Inn would be the most logical place for Siraj Razzaq to meet with his men."

"It makes sense. It's what I would do if I were a terrorist, although that's just my uninformed opinion. The Silver Hill Inn is quiet and remote, and the owners are just an old couple who wouldn't offer any resistance. But if we go in there with guns blazing, we might end up with a standoff and possibly even a hostage situation. How do you plan to get around that?"

Bolan shook his head. "I'll just have to cross that

bridge when I come to it. For now, I hope your men have strict instructions not to go anywhere near that place. I want them strictly controlling the perimeter, nothing else."

"Those were my instructions and your friend Brognola even reinforced the point. Those are good guys we've sent up there. They'll do the job. But what about you? How do you plan to take out an army of terrorists all by your lonesome?"

"Very simple," the Executioner replied. "It's called a blitz."

Yeah, the Bolan blitz.

CHAPTER TWENTY-SIX

With a coordinated effort that involved the Georgia governor's office, state police, the U.S. Fish and Wildlife Service and three local agencies, the tiny community of Silver Hill was unaware that it had been quarantined.

But this quarantine effort wasn't the result of any physical disease; it was the disease of terrorism and violence that had run rampant through the great state of Georgia for the past six months; a disease with tendrils that stretched across three states all the way into the nation's capitol and across a great body of water into the island politics of Puerto Rico. And standing in the middle of this great epidemic of wanton bloodshed and terror was one man, a veteran of such epidemics as this, and the most qualified man on Earth to stand against the hydra of terrorism.

It was in Silver Hill, Georgia, that Executioner Bolan intended to rid America of this disease calling itself the New Revolutionary Justice Organization once and for all. Yes, Bolan had his own brand of justice for the NRJO. He stood in the shadow of the Black Hawk helicopter, one foot propped on the edge of the fuselage, bent to tuck the pants of his urban combat fatigues into the speed-lace boots. Fresh weapons of war dangled from the new load-bearing equipment harness. Prominent among them were six M-69 blast grenades and a Ka-Bar fighting knife.

Once Bolan had finished blousing his fatigue pants, he checked the actions on the Beretta 93-R and .44 Magnum Desert Eagle. That accomplished, he strode over to the command tent that had been erected in a park two blocks from the Silver Hill Inn. An attempt by the local sheriff to call the inn resulted in the operator reporting trouble on the line. According to the phone company, the Silver Hill Inn's owners hadn't reported a problem, nor had they requested a repairman.

Inside the tent, Brognola and Grimaldi stood over a table alongside Wharton and one of his coworkers. They were joined by the Charlton County Sheriff—a hulk of a man named Roger Faust—and Second Lieutenant Kent Masterson of the Georgia National Guard. Two Georgia State troopers who had taken up guard posts at the entrance to the tent relaxed visibly when they saw Bolan enter. All eyes turned toward the Executioner, each man silently expectant that this man had a plan. In times like these, Brognola knew that ego and jurisdiction went out the door in favor of listening to those who knew best.

Mack Bolan was one of them and calm authority, confidence and assuredness emanated from him as he stepped up to the table.

Brognola immediately opened the briefing. "We all know why we're here, so I'll keep this short and simple. There are two roads into Silver Hill, and the state police have both of them blocked off. Nobody has gone in or out in the last thirty minutes other than official vehicles, and all of those were inbound only."

Bolan nodded. "And we're fairly confident at this point that Razzaq and his people have commandeered this bed-and-breakfast?"

Brognola looked expectantly at Faust, who said, "I've known Bob and Sally Walker, the owners of the Silver Hill Inn, going on thirty years now. In all that time I've never known them to take off for any length of time without calling my office to advise us they would be out of town, just so we know to keep an eye on the place. Plus, this is the eve of the tourist season, and I can guarantee you they wouldn't be going on vacation right now."

"We also have information from Bear," Brognola said. "He ran a trace on their phone line and he's convinced based on the way the line is acting that it's been cut at the source."

"Okay, that's all the evidence I need," Bolan said. "These are the blueprints here for the property?"

"Yes," Brognola said.

"It's a real nice place," Faust added, "big antebellum mansion actually. Three stories and about fifteen rooms inside that place, must be. You're going to have a real challenge on your hands clearing those terrorist rats out of there."

"The first order of business will be to get the hostages clear," Bolan said. "I'm hoping that since this is the off-season the Walkers are the only hostages and didn't have any unexpected guests."

"Well, Striker, I wish we could give you better intelligence on that, but there's just no way for us to verify that information up or down," Brognola replied. "The best I can tell you is that we know there are at least two bystanders inside that structure and possibly more. You'll also have to keep in mind that the Walkers are rather elderly so they won't be able to move too fast."

"Understood. Once I verified they're safe I may tuck them away until I've neutralized Razzaq and his people, unless I can find some way to get them away from ground zero before it *becomes* ground zero."

"It may seem like a funny thing to ask at a time like this," Faust said. "But if there's any way you can save that place from being blown to bits or burned to the ground, I know folks around here sure would appreciate that. That's all Silver Hill has going for it, all this town has left is that place really. Anything happens to it and people will just have to move away entirely."

Bolan nodded. "I'll do what I can to conserve life and property."

Faust simply nodded his appreciation.

"Are you sure you want to go this alone, Coop?" Wharton asked. "My boys and I are still willing to go along with you if you'll have us."

"I'm sure you would, Don, but this is between me and the NRJO now because it has to be."

"Our intelligence says that these terrorists are expecting a full-on assault by a law-enforcement team, not a single-man strike at the heart of their operation," Brognola added. "And I can assure you, Captain Wharton, that this man standing next to me has more experience and time and training in conducting these operations than anybody we know."

"He's right," Grimaldi added.

Wharton shrugged. "Oh, I have no doubt as to his

abilities there, gents. Don't forget that I've seen this guy in action and haven't ever seen anybody before who could fight like him. Frankly, makes me feel a little sorry for the terrorists."

Bolan looked at his watch. "It'll be dusk soon. Time to go."

THE EXECUTIONER made his approach to the Silver Hill Inn on its blind side. He reached the covered back patio of the antebellum mansion and crouched behind a column. From this position, he could see toward the double doors that opened onto the wide patio. Only a few tables and chairs provided obstacles in the direct path to the rear entrance. Bolan waited a full minute, watching each and every window in view for movement before he rose and made a silent rush to the double doors.

With his back to the brick wall, the soldier reached up to the brass handle of one of the doors and gave it a tug. Locked. He cursed his bad fortune before reaching up to his LBE harness and unclipping the Ka-Bar fighting knife. Bolan waited a moment to double-check his flank, then edged forward in a crouch-walk until he could get to the combat knife inserted between the two doors. With a hard outward shove of the 440-steel blade, the warrior was able to detach the door from the latch and pop it free.

Bolan sheathed the knife and unleathered the Beretta before standing and slipping through the opening. Once inside the darkened interior, he closed the door and latched it so a roving sentry wouldn't see it and raise an alarm. As his eyes adjusted to the gloom, the soldier realized he was in the dining area. A long, low table stretched across more than half of a dining room that was bigger than some apartments Bolan had stayed in. He looked up and saw a pair of ornate, crystal chandeliers span a good third of the ceiling.

Pressing onward, Bolan held the Beretta straight and steady in front of him, ready for any threat that presented itself. He had loaded the pistol with 147-grain, subsonic hollowpoint rounds. Unlike typical casings, subsonic rounds didn't expand the same amount of ignited gas and produced a muzzle energy of 330 feet per second or less. This facilitated a whisper-quiet report from the Beretta whenever the Executioner needed to operate in stealth mode, and because he usually took his targets at close range on such a probe, he had no use or need for a high-velocity round.

Bolan was nearly halfway across the dining room, having kept to the outside wall to protect his flank and minimize the possibility of tripping over an unseen obstacle, when the door to the dining room opened suddenly and the overhead lights came on. Two terrorist gunmen entered. They chatted quickly and aimlessly with each other in Arabic, oblivious to the intruder among them as they headed toward the kitchen, which was visible through an arched entryway on the far side of the dining room. Bolan didn't hesitate. He triggered two rounds, the first one striking one terrorist in the base of his skull while the second bullet took his partner in the spine. The terrorists collapsed to the carpeted floor, dead.

The Executioner moved quickly to the light switch and flipped it, blanketing the dining room in semidarkness once more. He quickly closed the door to the room until it was only open a crack and listened carefully for additional movement. He hoped the reports from the

Beretta, though quiet, hadn't been heard by the terrorists' comrades. He sincerely doubted they had come into the kitchen solely for the purpose of finding something to eat for themselves. If someone had sent them down here on a food run, the person would be expecting them to return soon and would send someone to check on them if they didn't.

The result was a push on Bolan's timetable.

The Executioner opened the door and slipped into the adjoining room, this one some type of sitting room. A light from the far side of the room illuminated a small portion of this area, enough so that Bolan could make out a pair of leather wingback chairs at the far end centered in front of a fireplace hearth. He moved along the wall, tracking the area with the muzzle of the Beretta, until he reached the edge of another archway where light spilled into the room. Now he could hear a dull buzz, and realized it was voices—not normal voices, but voices being produced electronically.

So Lebanese terrorists would stoop low enough to watch American television.

That suited Bolan just fine, because he planned to use their divided attention to his advantage. So far he hadn't found the Walkers, and he knew the only way to verify that bystanders wouldn't get in the way of his mission would be to conduct a room-by-room search. It didn't seem practical to Bolan, but he knew it was the only way to ensure the safety of innocents. He moved into the archway that opened onto a main hall and spotted a massive spiral staircase. It was a typical architectural design during the Civil War era, just like something right out of *Gone With the Wind*.

But Bolan's hope of finding the Walkers before encountering the enemy force was short-lived. He'd made some noise and the enemy was onto him.

Six terrorists emerged from the second-story landing and descended the steps, each armed with an SMG and hell-bent on eradicating Bolan. The Executioner ducked inside the archway just in time to avoid a maelstrom of hot lead that shattered the window of the sitting room and sent glass flying onto the front porch. Plaster and wood chips rained down on Bolan, and even as he yanked one of the M-69 grenades from his LBE harness he regretted he wouldn't be able to keep his promise to Faust.

Bolan yanked the pin on the first M-69, let the spoon fly and counted off three seconds before tossing it back and around the corner. He heard it skitter across the floor in the lull of firing a moment before it blew, but he already had the second one in his hand and primed, which he tossed overhand. Having cooked off a bit longer, the second grenade exploded in midair and Bolan was rewarded with screams of the terrorists that had been in its explosive path. The soldier emerged from the archway with the Beretta 93-R in his left hand and the Desert Eagle in his right. Only half of the original terrorists were still standing, and one of them sat on the stairs holding a shattered leg with bone protruding through the top of his thigh.

Bolan caught the first surviving terrorist with a 3-round burst from the Beretta that punched through the breast bone and punctured his lungs. The .44 Magnum pistol barked next, splitting open the other terrorist's skull with a 240-grain round. The wounded terrorist scrambled for his SMG, but he was too slow, and Bolan terminated the effort with the second round from his Desert Eagle.

Considering the power of the grenades the foyer held up well, probably due to the open space, and the destruction to property ended up minimal. As Bolan ascended the grand stairwell three steps at a time, he could feel the ache in his thigh muscles. He ordered his body to continue on despite its protests about the punishment it had taken during the mission thus far.

Bolan reached the top of the stairs. The landing opened onto a long hallway lined with medium-plush, scarlet carpet and decorated with brass fixtures. Dark, burnished wood trimmed the doorways of at least a half dozen rooms just on this side. Bolan wasn't gentle in his search as he kicked open every door, quickly swept the interior of the room and then moved on to the next one. Within a few minutes he had cleared every room on the second floor—except one.

It was in this room that Bolan saw the horror that one person could inflict upon another. He had found Bob and Sally Walker, but he was much too late to do anything about it. The elderly couple lay facedown on the bed, gagged, with their hands and feet tied behind them. But that had not apparently been enough to satiate the NRJO's thirst for blood. After binding this helpless couple, the terrorists then shot both of them in the back of the head.

A new, swelling fury rolled up from the pit of Bolan stomach.

The Executioner held back the bile generated by his anger, turning it to thirst for justice and revenge on the animals who had committed such barbarism. He barely remembered his ascent to the top floor, his fight with four armed terrorists barely registering in his psyche. The first target got three rounds of 9 mm Parabellum in the gut, and the second took a pair of .44 Magnum slugs in the chest. The remaining two terrorists brought their weapons to bear, only to find that at some point in the moment before, as they watched their comrades fall, they had lost sight of their target. And then they heard something clatter at their feet, watched a familiar shape as it wobbled to a stop between them. The M-69 blew a millisecond later with such force that it destroyed the terrorists' legs.

Bolan emerged from the room he'd ducked into to protect himself from the blast even before the smoke and choking dust had cleared. That brought the count of deceased enemy bodies to twelve, and Bolan figured that very little resistance remained. He still hadn't found Razzaq among the dead, and only one of the twelve he'd terminated had been unrecognizable. Still, he couldn't see Razzaq would have the courage to fight alongside his men. Razzaq would die only on Razzaq's terms, of this much Bolan was certain, and he would have considered a "common" death as somehow beneath him.

Once more, Bolan began searching each and every room until he eventually cleared the third floor. Razzaq was nowhere to be found; it was as if he had simply disappeared into thin air. Bolan descended to the second floor and made another search—still to no avail—before he descended the steps to the foyer.

It was then the Bolan heard the noise of someone approaching him from the rear.

The warrior turned just in time to step out of the path of the slashing knife blade, the edge of the weapon just catching the fleshy part of his shoulder. He followed through in his turn as he reached up to grab the wrist of his assailant to prevent a backward slash follow up.

Continuing in circular motion, Bolan managed to bring the attacker into a position that was parallel with his own, while simultaneously moving out of the line of attack. He then executed a foot sweep and yanked back to change his opponent's direction, a move that effectively knocked him off his feet. But the knife wielder was experienced and used his weight to drag Bolan down with him to the marble floor.

Like two titans embroiled in a battle for ultimate power, Bolan and his enemy struggled for control over life itself.

CHAPTER TWENTY-SEVEN

Although he was larger than the terrorist, Bolan realized his opponent had youth, speed and agility on his side.

But Mack Bolan had experience.

And in a case such as this, the soldier had learned it was the latter that counted most.

The terrorist made the mistake of letting Bolan regain his feet, and that only frustrated the enemy even more. As a result, he began to wield the knife in a sloppy fashion, losing confidence in his own ability as he circled his opponent. The Executioner might have risked drawing his Ka-Bar except for the fact that the extra seconds it would take him to do that might be all the distraction the terrorist needed to gain the upper hand. Besides, being unarmed did have one advantage in that it made his opponent feel like *he* had the upper hand. Surely he would underestimate Bolan, and he proved the point when he attempted a feint by trying an upper slash that he reversed at the last moment into a jab into Bolan's midsection. The moment it took him to change direction provided the big American with the opening he needed.

The Executioner stepped outside the attack and snaked his arm under the terrorist's armpit just above and beyond the elbow, giving him the leverage to bring the other arm up and back across the terrorist's neck. In a heartbeat, Bolan had the leverage he needed to stretch those two points in opposite directions. His muscles quivered as he applied all of his strength into a move that ultimately tore the man's shoulder from his rotator cuff while bending his spine in a direction it wasn't made for. The snap of the terrorist's neck followed a moment later and Bolan let the corpse crumple to the ground.

The soldier willed himself to stay on his feet while he tried to catch his breath from the combined exertion and adrenaline of the fight. Then he moved wearily to the front door and opened it wide. He stepped into the muggy evening air and took a moment to soak in the stillness, the peace and quiet. Crickets sounded nearby, and Bolan thought of how many nights people like Bob and Sally Walker had probably sat on this porch listening to them, watching the lightning bugs and chatting away the evenings, enjoying each other's company without a care in the world.

Siraj Razzaq had ended that for them, and now Bolan planned to end it for Razzaq.

He reached into his pocket and withdrew the small electronic device with a button set in its face. He pressed it and a moment later the area around him lit up with flood lamps. Armed SWAT teams and Army National Guardsman charged the property en masse, ignoring Bolan, who walked through the human waves of officers and soldiers. They had been the backup plan, the only alternative in the event Bolan had failed. The ironic thing was that in some sense the soldier felt he had failed. He had lost his chance to bring down Razzaq, and took little comfort in the fact he had eradicated the NRJO terrorist force.

It bothered him that Razzaq was still at large—still out there. And somehow he knew they hadn't heard the last of the terrorist leader.

"You okay, Striker?" Brognola asked.

Bolan looked blankly at his friend, knowing that Brognola had probably picked up on his mood immediately.

"Sarge?" Grimaldi echoed.

"I'm fine," Bolan said. "Thirteen terrorists confirmed killed."

"And Razzaq?" Brognola asked.

"He wasn't there. He somehow figured out how to slip through our net."

Before Brognola could respond, his phone signaled for attention and he answered it while keeping one wary eye on his friend. "Yeah, Barb."

A minute of silence followed. The change in the Stony Man chief's expression told Bolan that maybe they had finally caught a break. Bolan and Grimaldi stood by while the big Fed "yeah'd" and "uh-huh'd" a few times. Finally he thanked Price and disconnected the call.

"We may have another problem."

"What kind?" Bolan asked.

"It would seem the NRJO tried to take another shot at La Costa and Parmahel, and it sounds like this time they succeeded. Parmahel took a bullet, and he's in surgery now at the Hoffman Medical Center in Mount Airy, North Carolina."

"That's where we have that safehouse we occasionally share with the U.S. Marshals Service, isn't it?"

Brognola nodded at Bolan. "I figured they'd be safe there once we located the bug Miguel Veda planted in the little gift he'd given La Costa."

Suddenly, the whole thing came crashing down on Bolan like a tidal wave. The assault in the neighborhood in downtown San Juan; the attack at Andrews AFB; the interest Veda had taken in La Costa early on that could only have been triggered by Razzaq and his people; the torture and capture by Ad-Darr that had eventually drawn La Costa and Parmahel into this whole mess. All of it suddenly came to him in a moment of clarity such as he'd never experienced during this mission.

"That's it, Hal," Bolan stated.

"What's it?"

"This deal with La Costa. It's been about her the entire time. Everything that's happened up to this point we've assumed was about politics in Puerto Rico and the NRJO's desire to turn it into a base of operations by vying for its independence."

"Yeah…*and?* Even Veda confirmed that for us."

"But what he didn't know was why the NRJO was so adamant about using Puerto Rico. Why not the Bahamas or Mexico? They might even have been able to swing a deal with Cuba. Why specifically did they choose Puerto Rico?"

Brognola's expression changed and the Executioner could see his friend was starting to understand the direction he was going. "You're saying that their interest in Puerto Rico has to do with La Costa?"

"Why not? Her father served there in a diplomatic role for many years, not to mention his file said he was involved with certain operations for the CIA. Maybe he knew something, something the terrorists consider valuable enough that he might have passed it on to his daughter."

"And since we've now ruined their plans in Puerto Rico and brought her back here, she's their only remaining link to whatever it is they want."

"Right," Bolan said. "They're not trying to kill her, they're trying to kidnap her. Come on, Jack. We need to get to Mount Airy!"

"Right behind you, Sarge!" Grimaldi replied as he took off after Bolan, who was already sprinting down the sidewalk toward the Black Hawk.

Brognola cleared his throat, looked around and muttered, "Guess I'll stay here and hold down the fort."

THE CLOSEST AIRPORT where they could land their private plane on short notice was in Greensboro.

Siraj Razzaq had coaxed his pilot to try to convince them they needed to make an emergency landing, but he cautioned against drawing such attention because an emergency landing would automatically invoke an investigation by the FAA. They would be detained until investigators arrived and that would ultimately lead to their arrest. So they put down in Greensboro, didn't make any noise about it and drove the hour and a half to Mount Airy. At some point during their road trip, the homing signal started transmitting again.

Razzaq smiled at his good fortune. Normally he wouldn't have been so fortunate, but it seemed today was his day of reversals. In spite of his failure in Puerto Rico, he still had the possibility of returning victorious to Afghanistan. Maybe one day he would even be able to return to his own country. How he missed Beirut. And instead of Iskander taking his life, the man had shown himself brave and loyal by executing a brilliant stalling action that would certainly keep law enforcement occupied for many hours, if not days, while they tried to figure out what was really going on.

By that time, Razzaq would have the La Costa woman—or at least have the information she possessed—and be long out of the country.

The homing signal led them directly to a county hospital called Hoffman Medical Center. A quick check led them to the surgical waiting room where Julio Parmahel was still undergoing surgery. And was he family? No, but he was a very close friend who had been called by Guadalupe La Costa to come sit vigil with her. But of course, the nursing staff understood perfectly and wasn't it sweet of him to do that? It didn't take him any time at all to get directions to the surgical waiting room on the third floor.

What he didn't realize was that as soon as the elevator doors closed an entire unit of sheriff's deputies led by one Deputy Holcombe swooped into the parking lot where three Lebanese men waited in a rental car for their master. They took the men into custody without incident, whisking them away quickly and quietly. Moreover, Razzaq didn't know that this part of the third-story wing had been closed for remodeling and that ICU surgery had been moved to the second floor on the completely opposite end of the building. And most of all he didn't realize that all of this had happened with a certain phone call from a certain man sitting in a little place called the Oval Office for the purpose of clearing the area so the Executioner could do his work in peace.

So it wasn't really until Siraj Razzaq stepped off the elevator onto the dusty, deserted corridor on the third floor—a corridor lined with plastic and masking tape—that he realized he'd been duped. He looked down at the tracking device and, according to his signal, he should have been standing practically on top of the La Costa woman.

The glimmer of light shimmering off a metallic object caught his attention and he turned to see a tall, dark-haired stranger standing there in combat fatigues with weapons and ordnance hanging from every conceivable place. The man's icy-blue eyes glimmered as he held up something circular and gold in his left hand, the object that had reflected light. But it was the gleam of a sleek pistol in his right hand that seemed to demand most of Razzaq's attention.

"Looking for this?" the man asked.

"Wh-who are you?" Razzaq stuttered despite the fact he tried not show fear.

The man delivered a frosty smile. "That hardly matters now. The point is that I know who *you* are, Razzaq. And I'm here to tell you it's over. You failed and now it's time to pay the piper."

"I don't know what you are talking about."

"Don't you?" the stranger asked. "You're a murdering liar, Razzaq, a man who gets off on the suffering and destruction of innocent people. Many have died to accomplish your pathetic cause and some of them I count among my friends. But now that's over and the world no longer has to worry about you."

"You cannot stop me!" Razzaq roared. "I am not any ordinary man. I am the cause, the voice of the New Revolutionary Justice Organization. And if you kill me someone will rise to take my place. The West will fall one day and my brothers will be all powerful once again!"

"No, you won't," the man replied. "You're a lunatic and a criminal. And now judgment day has come."

And with that, Mack Bolan delivered the verdict.

EPILOGUE

"How you feeling, Parmahel?" Brognola asked as he and Grimaldi entered the hospital room.

"Not bad, Hal. Not bad at all."

The Stony Man chief nodded and then Grimaldi produced a bouquet of flowers he'd been hiding behind his back.

"Aw, shucks," Parmahel said. "You shouldn't have."

"They're from Stone. He was too embarrassed to deliver them in person," Grimaldi cracked.

Brognola harrumphed and said, "Actually, he's left for another mission."

Arm draped across the top of Parmahel's pillow, her other hand resting on his shoulder, La Costa said, "That guy doesn't slow down for anything. We barely got time to see him after Julio woke up in recovery before he had to split. I don't suppose you can tell us where he's going."

"I'm afraid not," Brognola said. "But he did want me to thank you for all your help and for risking your neck. Your father would have been proud."

"Did you ever find out why they were after us?" Parmahel asked.

"They weren't after you, specifically, they wanted Guadalupe here. It seems your father scammed the Hezbollah on an arms deal some twenty years ago and the terrorists wanted those weapons. In fact, in light of this new information I'm probably going to open an investigation into the circumstances surrounding his death."

"Well, much as I hate to be the bearer of bad news, the joke's on them, Hal," La Costa said.

"You mean you *did* know about the weapons cache?" Grimaldi asked quietly.

She shrugged. "Of course, but I never would have thought that's what they were interested in. My father dumped those weapons into the ocean somewhere off the shores of Puerto Rico. Once he found out they were for terrorists he decided he didn't want to have any part of it. You see, my father knew that the support the CIA was lending terrorists in that day would eventually come back to bite us in the ass. And it did."

"It did at that, La Costa," Brognola said with a laugh.

"Well, it looks like you're going to have one hell of a story to tell," Grimaldi said.

"I don't think so, Jack," La Costa replied. She looked at Julio Parmahel, squeezed his hand and said, "I'm taking some time off from the reporting biz. I've decided there are more important things in life right now."

"Yeah?" Grimaldi replied. "Imagine that."

The Executioner

Don Pendleton's ®

SALVADOR STRIKE

A WARRIOR'S PLAYGROUND

The star witness and the prosecuting attorney for the case against the lethal MS-13 gang have been murdered, leaving the trial in shambles. With the situation critical, Mack Bolan is called in to fight fire with fire. MS-13's leaders have a plan to terrorize suburban America and it's up to the Executioner to stop them—showing no mercy.

GOLD EAGLE ®

Available February 2010 wherever books are sold.

JAMES AXLER

DEATH LANDS

Blood Harvest

Welcome to the dark side of tomorrow. Welcome to the Deathlands.

Washed ashore in the North Atlantic, Ryan Cawdor and Doc Tanner discover two islands intact after Skydark, but whose inhabitants suffer a darker, more horrifying punishment. When the sun goes down, mutants called Nightwalkers manifest to unleash a feast of horror…which Ryan and Doc must struggle to survive.

Available March 2010 wherever books are sold.

TAKE 'EM FREE

2 action-packed novels plus a mystery bonus

NO RISK

NO OBLIGATION TO BUY

GE09